THE LAIRD

THE
LAIRD

Juliana Garnett

JOVE BOOKS, NEW YORK

THE LAIRD

A Jove Book / published by arrangement with
the author

PRINTING HISTORY
Jove edition / October 2002

ISBN: 0-7394-2965-5

A JOVE BOOK®
Jove Books are published by The Berkley Publishing Group, a division of Penguin Putnam Inc., 375 Hudson Street, New York, New York 10014. JOVE and the "J" design are trademarks belonging to Penguin Putnam Inc.

PRINTED IN THE UNITED STATES OF AMERICA

To Rob and Lisa

Campbell Keep

✝

LOCHAWESIDE, SCOTLAND
1327

DEATH WAITED JUST beyond the keep. It crouched in the black hills and in the devil's own mist that shrouded trees and marsh beyond the safety of Lochawe's walls. Robert Campbell of Glenlyon was familiar with death, and he felt its breath in the heavy March fog that rolled into the muddy bailey.

A ghostly hush muffled the impatient stomp of horse hooves and the metallic clink of swords. Torches sputtered and spit in sconces on high stone walls, the dancing light a misty haze that did little to dispel the predawn gloom. The creeping dampness penetrated leather and wool, ignored by the men gathered in the center of the courtyard.

Tall, dark, lean, Rob blended into the shadows as he watched them. He stood with his back braced against the battlements, his injured leg a constant ache save for moments of jarring agony when he moved too swiftly or too unwisely. The wound was either curse or blessing, but at the moment, it mattered little which kept him from join-ing—or preventing—his father and brothers' foolhardi-ness.

Cold seeped through the dark blue wool of his trews, even through the thick folds of the blue and green plaide swathing his chest, a knifing chill that made his thigh ache even more. Still, he waited, watching them prepare, anger warring with a growing sense of futility. He waited until he could delay no longer, until they were mounted and the gates began to open. Until he knew there was no more time.

Then Rob hobbled from shadows into the torchlight and barred their path, his long legs splayed and boots firmly planted in the muck and mud of the bailey. A searing pain shot up his leg, and he ignored it, concentrating fiercely upon the men and horses. His back was to the half-opened gates as he brought up his sword, the lethal blade held high in a warning to the horsemen. And a plea.

A roan steed snorted, half reared, eyes and hooves flashing close to Rob in the gloom as the lead rider reined the beast to a halt.

"Move out of our way!" His father's growl was loud in the smothering mist as he leaned forward. The ferocity of his expression defined the name he had earned: the Red Devil of Lochawe. Hellish torchlight played over Angus Campbell's rugged face, and his eyes were narrowed, fierce beneath a bushy shelf of red brow flecked with gray. "Ye have said yer piece and made plain ye're set against us."

"Kill yourself if you will, but for the love of all that's holy, don't take innocent lives with you." Rob aimed his sword point toward his two youngest brothers. Wet, dull light gleamed on the naked blade as he jabbed it toward them. "Diarmid, Duncan, stay here. This is a fool's errand, and a deadly one. You owe Argyll nothing save sword loyalty in battle, not this. *Christ*—not this."

Diarmid and Duncan exchanged glances, their youthful faces creased with indecision and turmoil. So alike, with the same copper hair and blue eyes as their sire, nearly identical, though a good year separated them in age. Good lads, with good heads. Yet neither of them wavered, to Rob's despair.

"Och, Rob," Diarmid said at last, and had the grace to look sheepish, "we gave our word to the earl. We willna go back on it. 'Tis Campbell tradition to honor our pledge."

"Aye, but not tradition to die needlessly." Rob spared a glance toward his eldest brother, but Kenneth's jaw was stubbornly set. He would not argue with their father. That, too, was tradition. Rob was the only son to ever ignore it.

His sword wavered, then slowly lowered as he recognized the futility of more argument. None of his seven brothers had listened to reason, only to vain promises of glory from a feckless earl. His gaze shifted back to his father.

Angus sat erect on his mount, a bright glint like blue fire in his narrowed eyes as he regarded Rob. "If this is why ye came to Lochawe, ye should have stayed at Glenlyon." His voice altered slightly, became cajoling. "Robbie lad, put aside yer bitter hatred of Argyll. Ye're no coward. Ye were knighted by the Bruce himself. If ye were not wounded—"

"A wound I received in service to the king," Rob broke in harshly, "not to a craven earl. Argyll preys upon the weak, sends others to do his dirty bidding. As he does now. This is madness. It's certain death to ride into a well-defended keep to take a hostage. Do you think Clan Caddel will stand by and do nothing?"

The laird's eyes flared with anger. "They have all been

lured to Inverness, but d'ye think I have ever shrunk from a fight? We'll gain a fat purse, as well as the earl's high regard."

Their eyes clashed, blue against gray, both angry and unyielding. Rob's lip curled in a snarl. "Argyll has never kept a bargain in his life. He's not worth one of our horses and certainly not one of our lives."

The Campbell grimaced. "Ye've turned womanish. Christ above, it's enough to curdle my belly. Stay, then!"

Rob barely got out of the way as his father spurred his mount forward. Winch chains shrieked a protest as the wooden gates opened onto a bridge stretched over a marshy breach of stagnant water. Hooves struck loudly against bridge planks, marking a death knell as his brothers swarmed through the gaping yett, all without a glance at him save for Diarmid and Duncan, who flashed cocky grins of reassurance.

Rob nodded, unable to speak, caught between rage and resignation. He watched until the little band rode out of the growing light into deep shadows still blanketing the marsh. Then he turned to Fergal, who waited silently.

"Bring my mount."

"Ye're not able to ride," the old gillie replied, but he had already lifted an arm to summon a stable lad.

Fergal would never refuse him, for he'd served Angus Campbell since they were both lads and knew his lord's sons better than most.

"I'll ride." Rob said it grimly. This may well kill him, but he was damned if he'd allow his father and brothers to go to their deaths alone.

The old gillie stood by as Rob mounted. It was hard work, but Fergal wisely did not offer aid. Stiff with pain from an unhealed wound made worse by the ride to Lochawe, Rob was sweating when he finally settled atop the fractious horse and took up the reins. Heat and cold both swamped him, but he clenched his teeth against it and dug his heels into the mount's ribs.

The drumming of hooves on wooden planks was deafening as he crossed the bridge, and his horse leaped the last few feet onto more solid ground. Jarred by the leap, agony shot through his leg and into his belly so that Rob tilted forward clumsily to grab at his mount's neck. His ears hummed loudly; the world shifted, swerved alarmingly awry. There was the taste of coarse mane, then marsh and water in his mouth, and darkness swooped down on him like a raven.

In his last seconds of lucidity, he thought, *God help them. . . .*

Chapter 1

$\dagger$

*L*IGHT DANCED WITH shadows beneath enormous linden trees that edged the Cawdor Burn below Caddel Castle. Seated on a tussock of dead, dry grass in the sunshine, Judith Lindsay tilted her face upward. Her green eyes closed, and she drew in a deep breath of sweet, soft air that held the promise of spring. A fair day, after months of cold gray days—a day tailored for sitting outside instead of in the dank confines of the stone keep. It was cool but peaceful, with the burn rushing past in a soothing melody. So quiet . . .

"Lady Judith, look at the fuzzy worm!"

Opening drowsy eyes, Judith turned to view the slow-moving caterpillar her young niece had discovered. Red hair like a flame curled haphazardly over Mairi's head, and the long-lashed blue eyes regarding the caterpillar were intent and serious. The child's Gaelic held a tinge of Fyfe dialect that must come from the servants.

"The unseasonable weather has lured it out. If you do

not touch it, Mairi," Judith said softly in English, "it will turn into a beautiful butterfly."

Mairi looked up. *"Dealan-de?* Will it fly?"

"Yes, one day. But you must be kind and not harm it, or the butterfly won't sprout wings."

Mairi's eyes widened. One chubby finger moved aside a twig from the caterpillar's path. After a moment, she looked up at Judith, her round little face solemn.

"Edith said Mama and Papa grew wings in heaven. Did she mean that they are flutterbyes, too?"

Judith smiled. "No, Edith probably meant that they're like angels."

"But maybe angels can be beautiful flutterbyes instead. Do you think they can, Lady Judith?"

The small, lisping question struck Judith dumb for a moment; inherent in the childish mind was an innocence that she was reluctant to crush. Edith really shouldn't fill the child's mind with such nonsense, yet how could she take away any crumbs of comfort Mairi might find in such tales?

When she found her voice, she answered gently, "It's said that angels can take on many forms, so they could choose to be butterflies, I suppose."

Her reply seemed to satisfy Mairi, and the child's pensive expression altered to a sweet smile.

"Then we should take special care of caterpillars and flutterbyes, shouldn't we, Lady Judith."

"Yes." Judith lifted a strand of the child's soft red hair. It felt like silk in her hand, fine as a spiderweb, gossamer strands gleaming in the sunlight. Her hand stilled on the small head. "We should take special care of all living creatures."

"Do you think my uncle Kenneth is a flutterbye, too?" Mairi turned an artless gaze up to her, sunlight reflected in the brilliant blue of her eyes.

"That's a nice thought," Judith managed to answer. The mention of her husband summoned a mix of emotions. Kenneth Lindsay was a vague memory. Six—almost seven years now since he'd died, and she was still widowed, with no offers for her hand, no hope of a family of her own. A widow, a barren crone of twenty-six years in a land and family that resented her presence.

If not for the unfettered love of this child, she'd not have been able to bear the past years of exile from her home and family. From England. She would have returned, but it had been made plain to her that she was unwanted in her father's house. By terms of her marriage contract, her lands would be forfeit should she leave Scotland.

A cool wind blew, stirring strands of Judith's pale blond hair in a light caress against her cheek. Woodsmoke was rife on the brisk currents, a sharp tang that reminded her of waiting housekeeping duties. She had lingered too long in the sloping grounds below the keep. With regret, she decided it was time they returned to the gray safety of stone walls that jutted up from the flat escarpment.

At this time of the day, Caddel Castle cast long shadows down the steep, rocky bank that led to the burn. On the side away from the burn, a dry moat kept enemies at bay and gave the inhabitants a sense of security.

Judith rose to her feet and brushed dry grass from her skirts, then stretched lazily, loathe to return yet knowing she must. It was washday, when all the linens and clothes were scrubbed in huge tubs set beneath the giant hawthorn tree that grew in the bailey. She should be there helping, though her presence was not always welcome. She was still considered an outsider after so many years here.

"Come, Mairi," she said and knelt beside her small charge, smiling a little at her absorption with the busy caterpillar. She gathered the plaide Mairi had discarded and put a hand on the child's head, a soft touch that snagged Mairi's attention at last and made her look up.

"I don't want to go back in yet, Lady Judith. I want to wait for wings."

"Ah coney, wings take a long time to grow. And some things are best done alone, without prying eyes to watch."

"Och, aye," Mairi sighed, sounding very much like old Edith when she did, " 'tis a sad thing tae be alone."

"At times, my love, but not always." Judith smiled as Mairi still gazed wistfully at the heedless furry creature inching along a gnarled tree root. "Perhaps the next time we see it, it will be a beautiful butterfly," she said and was rewarded with Mairi's bright, hopeful grin.

"Och aye, 'twould be a lovely thing, dinna ye think?"

"Yes, Mairi, I do think it would be a lovely thing to happen," she said, carefully enunciating her words in a subtle reminder for Mairi to watch her diction. It was part of Judith's duty to teach her proper English, a task made more difficult by the resentment of Mairi's Scottish nurse and others who cared for her. The English were still hated by those who lost loved ones in the savage conflict between King Edward and Robert the Bruce. Not even the recent abdication of Edward II as king of England had eased the sharp bite of war's atrocities and losses.

"The apple doesna fall far from the tree," old Edith predicted sourly, "mark me on tha', if ye will. The lad isna better than his da, just younger. It'll be muckle war yet."

Too soon to tell, but Judith suspected Edith was right. England was not yet done with Scotland, for all that Robert Bruce was now recognized as the rightful king. Escalating conflicts and the English penchant for attacking Scottish trading vessels in the Low Countries in defiance of the Bishopthorpe truce had earned a sharp retaliation by Robert Bruce. On the day young Edward III was

crowned king of England after his father's abdication, the
Scots attacked the castle of Norham to make their point.
Now Ireland was under threat, with the Scots rallying in
her defense. The shadows of war still hovered darkly
overhead.

Kneeling, Judith pulled the dark red plaide around
Mairi's shoulders, giving the child a teasing shake that
made her giggle. As she rose, the thundering sound of
hoofbeats snared her attention, and Judith turned to glance
down the rocky slope, faintly surprised that the Caddel
men were returning from Inverness. Mairi's uncles had
left the night before, intent upon finishing their business
quickly. But surely they could not be back so soon? It
was barely midday, and Inverness was a good distance
away.

Shading her eyes with one hand cupped above her
brow, Judith scanned the road that wound below the keep,
a brown ribbon of packed-down dirt half hidden by tree
limbs and bracken. Flashes of color appeared and vanished, the blur of riders visible for only an instant, but
just long enough for her to recognize that it was not
Mairi's uncles approaching. These riders came at a fast,
furious pace that sent warning tremors through her entire
body.

"Come, Mairi," she said calmly, and took the child's
hand tightly in her own to urge her toward the keep without causing alarm, "we must hurry, or Mistress Edith will
give us a scold for tarrying so long."

"Aye—oh wait, Lady Judith! You nearly stepped on
the wee worm."

Mairi broke loose from her grip, bending to move the
fuzzy creature aside, and Judith quickly scooped the child
into her arms. The sense of urgency increased, for now
she could see that the riders were strangers to her, coming
far too swiftly to mean any good. There was an air of

purpose about them that made her throat close with apprehension.

Startled at being snatched up so rudely, Mairi cried out
softly as Judith began to move toward the keep at a run,
stumbling over her long, dragging skirts, intent upon
reaching the safety of the postern door. So far ahead . . .
the climb arduous as Judith struggled beneath the child's
solid weight. Her breath huffed in front of her face, dis-
sipated in a gauzy fog. She lost a shoe but did not falter.

Panic seized her as Judith felt the ground shudder beneath the force of so many horses—six? Seven of them?
Oh, they were coming so swiftly now, she could hear the
labored wheeze of winded mounts, the excited, guttural
urging of the riders, and the entire world seemed a blur
of thundering horses and pressing danger, and the door
still so far away. . . . Only yards now, an uphill climb with
Mairi so heavy in her arms, but Sweet Mary, the men
were fast upon them, shouting in Gaelic, curses, laughter,
surrounding them and cutting her off from her path so
that Judith had to swerve, dodge outstretched arms to dart
into the shelter of thick hedges on the soft rise above the
meadow. Mairi sobbed, baby arms clinging tightly to Judith's neck as she ran, panting and helpless, like a caterpillar at the mercy of beings far larger and omnipotent.

And then the muscled sheen of a horse cut her off as
she turned and twisted, and a brawny arm swung out,
snatched at Mairi, the man cursing when Judith held
tightly to the child, her fists tangled in the folds of Mairi's
gown.

"Give up the lass," a hoarse voice snarled in Gaelic,
"or ye'll rue it, by God's teeth!"

A meaty fist knotted in the wool of Mairi's gown; red
gold hair curled over the bare arm, and without hesitation,
Judith sank her teeth into the muscled flesh. A pained
howl rose above the chaos, something slammed against

the side of her head, and still she clung to him fiercely, like a dog with a bone, as the taste of sweat and blood filled her mouth and desperate terror filled her world.

And above howls of pain, she heard snorts of laughter, and a note of urgency in one voice that said, "Bring them both, or we're like to be trapped! They come!"

Caught in the midst of jostling horses and determined men, Judith heard muffled shouts. Without seeing them, she knew that Caddel servants were coming to their aid; if only she could hold on a little longer, delay these marauders until help arrived.

Mairi clung still to her neck, a strangling hold as Judith kept her tenacious grip on the man's arm. It was hard to breathe, impossible to see more than the shifting horse and a man's bare leg . . . then the bloodied arm jerked free. She gulped in a breath of hot, dusty air that tasted rusty and thick. With her last bit of strength, she wrapped her arms around Mairi's frantically squirming body. Then another blow rocked her, lights exploded in front of her eyes, a whirling darkness spun her round and round until the world tilted and shifted beneath her feet. A keening cry enveloped her, and she recognized it as her own as Mairi was torn from her arms. Then all went black.

Chapter 2

✟

"**Y**E SHOULD HAVE killed the bloody bitch."

Harsh Gaelic penetrated the fog surrounding Judith, and she squinted against the dull, thudding ache in her head as she opened her eyes. It was dark, but she saw shadowy forms outlined against misty shafts of brittle moonlight.

The man who had spoken grunted in pain as the contents of a small flask splashed over his torn flesh. He sat upon a tree stump, and the pale-haired man who knelt beside him chuckled.

"She was too pretty to kill," was the reply, and when he glanced up, Judith could see in the sharp light that he was much younger than she'd thought. He was grinning, teeth a white flash. "And she fought too bravely, you must admit."

"What kind of son are ye, to laugh at a father's pain." It was not a question but a sour comment that earned more laughter from those around him.

The night smelled damp. It must have rained, for her wool gown was sodden and cold. Judith shivered. Her breath was a frost cloud. She remained still and quiet, aware of young Mairi next to her; the child's breathing was rasping and soft, an exhausted slumber. Beyond the wooded clearing, velvety blackness swallowed the forest and tethered towering trees to the earth. It was late. She had been unconscious for a long time. How far had they come? Too far for pursuers to find them? The beat of her heart was loud in her ears, blood pulsing through her veins as fear coursed through her body. She breathed more deeply in an effort to remain calm. It wouldn't help now to panic.

Muted voices penetrated the last shreds of fog that clouded her brain. They argued, discussed whether or not to discard her or keep her with them. Her value seemed to barely outweigh the inconvenience.

"She calms the child," the younger man said, and he indicated Judith with a jerk of his thumb over one shoulder. "And 'tis one more hostage to use against Clan Caddel if need be."

The older man, with bushy red hair sprinkled with gray, scowled as he nursed his chewed arm. "Mark me, she'll be trouble."

"Not as much trouble as a screaming bairn would be," another of the men said practically. "I've no stomach for gagging a wee lass. She might strangle on it. It's best we take the woman. Christ's blood, we brought her this far. A bit farther willna hurt. And God must be on our side. Why else would they have been outside the keep, almost waiting for us? Good fortune rides with the right, 'tis said."

Silence fell, then the leader gave a jerk of his head. "Aye, we'll keep the woman with us then, but if she gives me any more trouble, I'll slit her throat myself."

No one offered an argument, and a chill shivered down Judith's spine. Her fingers clenched convulsively into the green wool folds of her gown. She was cold, the damp wind knifing through the wet wool. Someone had covered Mairi with her own plaide; the child still slept, and she was grateful.

There was more talk, most of it a laughing reliving of the successful raid on Caddel Castle. What manner of men were they, she wondered, that dared ride so boldly into the very heart of enemy land to abduct a hostage? Two hostages?

And why?

She tensed when one of them, the young, fair-haired lad who had dared laugh at his father, stood up and came toward her. She had a vague impression of height and bare legs covered only in leather boots and a short tunic before he knelt, and his touch was insistent but gentle as he shook her.

"Wake, mistress," he said softly, "and gather the wee lass. We maun ride."

Judith forced herself to meet his gaze, the pale blue glint of his eyes moon-silvered and shadowed. Oddly, she felt no animosity in him, but even a kind of sympathy. With an effort, she swallowed the taste of fear that clung to her tongue and nodded.

"Where do you take us? The child is exhausted and could die in this cold night air."

She had spoken English, she realized, reverting to her natural tongue, and she saw his brow lower in confusion.

"D'ye have the Gaelic?" he asked before she could re-phrase her question, and she nodded.

"Yea. I asked where you take us. Mairi could die if not protected."

His youthful mouth pursed, but his reply was firm. "We

shall not let her die, mistress. Nor you, if ye dinna fight us. 'Tis a long way to Lochaweside."

Her eyes widened. Lochaweside—Holy Mother, it was near two hundred miles away on the west side of Scotland!

Judith sat up, shivering, and the youth noticed. He rose to his feet and stepped away, then returned with a dark length of plaide. It was faded and smelled of woodsmoke and things she'd rather not think about, but was warm as he pulled it around her shoulders.

His kindness gave her the courage to ask, "What do you intend to do with us?"

"Ye'll not be harmed," he said and held out his hand. "Come, mistress. We cannot tarry longer."

There was a gentleness to him that was reassuring, and Judith allowed him to lift her atop a mount and hand Mairi up to her. Drowsily, the child snuggled close as the youth tucked the end of Mairi's red plaide around her sturdy legs.

As the day wore on, they rode at a furious pace that gave Judith hope they were being pursued. Loch Ness was behind them now, the misty waters no longer visible. It was wild country here, climbing higher, with harsh crags still white with snow and the air breath-stealing, chilling hands and lungs with brisk efficiency. The sky was so blue and bright her eyes stung. The horse was a steady rhythmic pounding beneath her, and the world was a blur of trees and sky and steep green slopes broken by humps of gray rock as they rode relentlessly onward.

Mairi clung to Judith, a warm weight against her body. They rode from sunlight into the misty shadows of a forest in the valley, where little light penetrated the dense needles of pine and fir. Hooves were muffled on eons of deadfall cushioning the narrow track that wound through towering trees, budding oaks vying with the spicy-scented evergreens, wind soughing through shifting branches. Judith shivered. It was so quiet, only the sound of birds and horses broke ancient silence as they traveled at a pace made slower by the twisting path. No one spoke until they were out of the forest and into the sunlight again, where warmth wrapped around them like a welcome wool cloak.

When they paused at the crest of a hill, her young guard turned in his saddle to look over his shoulder at her, flashing a grin. "Rob prophesied doom. He'll be surprised we've had no trouble."

Judith lifted a brow in response. It was disconcerting that no one had pursued them. Surely, Mairi's uncles cared about their young heiress enough to go after the men who'd abducted her. Yet as the day wore on, there was still no sign of pursuit. Curse them. Were they too cowardly even to rescue their own? If only her abductors would lower their guard, she would take Mairi and steal away into the night.

Yet no opportunity arose, for the youth—whose name she learned was Diarmid—kept sharp eyes on her, and especially Mairi. Snatches of conversation revealed that the older man was father to all seven of her captors, and that the earl of Argyll was responsible for Mairi's abduction.

Argyll was a brash man, she'd heard, who held a firm grip on his lands and the lairds who gave him their loyalty. Her heart sank. There was scant hope of escape.

The country was too wild, her guards too many and too wary.

Late in the afternoon, when purple and rose shadows filled valleys and shrouded the hills, one of the men cursed loudly. Judith glanced up, her heart thumping madly as she turned to see the cause of his concern.

Riders! Mairi's uncles following them? *Oh, pray God it is true,* she thought fiercely.

The leader shouted encouragement, and horses were put to the spur. Judith clung to Mairi and the saddle, careening with them in a hectic race as her horse was pulled along. Trees flashed by in a blur, and cold air lashed her face. Then they came to an abrupt halt. Just ahead lay an abandoned croft with no roof or walls, only the bare bones of its foundation left. It squatted amid a tangle of bracken in a clearing surrounded by thick woods. The laird snapped out an order for everyone to dismount, turning to Judith to point a thick finger at her and Mairi.

"Ye'll stay where ye are," he growled. "Hold her horse, Diarmid. I've a plan to outfox Clan Caddel."

"We can outrun them," one of the men argued. "There are too many to fight against here. We've not enough shelter for an ambush, not enough men for a victory."

"I will not risk capture now," the laird shot back. "Do what I say, and we may yet win the day."

Judith hugged Mairi tightly to her chest, watching numbly when an old cooking pot was dragged from beside the ruined hut. It was a huge cauldron, large enough to boil an entire hog. The men struggled with it, inverting it so the iron feet stuck into the air like a felled dragon. It lay in the middle of the clearing, a rusting dome.

After a swift discussion with his sons, the laird took up his mount's reins and glared at Judith.

"We ride, and I'll have no trouble from ye," he growled, "or 'twill be just me and the bairn that rides on." Then he turned to Diarmid hovering close by and put a hand on the youth's shoulder, his tone gruff as he said, "God be with ye, lad, and give ye victory."

His voice trembling ever so slightly, Diarmid asked his father's blessing. "If we're granted victory, I'll see you again in Lochawe."

"Aye. The Argyll has asked much of me. I pray 'tis not too much. Kenneth . . . lads, guard yer backs."

The youth gave him the reins to Judith's horse. Despite his bravado, it was easy to see he was frightened.

"Do not stay," Judith blurted, startling the boy and drawing a fierce glare from his father. "There's no need to risk your life!"

"God's mercy, my lady, for your kindness, but I'll not flee from a fight. Take care of the lass and bide your tongue, for Lochawe doesna gladly tolerate willful females."

"Heed yer tongue, woman," the laird snarled when she started to speak again, and gave a harsh tug on the reins so that her mount lurched forward.

Judith glanced back at the clearing as they rode away. Seven men circled the cauldron as if guarding something precious, and she saw with a start of surprise that the tail of Mairi's red plaide stuck out from beneath the pot. Then she understood; it was a clever ruse to lure the Caddels to fight over an empty cooking pot that hid nothing but dirt, twigs, and an empty plaide.

A ruse to gain time. A ruse that would slaughter the men left behind. The sheer calculated sacrifice took away her breath. She must be mistaken. No man would sacrifice his own sons for two hostages, not even for his overlord. Yet the old man did not waver in his path. They skirted the ragged banks of a deep loch, moving swiftly now, climbing into the foothills with the loch a shimmering jewel below.

A cold chill shivered down her spine when she heard the unmistakable sounds of battle joined; across the water came the harsh clang of sword meeting sword, the shouts and screams of men and horses. The clear waters of the deep loch carried sound as if it was a yard instead of a mile away, and Judith glanced toward the laird.

He rode a horse's length ahead of her, his back stiff and straight. But she heard him mutter what sounded very much like a prayer.

Chapter 3

✟

ᴴURTING LIKE THE very devil, Rob climbed the circular steps to the tower again. It had been over a week since his father and brothers had gone, and this was the first day he'd been lucid enough to leave his bed.

A fever, Fergal had said, that should have killed him quickly. Yet it had not. It had merely left him tossing and turning in fevered delirium for near a sennight.

He reached the top of the stairs and limped to the parapet. With hands clenched atop harsh stone, he watched the horizon beyond the undulating green of firs and marsh below. A brisk wind rife with peat smoke and desolation snapped the edges of wool plaide slung carelessly around his shoulders. Nothing moved but birds wheeling beneath dreary clouds. There was no sign of approaching riders.

He swore softly under his breath. Damned fools . . . his father especially. Argyll wasn't worth risking life and liberty for, not in this manner. He knew that well enough, by God. Aye, and a damn fool *he* had been for ever thinking a man's honor was armor enough against treachery.

One hand curled into a fist, the edge of his palm resting against stone as cold and gray as his mood. He should have stopped them. Or been with them. Curse his father for feckless pride, and curse Argyll for demanding honor when he had none of his own. Crafty devil. He knew his man well, knew the Campbell of Lochawe would not refuse him.

Just as Rob knew well enough that it was not only honor that made Angus Campbell heed the earl's demands. It was tradition. Campbell chiefs had always sworn fierce loyalty to their overlords. His father was not the man to spit in the eye of tradition. He was laird, and he would do as the lairds of Lochawe before him had done.

It was tradition.

Rob swore softly. The wind was keener now, wailing like a demon around towers, pushing black hair from his eyes only to capriciously whip it back into his face. He raked an impatient hand through his hair, narrowed his eyes on the spires of pine and fir in the distance, as if by sheer will alone he could summon his family home.

Once they were safely back, he would go to Kenneth and speak his mind. As the eldest, Kenneth had been reared to accept the responsibility and honor due the leader of this Campbell clan. It was his due. It was Kenneth who would continue the tradition. Or have the courage to break custom and do what was right instead of what was expected. Kenneth was no fool. And more, he knew Argyll for what he was.

This site had been held by Campbells for longer than anyone could recall, save perhaps the bards of long ago. Tales were told round the fires at night of the first Campbells to come to Lochawe, following the first Argyll, though he'd not been known by that name in those ancient times. These lands had been wrested from the Mac-Gregors at great cost in lives. Feuds still simmered beneath a thin veneer of cooperation against the English. Raids on sheep and cattle were common, deaths more so.

Rob had cut his milk teeth on those old tales, heard time and again of how the firstborn Campbell was always given the hilt of a sword to suckle, as were all males born to the clan. But it had been Kenneth who was given the laird's sword hilt to pacify his infant cries. It was an honor and a burden that Rob did not envy him. He preferred his own path, and he had done well enough, despite Lochawe's prophecy of doom.

"Monkish," his father had once called Rob, an intended slur that hadn't gone unnoticed for all that he'd ignored it at the time. Eight sons, and Rob was the only one to pursue studies Lochawe considered an unnecessary waste of time, his schooling cut short through no fault of his own. A dream, to study at a Glasgow university, a dream rendered impossible by the war between England and Scotland. He'd stayed home to fight.

And spent three years in an English prison for it. Hard years, when he'd thought each day would be his last, that he would follow so many who had gone before him to the scaffold or block. If not for James Douglas, he might be there still.

Betrayed by Argyll, redeemed by the Black Douglas.

Home now, and his father still unaware of the reason his son had spent years in an English prison. That was a private matter, to be settled with Argyll himself when the time came. And the time would come.

Restless, angry, and uneasy by turns, Rob glanced again over the walls. He paced the narrow space in a halting gait. Too much time had passed. If all had gone as Angus planned, they had more than enough time to return. This delay boded ill, an omen he misliked.

"Will ye be going after them, lad?"

The question snared Rob's attention, and he paused, turned toward the stairwell.

Fergal stood on the top step; his gaunt face was sharp as an ax blade, his cheekbones stark, black eyes deep-set and penetrating. Wind whipped at his tattered blue and green wool plaide, ruffled his gray beard. He stepped forward to lean against the weather-gnawed stone and squint into the verdant distance. The familiar shade of a half-blind old hound trailed behind, nose snuffling a wet path to find Rob.

"There may be no need for it," Fergal said before Rob could reply. He lifted a bony hand to point. "Riders."

Rob wheeled around to look, cursing at the sharp pain his sudden motion summoned. Leaning forward, his body tensed with expectation at the blur of motion glimpsed among dense firs. Then he saw them, two horses, one heavily burdened, approaching on a thin track that ran through woods beyond the marsh. There was a brief flash of color beneath whitened bare branches that shifted like dry bones in the wind, then they vanished into a copse. He waited, but no other horses followed. Behind him, he heard Fergal's sharply inhaled breath.

"Only two horses," Fergal muttered heavily.

"The others will follow."

Fergal didn't reply, but his silence was eloquent. He trailed behind Rob on the tightly winding stone steps that led down to the great hall, a slow progression of two men and an old hound. Musty rushes squelched beneath his boots when Rob reached the hall, and melancholy seemed to hang from the blackened timbers of the high ceiling. The fire was nearly out, only a few sullen coals glowing like red eyes among gray ash.

Rob paused, his scowl earning the attention of one of the servants who lounged on a long bench. With a guilty expression, he sat up straight and nudged his companion, who turned and saw Rob and did the same. Both men lurched to their feet, mumbled excuses that Rob didn't bother to acknowledge, and began to tend their tasks with an alacrity that was as unusual as it was unbelievable. Chaff hazed the air as dirty rushes were swept to one side of the hall.

Fergal glowered fiercely. "I leave for a brief time and they lie down like sheep. Curse them. They'll move lively enough now tha' the laird ha' come back."

The bailey was near empty, mud sucking at Rob's boots as he limped to the closed gate. Gears creaked, strained, chains rattling and cogged wheels slowly churning, almost drowning out his father's demand: "A Campbell!"

Working the thick oak levers, his muscles straining, Rob opened the heavy doors. They swung wide, and almost immediately, the Campbell clattered across wooden planks, tugging a horse behind him. The rider of the second beast was fair-haired, with a Campbell plaide slung around slender shoulders, but it wasn't Diarmid or Duncan who held the small heiress in tight arms. It was a woman.

Rob gave her only a cursory glance before turning his attention to his father. Bareheaded, Angus Campbell reined his weary, lathered horse to a halt and dismounted. His shoulders were slumped, his head bent. Tangled red hair clung to the nape of his neck, and his hands shook slightly. Angus didn't meet Rob's eyes but turned to Fergal. His jaw was set, his eyes shuttered beneath the shelf of thick brow, his voice gruff when he spoke to his old gillie.

"Fergal, take the woman and child to the topmost tower. Guard them well."

"There be only the two o' them, hey."

It was said heavily, and after a moment, the laird's head

jerked an acknowledgement. "Aye. Only the two of them."

Rob lurched forward, unable to hold his tongue a moment longer. "And the others? What of your sons?"

Without looking at him, Angus replied tersely, "They gave me time to escape with the hostages."

"They follow you, then."

Silence was the reply. The tightness in his chest clutched more deeply, left him breathless so that he could not utter another sound. His throat ached with the effort. His tongue would not form the questions that his mind screamed, even the hope they were being held for ransom.

Rob sucked in a sharp breath that tasted of mist and mud and despair. His gaze shifted to the woman who held the little heiress. She stared back at him with something like pity gleaming in soft, green eyes, shattering any hope and effectively loosening his tongue.

"Curse you for an old fool," he said softly to his father and saw him stiffen angrily. "You've killed them all with your damned pride and greed. Is the life of this bairn worth that of any one of my brothers? Is Argyll's arrogance worth Diarmid and Duncan? Damn you."

"Guard yer tongue," Angus finally growled. "I did what had to be done—as did yer brothers. If ye were man enough, ye'd have come with us, not stayed behind like a cowardly dog!"

Fergal's head lifted and he started to speak, but Rob put up a swift hand to stop him, bitter grief nearly choking him as he said, "Aye, think what you will. Your judgment is no longer important to me."

"It never was." Angus looked down at his bare hands, studied old calluses on the hills of his palms for a long moment. "Would to God it had been ye who—"

He stopped, his intent plain, and Rob finished for him, "Died rather than them. Aye, we agree on that one point."

"If ye had gone with us, it might not have ended like this!" Angus looked up to say fiercely.

"Yea, you're right about that, for I would never have let you sacrifice my brothers just to indulge Argyll like a preening cockerel!"

Angus lashed out a balled fist, all his weight behind the blow. Rob managed to duck, stumbling to one side so clumsily that a sharp pain nearly sent him to his knees. The momentum of his swing sent Angus sliding in the muck of the bailey, and he was unable to catch himself, crashing heavily to the ground.

When Fergal offered a hand, Angus knocked it aside. On his knees, he spread his muddy hands on splayed thighs, not looking up at his son. A tremor of shock skittered down Rob's spine at the sight of his father brought to his knees. Helpless, anguished, he could not bring himself to move.

Emotion clogged Rob's throat, anger and misery such a tight knot he didn't try to speak. It fell quiet in the bailey; the gillies and hostages seemed frozen in place. Even the horses made no sound but stood as still as if carved in stone.

Rob watched his father's bowed head bend lower, saw the broad shoulders shake. Horror trammeled his soul. The laird never wept, never betrayed weakness. Not in front of servant and hostage—not like this, Sweet Mary, Mother of God—not like this!

Slowly, Rob sank to his knees in the mud and muck, so close to Angus he could feel the heat of his breath. No words came to him. He had no comfort to offer. Rage, grief, and helpless frustration scoured him, held him captive so that he could do no more than crouch silently.

Angus looked up. Unshed tears washed his blue eyes, red-rimmed with suppressed grief, and his lips trembled on words that seemed to come without volition, tumbling over one another, a whisper of Gaelic and pain.

"There was naught I could do to help them, Robbie. God's heart, there were too many Caddels. We saw them coming around the bend, knew they would be upon us before we could escape. . . . I did what had to be done, but I could hear it behind me, hear it across the loch, the shouts and swords and my dyin' sons—*my sons!* Ah Mary, Mother of God, ye're right when ye say I killed them. . . ."

His whisper trailed into a choking sound like a sob, and Angus put a broad hand over his face. Rob stared at the pale reddish hairs on the back of his father's hand, the tiny brown freckles dotting strong sinews and bones: a hand he knew so well could wield a lethal sword, discipline an unruly son, lie gently on the head of a wee bairn. He tried to summon forgiveness, to find words of comfort, yet found only a black, vicious ache that held him in a vise.

The heavy oppression took on ominous form, weighed down on the bailey in a dark cloud that obscured everything from his vision. Rob tried to focus, but his father blurred into a vague outline. Residual weakness from his fever swamped him, and he fought it.

Soft words barely penetrated the haze that threatened to swallow him, but he slowly became aware of a husky voice that was rich and full, seeping into him and bringing him back from the void. Gaelic words in an unmistakable English accent drifted to him from above, and he looked up.

". . . They chose their own path," the hostage was saying. "If they died, 'twas for their own decision, not one man's pride."

Rob's gaze sharpened. She was still mounted, sitting erect upon the shaggy Highland pony, holding the red-haired child against her breast. The gaze that met his was direct and honest, wide green eyes that didn't flinch away. Unexpected composure and compassion from a woman who had been brutally torn from her family. . . . He looked at her more closely. Weariness etched around her eyes, and one foot dangling at the side of the pony was bare, stockings torn and dirty. Yet despite disheveled hair clubbed into a loose knot on the nape of her neck and smears of dirt on one cheek, he could see that she was bonny. Her hair was the soft color of corn silk, tumbling over finely arched eyebrows, and her lips were generous beneath a patrician nose. An elegant face.

He was on his feet without recalling the impulse to stand, staring at her. The little girl in her arms peeped out from a fold of plaide, face muffled by the protective embrace. A mop of red curls cascaded into childish blue eyes that regarded him with terror. It took him back.

Rarely in his life had a child viewed him as a threat. Not even against the English had he ever been craven enough to harm a child. Yet this wee lass stared at him with round eyes filled with fear and apprehension, and he was suddenly, bitterly, ashamed.

His gaze shifted to the woman again, but instead of condemnation he saw wary expectation. It was as unnerving as the child's fear. What did she expect of him? She was a hostage now, as well as the child. There was naught he could do for her, not now. Not ever.

Abruptly, he turned away from them, from the hostages and his father and the searing knowledge that he had failed to protect those he loved and that he could not protect two helpless females. There was nothing he could do or would do now, for the die had been cast. Argyll had won again.

With a limping gait, Rob moved across the ruts and muck in a silent retreat to the keep. Only the old brindle hound had the courage to follow.

✝

SILENCE CLOSED UPON the grim tableau in the bailey when he disappeared within the high gray walls. An air of gloom settled like a shroud over the muck and mud and immobile figures. The wind sighed, a moaning current that tugged at horses' manes and wool plaides. Judith clutched Mairi to her more tightly. The child's small fists were tangled in the folds of plaide wound about their bodies, and while she made no sound of protest, the whisper of Mairi's shallow breathing feathered over Judith's neck like a plea for safety.

For a moment, she'd had hope they would be safe here, that the laird's son would offer reassurance. She'd seen in his eyes the pain he felt, heard his bitter condemnation.

Yet that hope was now banished, and the full import of their situation was upon her, for she knew where they were: the infamous home to the Campbells of Lochawe, that wild, unruly clan fiercely loyal to Argyll.

The man who'd brought them here must be Sir Angus, the Red Devil by name and reputation, and the man he called Robbie could only be the Robert Campbell of local legend: the Devil's Cub, he'd been called, laird of Glenlyon and a man knighted on the battlefield. A shiver tracked her spine. They had fallen into the lion's lair, it seemed, and a more forbidding place she could not imagine.

It was a dour keep, a fortress built on a promontory thrusting into the very waters of Loch Awe, crouched as if poised to dive beneath the headwaters that scrubbed past the craggy shoulders of Ben Cruachan and the Pass of Brander. A peel tower soared high and stark toward the sky, rising in four levels of solid stone, a formidable

spear jabbing at clouds scudding past. Gaunt windows
pierced the stone like sullen eyes brooding down on stout
barnekin walls. A smaller tower stood to one side, and a
massive gate yawned open. The keep stood at the end of
a straight, dun road sweeping over clear marshland for
nearly a mile. Any riders could be seen quickly from cren-
ellated parapets atop the peel tower.

Numb now with exhaustion, fear, and futility, she
watched the laird struggle to his feet and turn to his gillie,
a man with a sharp face and deep eyes. A potent look
passed between them, but the laird spoke calmly.

"Fergal, take them to the topmost tower. Send word to
Argyll that the task is done . . . at great cost."

The last few words were hoarse, almost a whisper like
a rusty hinge, grating and empty. Judith closed her eyes
against such anguish, let herself feel sympathy for the
torment of his loss. She thought of the lad, Diarmid, who
had been so full of life, so confident and triumphant, and
she offered a prayer for all of their souls.

Then she offered a prayer for little Mairi, whose fate
was in the hands of this man. A shudder traced her spine,
and she closed her arms protectively around the child.
There must be a way to free both of them before they
were taken to Argyll.

Chapter 4

✝

A WOOD FIRE burned in the center of the hall. Rob gazed into leaping orange and gold tongues of flame that licked at bleak shadows scouring high walls. The hall was near empty. Tables were against the walls, benches scattered. The stench of old food fouled the rushes, and lamps of fish oil reeked. He barely noticed. A dram of whisky filled one hand, his fifth in as many minutes. It didn't ease the ache inside him, did nothing to fill the cold emptiness that gnawed his belly.

Barren days, eroded nights had passed in the week since they had retrieved the bodies . . . a grim task. Women weeping and wailing when they returned with carts laden with the weight of the dead. Ah God . . . grim indeed. Just as grim as the funerals. He closed his eyes against the unbidden vision that he could not banish with whisky or sleep.

The first cortege, solemn and swelled with widows and children of the slain, then the mournful tolling of the deid

bell, the eerie wailing of the pipes in the dead dirge, the
bell pennies, the men walking to the graveyard, and the
deid dole handed out to beggars to pray for the souls of
those slain . . . familiar rituals, haunting and sorrowful.

In the fire, a charred log popped, collapsed, sending up
a shower of sparks like tiny glowing stars soaring to the
rafters. Rob's gaze riveted on the fire, yet he saw not
flames but strong, laughing young men—now entombed
in stone for an eternity, leaving behind those who loved
them. But he still saw them in a trick of light among
shadows that made him turn to seek Diarmid or Duncan,
or heard them in a burst of laughter that lifted his head,
expecting to see Kenneth.

His hand tightened on the whisky. His eyes and throat
burned with grief. Death was not uncommon, yet never
had he dreamed it would take them all at one time, leaving
the keep in a ghostly pall, servants treading softly as if
afraid to wake the dead. Or afraid of attracting attention.

It was not just Lochawe they avoided. Rob had seen
glances in his direction, from the corners of their eyes as
if expecting him to rage or bellow. He could have told
them they were safe; he felt nothing save grief. He was
cold, empty inside as if he had died along with his brothers.

A soft whine snared his attention, and his hand moved
to caress soft ears on the old hound, a constant companion
at his side. His hunting days were gone, the pace too fast
and painful for old bones, but courage and will still
burned in Caesar's heart. Only his body failed him. More
time was spent by the warm fire than in the field now,
while younger dogs gave chase to fleet-footed deer and
ferocious boars.

If Caesar's place was by the fire, so was his, of late. A
frown settled between Rob's brows at the thought.

Turning the cup in his hand, he watched the tawny liquid slosh against the sides, aromatic and potent. A balm to ease his days, obliterate his nights. A temporary remedy. He knew better than anyone that he must face the empty days soon enough. Life went on for those still dwelling inside Lochawe.

As life went on at Glenlyon, left in the dead of night upon receiving his father's summons, riding injured over crags and heaths to stop Lochawe from disaster. A futile act that had near killed him as well. And now he must return to Glenlyon with the sorrow of his failure heavy on him.

Glenlyon: reward won on the battlefield at Sutton Bank where the great seal of England had been abandoned by King Edward II, where English knights taken by surprise fled like hares before the greyhounds, leaving the Earl of Richmond and Sir Henry de Sully, grand butler of France, in the hands of the Scots. Sweet triumph, wrested for Bruce by his own Highlanders.

And Bruce, generous in victory, bestowed upon him the lands of Glenlyon for his service. Laird of Glenlyon—a lengthy vale, but so narrow in places that the mouth of the glen where the river tumbled over a small waterfall was only twenty feet wide. It was home now, his by right of might, though he had spent little time there. Three years in an English prison, hostage to his own foolishness. He knew well the plight of hostages.

His thoughts drifted to the heiress and the woman. He'd not seen either of them since the day they were brought to the keep. Argyll had sent word to hold them until it pleased him to retrieve them. Curse him. It had been a careless acknowledgement of an abduction that had cost Angus Campbell so much . . . so much, and Argyll had not the decency to remove the cause of all their sorrow.

The child would be wed to Argyll's son, sealing the ties to Caddel lands, but she was only five. It would be years before she would marry. For now, she would remain here with her nurse. Ah, the nurse, the widow of Kenneth Lindsay.

The widow, Fergal reported, had fought like ten wolves to keep her charge safe, and so they had brought her with them. It was easier and calmed the child, an argument he was willing to wager his brothers had made, not a point Angus would normally consider. Yet it made sense. This one hostage could be bartered, perhaps, for Clan Caddel concessions. A letter had been composed to begin the ne-gotiations. Soon, the woman would be ransomed by her kin.

Auld Maggie had sworn she'd seen her walking wid-dershins in the tower chamber, taking a leftwise path op-posite the journey of the sun—a sign of evil. It was the way of those who dealt in black magic, Auld Maggie in-sisted.

Fergal snorted derisively at the suggestion, insisting that the widow was too fair to be a witch. There had been a lively argument between Maggie and Fergal, with Rob a weary spectator. The two of them scrapped like dogs over a bone most of the time, bickering about trivial events nearly as much as they did the more serious matters like witches.

Stretching his long legs toward the fading fire, Rob watched the flames through narrowed eyes. Witch or not, the woman provoked an odd mix of emotions in him, an aversion and fascination. He recalled too well the elegant turn of her head and those gleaming green eyes like a cat's that had regarded him with what he'd recognized as hope. Or perhaps accusation.

Another sip of whisky burned down his throat into his belly. He regarded the cup with a bitter twist of his mouth.

I should have been with them. . . .

The familiar refrain exploded inside his head with all

the force of crashing thunder. He flinched from it. It would have made little difference if he'd been with them, only one more death.

He knew it. Fergal knew it. Only Angus Campbell refused to believe it. The auld laird was like a wounded bull since his return, snarling and bellowing at any unfortunate who crossed his path. Accusation hung in the air when he looked at Rob. He hadn't said it aloud again, but it was in every glance, every movement.

Glenlyon should have been with them.

Even though logic and Fergal reassured him that he would have only died with his brothers, Rob could not help but agree with his father. He should have been there.

Pain pounded in his skull, a steady throb that never seemed to ease. Not even whisky relieved it.

"D'ye intend to drink yerself into oblivion again?"

Rob looked up with a rude reply on his lips, but it died in the face of Fergal's pained regard.

"Aye, if I can," he retorted and lifted the cup. "*Slainte.*" He drained it and looked back at the fire.

"Health, is it naow. No' good health, I warrant. 'Tis no' like ye—ye've never been a drunkard."

"Perhaps I've become one now."

"I've always thought drunkards were cowards afraid tae face life. Is that wha' ye've become?"

Rob's hand tightened on the empty cup. "That seems to be the general opinion now."

"I've heard no one say it."

"There's wisdom in knowing when to keep your mouth shut." He waggled his empty cup in an ironic salute. "Only Lochawe dares make his judgment plain."

Fergal fell silent. His gaunt face closed. When he spoke, his tone was even.

"A messenger from the village brought word from Clan

Caddel. There's to be no ransom o' the widow unless the bairn goes wi' her."

"I'm not surprised. What did my father think? That they would welcome negotiations?" Rob set down his cup. "I find it amazing we haven't yet been attacked and sacked."

A shrug lifted Fergal's shoulders. "The Argyll wa' granted authority by the king to arrange a marriage for the wee heiress. 'Tis his right, and a certainty Clan Caddel knows tha' well enough."

"Even more certain that Argyll covets Caddel lands more than he does the hand of the little heiress."

" 'Tis the way of the world, lad, but tha' is not why I ha' come to ye. Ye're to talk to the Sassenach and learn wha' will earn her ransom from Clan Caddel."

"Am I." His brow slanted upward. "I prefer that you do it, Fergal."

"It's no' my place. As the next laird of Lochawe, 'tis yer task."

Rob stiffened. *The next laird . . .*

"It is not required that I be laird after my father," he said and rose to his feet in an impatient surge. "I am laird of Glenlyon. He will name whomever he chooses when the time comes. Kenneth left sons behind."

"Nay, lad," Fergal said when he turned away, " 'tis you he will name to succeed him here. Ye must know tha'."

Rob turned back to glare at him. "I don't want Lochawe. You know that!"

"Aye, ye ha' made it clear enough, but it doesna change yer duty. Ye are the only living son now of the Campbell of Lochawe, and 'tis yer duty to do wha' must be done. Lives depend upon ye, lad."

It was the phrase he dreaded most; *lives depend upon ye* had been used like an ax on him before. It was what had sent him to fight against the English, to perpetrate death and destruction—to become someone else. He knew what he became when there was a fight, didn't recognize that part of him that rose up to extinguish civility and humanity. It was as if he became another man.

"I'll talk to her," he said abruptly and bade Caesar stay as the dog struggled to his feet to follow. He turned toward the circular stairs that led up to the north tower. "But I doubt she will yield up the information you seek. It's been my experience that most females never recognize imminent danger until it's too late."

"Remember, Auld Maggie claims she's a witch."

"If that is meant as a warning, save it for the more credulous. I've yet to meet a woman who does not have some sort of power of enchantment over a man, whether it be by persuasion, trickery, or beauty."

He heard Fergal's derisive snort behind him and ignored it, climbing the curving stone steps two at a time. Lamps set in niches lit the circular staircase, flickering light dancing with shadows. He was in no mood for this. It was too soon, the woman a harsh reminder of why his brothers were dead. It wasn't just, but he cursed both woman and child for their very existence.

Three flights up, the heavy oaken door to the tower room loomed at the end of a long corridor. A single torch tilted outward from a cresset holder, shedding sparks. The key hung on a peg outside the door, and Rob took it down with a jerk. It fit easily inside the huge lock, tumblers turning with a metallic grind as he unlocked the door and shoved it open with an impatient push.

The tower room was small, circular, with only the bare necessities of comfort: a narrow cot half hidden by a frayed tapestry on one wall, a small table and stool, a privy close in an alcove. Cut into a recess, the only window was an arrow loop that looked onto the bailey below, a restricted view.

Despite the frugality of furnishings or perhaps because

of it, the room was tidy. A sparse fire burned on a charred hearth, the peat smoking so that an acrid pall hung in the air. The widow stood before a polished steel shield mounted on the wall, brushing her hair as if before a mirror of the finest quality. She was garbed in garments of English style, not the léine and brèid most Scottish women wore; this gown fit her form closely, green wool smoothed from breast to hip over an undertunic, torn in places and dirty, but obviously of good quality.

At the intrusion, she turned toward the door and regarded him silently. Had she expected him? There was no sign of surprise on her face, only a wary anticipation.

Loose hair settled around her shoulders in a glossy cape that made her look younger than he recalled, softer, but the green eyes were the same, watchful as a cat's.

A perverse urge to elicit a reaction other than this calm wariness prompted him to slam the door closed with a deliberate violence. It shuddered loudly, a thunderous bang that echoed in the tower room.

"You'll wake the child, sir."

Her response was not what he wanted from her, from this woman who had inadvertently caused the deaths of so many, and he leaned back against the door. A glance at the small cot tucked into the shadows of heavy tapestry revealed the sleeping child, copper hair rioting over the mattress, but she gave no sign of waking. He cocked a brow in disbelief.

"She sleeps soundly enough." When there was no reply, he pushed away from the door, took a step closer, and saw the woman's nostrils flare as if a wild doe scenting danger. Her knuckles whitened on the handle of the hairbrush she still held like a weapon in front of her.

At last. An honest reaction. He smiled.

"I've come to persuade you to write a letter to your Caddel kinsmen to ransom you."

For a moment she just stared at him, wide eyes dark with something he didn't recognize, then her lips curved in the suggestion of a smile.

"That is impossible."

"It would be to your advantage," he snarled, any claim to patience he still possessed evaporating in the face of her refusal. "Are you so foolish as to think we welcome your presence here?"

"Are *you* so foolish as to think they would expend one gold coin to claim an unwanted possession? That is what I am, you know, a stranger in that household, unwanted since my husband's death, an enemy in an alien land. Surely, you know who I am?"

"Lady Lindsay, widow to Kenneth Lindsay, the nephew of Iain Caddel."

"Yea, and with my husband's death, my value died as well. My father would not yield so much as a hide of land for my return, so I became a stone around their necks. Only little Mairi has required anything of me."

It was said calmly, without self-pity, a bald statement of facts. He frowned.

"Then your own family will be willing to ransom you."

"Perhaps. Perhaps not. A barren daughter brings little to the family coffers."

Now he detected a trace of bitterness, but it was quickly gone, her composure returned.

"Then you will write a letter to your father," he said irritably, "pleading to be ransomed."

"I will not plead." She paused, then added softly, "I refuse to humble myself."

"Stubborn pride may find you left to uncertain mercy, my defiant lady."

"I was left to that long before your men came to snatch us away, sir. Do not deceive yourself that my father will

be swayed by threats or pleas. He is not a man to yield
to such paltry tactics."

"Nor, it seems, is his daughter." Rob regarded her with
a new perspective. This was not a woman who would be
easily intimidated.

"Fate has left me with few options, sir. I do what must
be done."

"Then you will write the letter."

After a brief pause, she said quietly, "No."

"No?" He moved closer, using his size and anger as a
weapon. "You are in no position to defy me."

The hairbrush she still clutched in her hand quivered
slightly, but her gaze did not waver. "Yet I must, sir."

"You would risk your liberty for a whim?"

" 'Tis no whim." She inhaled sharply when he moved
so close that there was only a handbreadth between them,
but she did not retreat. "I will not leave Mairi."

"Mairi?—The bairn. Do you think we mean her harm?"

"Oh no, 'tis certain you mean her only peace and good-
will. Why else would you have torn her from her home
so rudely?"

He scowled. "Your mockery is insulting."

"Your stupidity is more so."

"Stupidity!"

"Yea, do you think I am so inhuman as to leave a child
to men such as you, who want only to use her as a piece
of goods, like no more than a bolt of cloth to be haggled
over? No, I will not leave her in your careless custody
with no one to watch over her!"

Tightly, he said, "She is safe enough here."

"She was safe enough in Caddel Castle, yet here we
are. Your own brothers were not kept safe. Why then
should I have any reason to think a child who means
nothing to you would be cared for any better?"

The sheer scope of her reminder stunned him. Worse,

he could not deny the truth in it. The air between them quaked with tension.

"Milady treads on dangerous ground," he said at last.

"I am accustomed to navigating quicksand, sir. I'm just not foolish enough to build a house upon it."

"Your meaning escapes me."

"I know better than to trust in promises. Men's oaths are made only to be broken, honor tarnished and lies mended. You have given me no reason to trust your word."

"I have not lied to you."

"That is only one more lie."

Anger fueled by whisky and her defiance scoured him. "Name me the first lie I told."

"When you said Mairi is safe here. She is not. It is not safety to be held prisoner."

"That is beyond your control, or even mine. She is here and will stay. Your fate, however, is undecided."

"I am all Mairi knows in this dismal keep. She is only a child. I will do what I must to stay with her."

"Will you?"

"Yes." Her head tilted back, lips pressed rebelliously tight. "I will not write that letter."

It was time to point out the precariousness of her situation, that she was in no position to refuse him.

"You have said only what you will *not* do. That does not say what you *will* do to stay with the child."

He meant it as a mocking illumination of circumstances, but to his astonishment, she took him seriously.

"I will do anything else that is required of me."

"Anything?" *Christ above!* His brow rose. Foolish lady, to present him with such a challenge. He smiled. "That could be interpreted to mean a broad range of deeds, Lady Lindsay."

"Interpret it as you wish."

His smile faded. He stared at her. A faint fragrance emanated from her, teasing him with elusive memory. He was so close he could see striations in the pupils of her eyes, the gold flecks gilding deep green. Riveted by her gaze, he found himself reaching for her, his hand closing in a skein of hair softer than he'd imagined it. His fingers curled into a fist and let the feathery strands slide across his palm slowly, pale ribbons trickling free to lie upon her breast.

Silent, she stared up at him, only the small pulse that beat a rapid tattoo in her throat evidence of reaction. Pallid, brittle light streamed through the arrow loop to play upon her face, glinting along the high, sweet curve of her cheekbones. She was bonny, this fair lady from Caddel Castle, bonny and foolish indeed.

When he put his hands upon her shoulders, his fingers digging into slender bone and muscle, she murmured a protest that he swiftly overrode.

"Sir—"

"Ah no, you swore compliance, sweet lady. It is only my duty to test you."

He closed his hand along the curve of her jaw, holding her still. His head bent, and he brushed his mouth over her lips, felt them tremble. It sparked an unexpected heat in him, just the taste of her a teasing lure to unanticipated bounty, her fragrance a subtle, delicious temptation.

Heather, sweet and spicy . . . she smells like the spring meadows.

She quivered beneath his touch, a faint tremor that was a betrayal. Loosening his grip on her chin, he skimmed the backs of his fingers down the curve of her throat, pausing on the dip between her collarbones. The pulse beat fluttered, a frantic thrum like the wings of a trapped bird. There was a seductive vulnerability in the way she

closed her eyes and leaned away that prompted him to
test the limits.

Soft female curves fit snugly against him when he drew
her close. Her fists were still held against her chest, the
hairbrush an uncomfortable intrusion that he gently removed and tossed aside.

Closing one hand in the wealth of hair at the nape of
her neck, he slowly drew her head back so that her face
was tilted up to his, his other arm curved behind her to
hold her tightly. In blind obedience, long brown lashes
lay on her cheeks in soft shadows, her lips parted slightly,
moist from the drag of her tongue over them, and his
hunger grew sharp and urgent. It coiled in his belly,
moved lower, an aching fullness that startled and unsettled
him.

Curse her for her folly. He should halt now, before he
took this further than he'd first meant. He should . . . yea,
he should, but the weeks—nay months—of empty nights
stretched his resolve to its limits, his self-imposed absti-
nence an evil reminder now, with temptation so soft and
sweet in his arms. Whisky urged persistence, reason bade
him resist.

"Open your eyes," he said then, and she complied.
Brown lashes still veiled her eyes, her gaze averted so
that he had to tilt her face even more. "Look at me, milady."

When she did, he recognized the hazy uncertainty and
confusion in her eyes and regretted his insistence. The
irresolution in her gaze only inflamed his need, whispered
to him of compliance if he would but persist. He kissed
her, this time a lingering kiss that left no doubt of his
intentions. His mouth moved over hers with insistent pressure until her lips parted for his tongue. She tasted of
something sweet, a honeyed comfit, perhaps, or sweet
wine that was heady and potent, a powerful snare to a

man long starved. It took all his resolve not to toss her skirts and thrust himself inside her without preliminaries.

She was limply acquiescent in his arms, her hands still folded between them like pale doves, clasped in an attitude of prayer that was unnerving. This had become a test of his own fortitude more than hers, it seemed. She made no protest nor resistance but no response, either. Frustration roiled in his belly, until at last he found the control he sought.

He set her back from him, his tone cooler than he felt. "You are not keeping your word. I expect participation, not just compliance."

She met his eyes calmly, a limpid gaze. "I offered you compliance, but you cannot command emotions I do not feel."

"Do you think I want vows of love, or even your regard, milady? You are much mistaken." Her eyes widened slightly, a startled green beneath her lashes, and his mouth curled into a smile. "I expect more enthusiasm from a woman who barters her body for favors. Disrobe, my lady, if it is your intent to purchase my sanction of your freedom."

A last chance, an insult designed to prove how reckless she had been; no woman should allow such an offer, and not a woman of gentle birth, certainly. He waited for her retreat, an admission of fraudulent purpose to wring concessions from him, a confession that she had no intention of pursuing or allowing intimacy. He was rarely wrong about a woman, and this lady was no common harlot.

Lady Lindsay stood still for a moment, shock written on her fine features. Light through the arrow loop shifted, caught in her hair, a hazy glow. She looked like the church's depictions of the Madonna, with hands still clasped upon her breast, a halo of light above her head, the perfect symmetry of her face—until he recognized the unholy light that sprang into her eyes, the almost feral gleam. For an instant, he thought he'd erred in his evaluation of the lady and the circumstance.

Then she tossed back her head, the glossy spill of her hair sliding over one shoulder as she stepped away from him. This was the expected reaction, this retreat from an offer she had obviously made out of desperation. He accepted it, though his body still throbbed with aroused need. Jesu, but he was glad of the long tunic over his trews.

But then the lady's hands moved to the laces of her bliaut, fingers tugging at the fine linen while her gaze held his in cool contempt. A faint, elusive smile touched the corners of her mouth, a mysterious curve that betrayed them both.

Heat swamped him, renewed reaction a rapid surge to his groin, an inevitable response to her silent suggestion. He stood with narrowed eyes and clenched jaw, his body raw and throbbing as she untied her laces.

The cloth fell away, pale drifts against skin of creamy white, a shadowed cleft separating twin globes barely visible beneath the linen garment. Rents in her green kirtle rendered it nearly unwearable, frayed threads barely holding it together over what had once been fine white linen of her bliaut. Gilt embroidery was unraveled, gold threads sparse on bodice and sleeves, reflecting light in tiny splinters.

A challenge answered, surrender hovered, yet not even the fierce urges of his body could ignore the contempt in those cool green eyes that swept over him.

"Is this what you desire, sir?"

Chapter 5

✝

WITH HER TREMBLING fingertips still grazing the untied laces, Judith waited for his reply, tensing as he stared at her with hot lights dancing in his eyes. Oh, pray God that she had not misjudged him!

It would not be the first time she had mistaken decency in a man, but that had been a long time ago, before she had years of bitter experience to her credit. Now she listened to that innate sense of recognition that warned her which man she could trust and which she could not.

Bars of light weaving through the narrow window fell across him. Black hair framed features that were a fusion of strength and softness. His strong, square jawline was a stubborn angle, his nose straight and sculpted. A jagged scar was palely visible in dark stubble along the left side of his jaw, a badge of some battle, no doubt. But his eyes held a hint of humanity, smoke colored beneath thick black lashes, sober and piercing. He looked both fierce and noble, a contradiction she dared not explore at the moment as she waited to see what he would do.

Time hovered, a breathless eternity, an agonized delay as Judith's lungs expanded with pent-up air and doubts flew at her like bats in the night. Should she continue and hope for a reprieve? Refuse to go on? Oh he looked so . . . so savage standing there, that dark slash of his brow crowding eyes gone cold and narrow, and there was no hint of what to do, no sign that he would not take what she had so recklessly offered to give. A monumental blunder.

Indeed, she recognized the evidence of a man's desire in him, in the quick flash of light that had sparked in his eyes, in the way his gaze clung to the skin exposed by her open bliaut. Tension vibrated in the tall, lean body that was as finely honed as a steel blade.

She had seen him in the bailey the day before, stripped to the waist and only in his trews, slashing viciously at a straw-filled sack with his sword. It had been an exercise of some sort, for he turned with precise motions, hampered some by his injured leg, but still oddly graceful. A dance of war, she'd thought then, as if he fought enemies only he could see. A warrior, beautiful and deadly.

Fully clad now, in trews and a belted linen shirt open at the throat, he seemed no less intimidating.

His eyes flickered, moved upward to her face, a probing gaze that held her captive and immobile.

"Do not shame yourself, woman," he said in a grating voice that seared her to the bone.

Relief made her knees weak. "Am I to understand that you do not require submission from me, sir?"

"Not that kind."

His gray eyes were like Scotch mist, she thought, just as fluid. They shifted from pale silver to nearly black, from light-tricked to midnight velvet. Now they were dark and thunderous beneath jet-black lashes.

Bowing her head, Judith clasped her hands in front of her piously, though she could not bring herself to pretend a humility she did not feel. It was risk enough to tempt this Highland laird and escape unscathed, and there was no sense in ruining it now.

"You do not deceive me, milady."

His soft voice brought her head up, and her stomach twisted into a knot at the harsh expression on his face.

"Pray, sir, explain what you mean."

"You know well enough what I mean. This—" He reached out to lift a dangling lace in his hand—"is only a ploy. You betrayed yourself with your eagerness to retreat. Do not seek to deceive me like some callow youth."

Her chin lifted defiantly. "Some men prefer deceit."

"I am not some men. I am Robert Campbell of Glenlyon, and I will not tolerate trickery. Cover yourself, before I decide to take what you only pretended to give."

Heat scalded her cheeks, but she did not delay in retying the laces, albeit a little clumsily. His gaze on her was keen, piercing, and she felt suddenly stripped to the bone, not so much of garments but of pretensions, and yea, even hopes. This man was not one who would be lightly played as a minstrel's lute.

"I have but few weapons left to me, sir," she said flatly to cover her embarrassment, "and if I must use female trickery, then I will do so."

"So I have seen."

"I much prefer honesty, but you did not listen to that."

"I listened. My answer was as honest as I could make it, and as plain. A letter, or your mark if you cannot write, is required of you. Ransom is all that will see you quit of Lochawe."

She smoothed the stained sleeves of her bliaut, then ran her hands down the sides of her kirtle. "And my answer was as plain as yours. I will not willingly leave Mairi. I will not write a letter, nor will I put my signature to any of your letters."

"An impasse."

She looked up to meet his eyes. "Yea, so it seems."

"What are your terms?"

Blinking, she stared at him, saw the corners of his mouth tuck slightly inward, as if repressing a smile.

"I have no terms."

"We are in negotiations, are we not? A truce, a temporary cease of hostilities in order to reach agreement. What are your terms?"

Anger formed a tight knot in her throat, and she said stiffly, "My terms are as before: Send Mairi with me back to Caddel Castle, and I will write a letter. I do not leave her here alone."

"You will change your mind soon enough." He cocked a dark brow at her. "Make no mistake on that."

He was gone as abruptly as he'd come, the slamming of the door reverberating in the cold tower room like an oath. The taste of peat smoke and apprehension stung the back of her throat, and Judith sought the table's edge for support.

Leaning on it, she took a deep breath. A narrow escape. What madness had prompted her to provoke him thusly? She found it difficult to decide if he was dangerous to her. A cipher, indeed, for he had seemed very dangerous the day of her arrival, his tone and mood savage. Today, he had seemed even more ruthless, save that he had not taken what she had offered.

In truth, it had not been so great a risk for her to take. If he meant to have her, nothing she said or did would stay him. She was a hostage with few rights, a woman alone in a foreign land, for all that she had spent nearly seven years in Scotland. It wasn't home. Not *her* home.

There were times she yearned for the sweet hills of

England, for her father's estate where she'd been born and spent her childhood with a sister and four brothers. Gillian gone now, married to a Welsh baron, and two brothers dead in the struggle between Robert Bruce and King Edward. The same war that had taken her brothers had given her father power, more lands, another title. It was during the brief truce signed in December 1319 that she had been wed to Kenneth Lindsay, a ploy engineered by barons to gain enemy lands, for her dower was a manor house and lands near York, her bride's gift a Scottish estate in the Marches.

There had been peace in Scotland since 1323, though the negotiations at York in 1324 had ended in the usual impasse, but there had been no resumption of hostilities. It was a peace Judith had hoped would see her returned to England since Kenneth's death. That, too, had been a disappointment. Her father flatly refused to give up even a hide of land to have his daughter returned, and so she had been locked in a no-man's-land between two countries, belonging to neither, an outsider and transient. Bitter truth, that she found herself wanted by none except the little heiress.

Judith glanced toward the cot where Mairi lay sleeping. Another child to be used as a pawn, to be bartered and haggled over like wool or hides, just as she had been. There was a sense of betrayal in being used thus by family.

There was nothing she could do to stop it, but if at all possible, she would ease Mairi's adjustment to what was certain to be a struggle between two powerful clans. The girl she had once been would have given anything to know the comfort of a loving touch in times of strife and uncertainty, and she meant to give what she could to Mairi. It wasn't the child's fault she'd been born into a world of chaos.

Moving to the narrow window, Judith crossed her arms over her chest and gazed down into the bailey below. Life here was much as it was in Caddel Castle, even England. All had tasks to tend, beasts to care for, duties to perform for laird as well as family.

It must be true that idle hands were the devil's tools, for with nothing to do save amuse little Mairi, Judith found herself plotting strategies that would see them well and away from Lochawe. It was a crude, mean keep with little comfort about it, only mud and gray clouds to recommend it that she'd seen, and the people were brutal.

The woman who brought their meals was sullen, with small, squinty eyes and a short temper, contempt written on a face as wrinkled as wet wool stockings. Yet beneath that contempt lay fear that at first Judith hadn't understood. It was only when she'd made a leftwise circle in her pacing and had seen the woman's swift sign of the cross over her sunken chest that she'd realized why she was regarded as if she was dangerous.

Superstition was everywhere, even in England, but in the people of Scotland she had seen conviction in the belief that lives were ruled—and ruined—by witches. It was a risk. Any association with witchcraft could see her in true danger, but it was also a form of protection. It kept the old woman at bay, her insults few now. She left food and drink and departed swiftly, the amulet around her wrist worn openly to ward off evil.

Staring out the window, Judith saw an instrument for negotiation at hand, if only she had the wit and courage to use it well.

Chapter 6

✝

ᴍURKY ʟɪɢʜᴛ ᴄᴀsᴛ fitful shadows in the great hall. Long trestle tables were set up for the evening meal, benches set around the scarred oaken tables for visiting tenants and the inhabitants of the keep. There was no ceremony here, not as in the great halls of noblemen and kings. Food was brought from the kitchens, a communal pot with trenchers set out for the diners to dish their own meal.

Angus sat nearest the fire, his back to it, shoulders hunched forward, his face set in an expression of guarded courtesy as the visitor to his right carried on a trivial discussion about hunting wild boar. It was almost painful to watch.

At the far end of the table, Rob stared at his still full wooden trencher of meat and boiled turnips. Not even oatcakes could tempt him. His appetite waned. Conversation flowed around him, an ebb and flow of mostly petty remarks that barely penetrated his apathy. Then a comment caught his attention, and his head came up, eyes narrowed slightly on the speaker.

"Now that the Red Earl is dead in Ulster, the king intends to put the English to flight in Ireland. With his father-in-law's death putting Ireland into chaos, the Bruce is taking advantage of the disorder." Sir David smacked his lips as if tasting a comfit and grinned. "Mark me, he means to roust Mandeville from Ireland."

Angus nodded agreement. "It seems likely. D'ye join the fight?"

"Not in Ireland." Sir David glanced at Rob. "Rumor has it that the queen and Mortimer have begun to mobilize an army, for all that the truce has been prolonged. If Queen Isabella has her way, every mercenary in Europe will fight under the regent's banner."

Sir David addressed his comments to Angus, but his gaze also included Rob. His voice had been lifted to carry down the length of the table, and other conversation stilled. Rob did not reply, jabbing at his meat with the point of his dirk as he studiously ignored them.

Yet he had grasped the meaning at once, as no doubt did all those there. Queen Isabella meant to flout the truce, her lover Roger Mortimer goading her on as they acted in the interests of the young king. While Bruce was officially acclaimed king of Scotland, they still tested his will to hold the country. They would find his mettle strong, Rob reflected, despite the years of warfare and the promise of lasting peace that dangled so enticingly.

"Argyll has cast his lot with the Earl of Ross," Sir David continued, "as have others of the Highlands. Will the Red Devil of Lochawe be among them?"

"I owe fealty to Argyll and honor to Bruce. I will do as I am bid." It was the expected reply, given readily.

Silence fell, thick with tension. Rob stared down at his trencher. Grease congealed around the mutton, and the

turnips were colorless and unappetizing. Trouble brewed
in the kitchens again, apparently. No decent cook would
serve such food to guests or even to the laird without
expecting a harsh rebuke. He'd have Fergal settle the
kitchen problem, since Angus obviously cared less than
usual.

Aware that his name was being repeated, he looked up
to see his father scowling at him fiercely, and Sir David
looking a little bemused.

"Sir David asks about Glenlyon," Angus said again, his
voice near a snarl. "Will ye fight?"

"Not with Argyll." Rob met his father's gaze steadily.
"If Black Douglas calls me, I will fight under his banner."

It was as near an insult without being direct that he
could make and keep the peace, and he saw that Sir David
understood immediately. The man's brow rose, his mouth
went thin, and he gave a short jerk of his chin in recognition of Glenlyon's reply.

Without waiting for more discussion, Rob rose from the
table and gave a polite excuse for leaving.

A chill wind greeted him outside the hall, the bailey
fair quiet for the night. The usual sentries manned their
posts on the barnekin walls, horses in the roofed stables
stomped hooves, and chickens clucked sleepily. Sir David's train was camped on solid ground beyond the marsh,
save for a few men inside. He traveled heavily for a man
supposedly on an idle journey to visit old friends.

Rob suspected he'd been sent to ferret out information,
to learn who would fight on what side. Not all Scots were
loyal to the Bruce. Some still held close ties to England
through blood and marriage.

As the lady in the tower.

Lady Lindsay's father was the Earl of Wakefield, a
powerful English baron with a foot in both camps. It was
said he straddled countries as he straddled loyalties, and

there was little reason to trust him. Or to believe that he would ransom his daughter. Perhaps she would get her desire after all, for it seemed that she would be in Lochawe for a long time unless she convinced her father to pay the ransom.

Another slight possibility.

The wet wind smelled of horse and sheep, and he turned to go back into the keep. Drawn by thoughts of the widow, an upward glance found the narrow window of her tower chamber. A sliver of light indicated the shutter was open; through the small opening, he could pick out vague shadows and knew she was awake yet.

Did she pace, wondering what to do, or was she plotting a new strategy? Sweet Mary, but she had almost won out with her last ploy, for he had wavered dangerously close to following the urges of his body instead of the warnings that rang loudly in his head. It had been cursed plain that Lady Lindsay's reaction to his kiss was decidedly different than his reaction, an inescapable fact. She had remained coolly calculating, while he'd been ready to tumble her on the floor.

It had effectively dampened his ardor, he thought wryly, and it left him feeling like a fool.

Voices drew his attention from the window, and he heard Auld Maggie and Fergal quarreling just inside the arched door that led to the granary. Another heated argument about the hostage, from the sound of it. Maggie's voice was lifted to near a screech, while Fergal's tone was a muted growl. Unabashed at eavesdropping, Rob moved closer to hear.

"I tell ye," Maggie was fair shouting, "she be a witch! 'Tis obvious to a dolt, so ye should see it well enough."

"She's Sassenach. All know they're a daft lot, given to odd habits. Witches are evil looking, no' fair as the lady in the tower."

Rob leaned against the stone wall beside the open door, half amused, half pondering, as he listened.

"Och, ye're addled if ye think she doesna know well the black arts, Fergal of Kenshire, for I tell ye tha' she was walking widdershins—an' when she passed by the shield hung on the wall, there was narry a hint of her to be seen in it. Is that the way of a Sassenach? Even Long-shanks himself casts a reflection, by all the saints!"

"Aye, woman, ye're fair addled yerself. Ye think to blame a lame cow on the evil eye? Blame it instead on tha' fool of a grandson of yours, for letting his cur nip the beastie's hind leg too hard."

"Tam's a good lad! D'ye think tha' would sour her milk, too?" Maggie snorted derisively. "Ye willna see wha' is right in front of ye, Fergal, and mark me, ye'll regret it."

Irritation raked Fergal's voice as he snapped, "How did she cast an evil eye, when she hasna been out of the tower?"

Maggie turned, jabbed a finger toward the tower where the light still glowed in the narrow window. "She has an eye on the bailey and gate through yon arrow loop."

There was a moment of silence, then Fergal blew out a sigh of exasperation. "How will ye remedy it, then?"

"Ashes of rowan wood need be scattered on the ledge, so she cannot cast her evil eye out of the chamber. 'Close the north window and quickly close the south, and close the window towards the west, evil never came from the east,' is the old saying, as ye maun know." She shivered. "A black wind blows, Fergal, and brings evil wi' it. Cast her out, I tell ye. Tell the laird. He canna know what disaster he ha' brought into his keep."

"I would think he knows well enough. He's lost seven of his sons," Fergal said softly. "His heir is dead."

"Aye, but 'tis as I always told ye. Kenneth wa' never

meant to be laird of Lochawe. 'Tis Rob tha' wore the caul when he was born, the only one out of all eight, a sign. He be the laird as the signs fortell.''

Rob had heard of Auld Maggie's prophecy before, and it amused him no more now than it had then. He straightened from his slouch against the doorframe and stepped into the faint light cast by torches in iron sconces.

"Lochawe is still laird," he said, and when Maggie's head jerked toward him, he added, "The lady is not a witch. She is a hostage here, but she will be treated as an honored guest until she is ransomed."

Auld Maggie's wrinkled face settled into deeper creases. Her mouth pursed into a knot of disbelief, but a glance at his face kept her silent. Only Fergal dared speak.

"There be a rumbling in the hall about the woman tha' has naught to do with witchcraft. The widows and bairnies of yer brothers willna regard her as a guest any more than does our timid Maggie."

"Timid!" Maggie burst out, glaring at him as she lifted a knotted fist to shake it in Fergal's face. "Ye'll be chewin' yer own teeth in a trice if ye dare say tha' agin!"

Ignoring Maggie, Rob saw the truth in Fergal's remark. He agreed with them and would not have said what he had if he hadn't been irritated by Maggie's repetition of her old prophecy. That prophecy had caused friction with Kenneth for years, though his older brother had never mentioned it to Rob. Why would he? He was firstborn. It was unlikely that the fourth-born son would ever be laird of Lochawe.

Yet here he was, the only one left, the Red Devil's heir after all.

Rubbing his chin, Fergal asked, "Did Lochawe say the woman is to stay?"

"No ransom comes. She will be with us a while. Unless one of you has a better suggestion?" He lifted a brow when Auld Maggie muttered an imprecation. "Speak up, Maggie, if you have something to say."

Fiercely, the old woman spat, "Test her! Put her in a sack, sew it up, and toss her in the loch. If she floats, she be a witch. Then ye can burn her."

"And if she doesn't float, she drowns," Rob said wryly. "Absolution by death, a difficult choice, to be certain. I'll think it over. But for now, leave her be. And keep any accusations to yourself. If I hear them, I'll know where they came from, and I'll be most displeased with you."

He pierced Maggie with a ruthless stare that made her take a step back. Her chin quivered slightly, and after a moment, she dropped her gaze and bobbed her head.

"Aye, I'll no' be warnin' t'others, but neither will I go near enow to be struck down!"

"Then stay away from her. That's your choice. Since the bairn is to stay with us until old enough to wed Argyll's son, she needs care. It might as well be the widow who tends her. I expect cooperation from everyone in this keep. She is to earn her own subsistence while with us."

Maggie's eyes narrowed on him. "Wha' does the laird ha' to say aboot it?"

"As you've just said so freely," Rob replied coolly, "I am the next laird of Lochawe. Keep that in mind."

Auld Maggie's lips pressed tightly together, and she fell silent.

Rob turned on his heel and stalked away, his temper raw from the reminder of what lay ahead. Angus wouldn't live forever, for if he continued as he was, he may not live out another year. Since the raid on Caddel Castle, he'd lapsed into days and nights of drunken stupor, save for the brief hours of courtesy when visitors arrived.

While he understood, Rob still resented his father's lapse. Angus Campbell was laird here. He should have done more to save his sons, should have refused Argyll, should not behave now as if it was Rob's fault they'd died.

God knew, if he could have prevented it, he would. It was a grim thought, the facing of the widow, knowing that if not for her and the child, his brothers would still live. But he had made his stand, and he would stay by it. That did not mean he had to ally with Lady Lindsay, however.

She was a constant reminder of all that he had lost.

Chapter 7

✝

JUDITH MADE HER way cautiously down the winding
stone steps to the great hall. Liberty was a fragile thing,
welcome and yet feared in Lochawe. While not free to
leave the keep, she passed the time more easily now, even
carding wool and mending garments. She cared for Mairi
and tidied the new chamber they'd been given in the east
tower. It was no larger but more comfortable, with a double bed instead of the narrow cot, and a hearth large
enough for a decent fire instead of the small, smoking peat
fire of the north-side chamber.

Glenlyon took pains to avoid her, she noticed, slipping
out one door when she came in another, his tall, lean
frame easily recognizable. It was a relief. And an irritation.

Why should he avoid her? It wasn't her fault she was
held here, nor was it her fault his brothers were dead. For
that blame, he need only look to his father. It was galling
that he considered her the cause.

But it was frightening that the old laird lay the blame at her door. She'd seen a ferocity in his eyes that made her draw Mairi close both times she accidentally encountered him in the hall. The smell of whisky was strong on him, the look on his face malevolent and ugly. The Campbell never spoke directly to her. He didn't have to. His feelings were obvious and frightening. It was a relief when she now passed through the hall without encountering the auld laird. Nearing the kitchens, Judith hoped she would not see him today. Mairi was napping in their chamber, and she had come down to scrounge up some kind of meal other than boiled mutton and turnips. Surely, even in April, there should be something other than such meager fare to eat.

Hitching up the trailing tail of the léine that dragged the floor, she adjusted the brèid that flowed over her shoulders, the dull-colored garment bulky but warm. It was a poor replacement for her own gown, but for the sake of modesty, she'd been forced to discard her kirtle. The rough journey had rendered it nearly to rags, and she'd been given these castoffs to wear, a miserable exchange for the soft green wool gown.

She disliked the garments these Scots wore and had clung to her English clothing during all her years in Scotland. It was a comfort and a reminder to her of who she really was, someone who couldn't be obliterated or subjugated. Now, here, in this dismal, dank, and dirty keep, she began to lose that sense of home that had kept her from despair.

'Tis God's grace, she thought, *that I have Mairi to keep me from going mad.*

The kitchens were dark, lit by cooking fires and only a single tattered torch, and they needed a good scrubbing. Soot-blackened pots with crusted food lay scattered on a long table scarred from years of use. Utensils were carelessly strewn on table and hearth. A few shriveled turnips had tumbled out of a frayed basket, lying on the stone floor beside a pile of spilled oats.

A slatternly scullery wench dozed in a corner, draped upon sacks of grain with her short léine flung up almost to her waist, exposing pale thighs to the world. Her mouth hung open, soft snores the only sound in the kitchen.

Accustomed to the scrupulous order in the kitchens of her childhood and the tidy state of the Caddel kitchens, Judith could only stand for a moment in horror. Then anger replaced disgust as the scullery wench snored even louder.

Judith strode forward and nudged her with the sole of her shoe. "Rise," she commanded, "and clean this unholy mess you've left lying about! Do you mean to serve your lord meals cooked in yesterday's filth? Get up, I say!"

Snorting awake, the scullery wench sat up, knuckling sleep from her eyes with one hand. She blinked sleepily and said in Gaelic, "Ye're no one to be ordering me about."

"It's plain you need someone to give you orders, for the place is worse than any sty. Where is your mistress?"

The girl's eyes widened slightly in belated recognition of Judith. "Gone," was her sulky reply, given after a brief hesitation and swift crossing of her chest as if to ward off evil.

Judith's lips compressed. It was obvious that silly old woman had spread her vicious rumors of witchcraft. While vexing, it could be useful.

She stepped forward, lowered her voice, and crooned in a soft mixture of English and French that she was certain this girl would not understand, "Slovenly bit, if I could lay a curse upon your head, I would!" The dark eyes widened with fear, and the serving girl scrabbled backward on the bags of grain, arms and legs flailing as she struggled to her feet.

Her efforts dislodged a pewter pot on a shelf over her head, and it tipped, spilling foul-smelling contents over the girl's head. Her sputtering wail was loud, cut short by Judith's uplifted hand.

"Do as I tell you, or it will go badly with you," Judith warned in native Scots, and she knew from the quick bob of the girl's head that she'd succeeded in gaining her co-operation as well as some measure of respect for powers she didn't possess. The accidentally tilted pot had ensured success.

"Clean yourself," she ordered. "Then heat water in yon cauldron to clean these utensils. There is scrubbing sand, I see, and some stiff brushes. Use them. Then sweep this floor until you can see the stones beneath all this muck and grime."

While the girl set about with an energy Judith would not have suspected, she began to prowl through the stores to find edible supplies. Surely there would be something else to eat beyond the eternal porridge, oatcakes, and turnips.

"What are you doing, milady?" a deep male voice said right behind her when she was bent over inspecting a crock of dried lentils, and she gave a yelp of surprise as she stood up, cracking her head against a heavy wooden shelf.

Glenlyon regarded her with a lifted brow, something close to amusement in his gaze.

Flushing, Judith massaged the back of her head and said with as much dignity as she could manage, "I'm searching for edible food."

"Our table is too meager for you?"

"Your table is too inedible for me. Look at this—" She swept out a hand to indicate the dirty tables and kettles.

"The kitchen looks as if you keep swine in it."

To prove her point, there was the audible snuffling of a pig just outside the open doorway, then a high-pitched squeal followed by the excited barking of a dog.

"Ah no," he said calmly, "Caesar keeps the swine well trained and out of the kitchens."

"Caesar?"

"My old hound. 'Tis all he can manage these days, and it keeps him content, so I allow it. Once, he was the finest alaunt in Scotland. Now he's reduced to herding swine."

"Is there a lesson for me in that allegory?" she said sharply, and a faint smile pressed the corners of his mouth.

"If you find one, milady."

A bit nonplussed, Judith just stared at him for a long moment. The sadness still etched his face, easily visible in his eyes, but it had lessened. Acceptance had settled in, a weary resignation that weighed on him like a heavy cloak. He was not as impenetrable as he'd like to believe, she thought then, for the face he presented to the world was too easy to read.

"I see you now wear our native garb, milady," he said, and she realized she'd been staring at him.

"Yea, though not without regret. I find the bulk a bit daunting." She plucked at the thick folds of brèid, the rectangular piece of woven wool thrown around the body and fastened on her breast with a brooch. This one was too long for her, dragging the ground along with the léine, the long shirt of unbleached linen decorated with what once had been a pretty design at the neck, but the embroidered red threads were now frayed and the design obscure.

"At least you have two shoes now," he said with a lift of his brow and a pointed glance at her feet.

Curling her toes inside the thin footwear, she glared at

him. " 'Twas hardly my fault my shoe was lost. If not for the rude manner in which I was brought here, I would yet be well-shod and garbed, sir!"

"Would you? If Clan Caddel cares so little for your return, I had not thought they would go to the trouble of seeing you properly clothed."

It was a scalding reminder of her situation. Judith drew in a sharp breath.

As if he had not noticed her anger, he continued, "Why are you down here terrifying Catriona?"

"Someone should terrify her. She's lazy. I found her asleep instead of cleaning, and it's obvious this kitchen needs a good scrub. I shudder to think of the food I've eaten being prepared in such squalor. Where is your mistress or chatelaine?"

Crossing his arms over his broad chest, he leaned back against the massive table slowly being cleared by Catriona, and surveyed the kitchen for a long moment. Then he turned his attention back to Judith. Heavy-lidded eyes regarded her silently, an appraisal that made her wonder if there was dirt on her face or a bird snared in her hair, and she grew uneasy. A faint explosion of light glinted in his eyes, then faded, and the hard line of his mouth curved into the barest of smiles.

"This humble keep is hardly large enough to merit someone as grand as a chatelaine, milady. No doubt, you are used to such at Caddel Castle. No? Well, certainly the earl your father employed such, and you are familiar with the duties. If you find our lodgings so lacking, perhaps you should take up the tasks that Maggie and Catriona failed to complete to your satisfaction. You may be a hostage here, but that's no reason why you should not use your—talents—to good effect. I give you leave to see to the kitchens and other such tasks that need a woman's touch. Perhaps you may earn your freedom since no one sees the necessity of relieving you of our company."

"Is it your place to make such an offer? I had thought your father to be the laird, sir."

"So he is. He does not concern himself with such small matters as the business of women, however."

Judith's cheeks burned with anger at his dismissive tone and gesture. Bending, she scooped up one of the turnips from the floor and thrust it close to his face, taking a small measure of satisfaction at how quickly his head jerked back from the fetid odor.

"The business of *women?* Do you truly enjoy rancid turnips for your dinner? If so, there are those aplenty here, and 'tis most like what we have all grown accustomed to eating if yon slattern is in charge of preparing our meals. I prefer decent food, and have lived in Scotland long enough to know it is plentiful, if one takes time and pride enough to use what God provides. Your larders are near barren, sir, when they should be well-stocked with provender more palatable than oats and spoiled turnips!"

They had been speaking in English, and Judith saw from one corner of her eye that Catriona had paused to listen, her mouth slightly agape and eyes wide. Their raised voices had summoned other spectators, and she saw that Rob was now aware of it as well.

Black brows snapped down over his eyes, and his mouth flattened into a straight, fierce line.

"If you seek to embarrass me in front of my own, I advise against it, milady."

It was said softly, but the menace in his tone warned her not to provoke him further.

Just as softly, she said, "Grant pardon, sir, if I have offended you with the truth."

There was a long pause, and she knew she had gone too far. Her belly clenched, and chill oozed through her veins as he stared down at her. What had possessed her to speak out so? She may well have endangered Mairi with her blunt speech, and she should have curbed her wicked tongue!

To her surprise, he laughed, a short burst of sound that seemed to startle him as much as it did her. Wary, she did not move as some of the tension eased and he shook his head.

"Milady, you dare much," he said wryly, "but I cannot disagree. It has been on my mind to set the kitchens aright, and now you shall have the task. Do it well, and we will all benefit."

Judith stared after him as he left the kitchens, his gait clumsy with the staff he carried to prop his injured leg as he walked. Glenlyon was more complex than she had first thought. This was not the first time he'd surprised her, and she had an inescapable feeling it would not be the last. He was unpredictable, swerving between ruthless and kind at an alarming rate.

The Red Devil's Cub was definitely a contradiction to all she had heard of him.

Chapter 8

✝

IN THE DAYS that followed, Judith created a routine that kept her busy. After the morning mass at dawn in the small chapel of the keep, to the first breaking of their fast, to the noonday meal, she scurried between duties with an agility that would no doubt have amazed Edith and all of Caddel Castle. They'd never given her the opportunity to lend her hand to their tasks, save for the most mundane they deemed a widowed English noblewoman capable of doing. But now Judith involved herself in everything from spices for the mutton stew to the proper warp in weaving cloth.

It surprised her that the widows of the laird's sons had no hand in the duties of the keep, for even at Caddel Castle, all the women were involved in the stewardship of daily life. Yet not even one resided at Lochawe, though they occupied residences beyond the keep, some walled and others just stone and thatch cottages.

Only one had visited in the past week, a hollow-eyed

woman with dark hair and two small bairns at her side. Her visit had been brief, and when she saw Mairi, she'd halted in her tracks, staring at the child.

Protectively, Judith moved forward, an arm going to lie upon Mairi's shoulder, though Mairi was more interested in the lad staring back at her with wide gray eyes.

"The heiress o' Caddel," the woman said in broad Scots, and Judith nodded. A bleak light glimmered in misted eyes, and she reached out to touch Mairi's red gold curls. "A fair bairn, tae cause muckle sorrow."

"The sorrow came when she was taken from her home through no wish of her own," Judith reminded softly. " 'Tis a great grief that you have lost so much because of it."

"Aye." Wet eyes flicked up, studied her for a moment. "I am Saraid, widow o' Kenneth, heir tae Lochawe—a braw callant, he wa', a bonny man." She paused, swallowed hard, then said, "Glenlyon will ha' it all naow, an' welcome he is tae it. 'Tis cursed, a de'il's lair. Me Robbie willna be sae cursed."

The lad at her side looked up at his mother, his face solemn. "Me da didna think it cursed."

"Aye, yer da didna think sae, Robbie lad." A weary sigh accompanied the shake of her head. "Daffin, he wa', and sae I told him more than once. Good day tae ye, lady."

Judith had watched them leave, Saraid walking beside a cart laden with bags of grain and a crate of chickens, her two bairns perched atop as it lumbered through the gates. A feeling of hopelessness swept over her. So many widows, so many orphans . . . Life was tenuous at best, enemies lurking in unexpected corners.

Old enmities were familiar. Here, it was Maggie who resented her presence, though she had not confronted her directly. She stayed in the shadows, a constant glowering presence muttering to herself in Gaelic. Only the arrival of Robert Campbell could render Maggie silent.

Robert Campbell of Glenlyon, the most difficult and alien of all males Judith had ever encountered. He remained aloof, for all that he watched her. She felt his gaze on her at times, and when she looked up to meet his eyes, he rarely spoke. It was as if he wanted only to observe her, even at the meals taken in the great hall. It was unnerving.

More unnerving was the fact that she found herself looking for him, unaware until she felt a peculiar jolt that she'd been waiting for him to arrive. What was the matter with her? How could she countenance even an instant's empathy toward the man known as the Devil's Cub? A name lent him for good reason, she was certain, though she'd had only glimpses of the ferocity for which he was famous.

"Lady Judith," an insistent whisper at her side implored, "may I play with Tam?"

Judith glanced down at Mairi, who was gazing across the muddy expanse of byre toward a lad who looked to be about ten years of age. He stood stoically waiting, though his eyes were downcast as if expecting a rebuff. She'd seen him at work, rounding up sheep and swine, a cheerful lad for all that he was Auld Maggie's grandson.

"Yea," she said after a moment, "but you must remain close enough that you hear me should I call for you."

Mairi's face brightened. "I shall, oh I shall!"

There was a little bounce in her stride as she made her way across the mud and offal to greet Tam, and Judith saw the boy's swift grin of delight. They immediately made for a large stack of hay at the far end of the yard.

"Are you not afraid the lass will be tainted by such close contact with a stable lad?"

Judith turned to see Glenlyon behind her. A light wind

blew his black hair back from his face, and his eyes gleamed with something resembling humor. Resting his hip against the side of the well, a sardonic smile curved his mouth as he watched her with a lifted brow.

"No more so than you'll be tainted by being close to me," she retorted.

" 'Tis worse than I thought, then."

"No doubt." Despite constraint at his close presence, she found herself smiling a little. "You may be cursed by just being this near me. I might bewitch you into a turnip."

"I'll take that risk. Auld Maggie's predictions are usually wrong."

"Are they?" She lifted the empty bucket to the side of the well and attached it to the hook, then lowered it. "Yet she manages to terrify most of the village with her grim prophecies."

"Ah. I suppose there's always the off chance that she might stumble across the truth. The people of Lochawe take as few risks as they must."

Eying him, Judith worked the well's lever, heard the muted plop of the bucket hit the water below, and paused. "What of you, Glenlyon? Do you take few risks as well?"

He moved forward, took the lever from her grasp, and began to haul up the heavy water bucket. She noticed the smooth flex of lean muscle in his back and shoulders as he worked, evident even through the loose tunic he wore over his trews.

"I take what risks I must, milady."

"Such as talking to a witch."

Amusement creased his eyes. "Fine witch you are. Why don't you conjure up a full bucket instead of go to this trouble?"

"I conjured you up, and you're doing it for me."

The wooden bucket clunked against stone as he set it on the well's edge. Water dripped, formed puddles that

ran down the sides of the well. He met her gaze for a
moment, some of the humor fading from his eyes.

"You don't belong here, Lady Lindsay."

"I agree. Set us free."

"And if I do? What then?"

Her heart thumped, an erratic lurch of hope that was
quickly squelched. He shook his head impatiently.

"You know that cannot be. The lass must stay. But you
are free to go." He swept an arm out to indicate the muddy
byre. "You were not born to be a servant and nursemaid.
Is this what you want for the rest of your life?"

"What I want is not always what's right." She drew in
a sharp breath of disappointment. "I cannot leave Mairi.
Who here would love her?"

"Love?" He seemed startled. "She's but a bairnie. Love
is nice, but unnecessary to survival."

"Tell that to the laird. He's dying before your eyes because of the loss of his sons."

Her barb hit its mark. His mouth thinned into a taut
line, and his eyes narrowed.

"You dare much, milady."

"Yea, those who have the least to lose dare what they
will because the risks are slight."

"You do not fear losing your life?"

"Do not confuse life with living." She indicated the
keep with a flap of her hand. "I do not live here. I exist
here as a prisoner. There's a vast difference."

For a moment he was silent, staring down at her with
an expression she couldn't interpret. There was no hostil-
ity in those eyes the color of new steel, or even suspicion,
only a thoughtful regard that made her more uneasy than
blatant rancor. She shivered, an involuntary reaction to
the moment and the brisk wind.

Around them the sounds of life went on, familiar yet
alien to her, the daily chaos of living much the same here

as at Caddel Castle. It was even similar to home, to the beloved soft gray towers of Wakefield where she'd spent her childhood, where she'd felt safe and loved. So long ago now, an eternity. Another lifetime.

It had been a lifetime since she'd felt protected, since she'd felt as if she belonged. She hadn't belonged in Caddel Castle, and she certainly didn't belong here. There were moments, almost every hour some days, when the sudden sharp yearning for home nearly overwhelmed her, when she wanted to cry out like a child, *I want to go home!*

How she kept from it was a mystery to her. It was so intense, almost painful to hold it back, to swallow the plea for something she'd never have again. And there was the despair and fear that she'd never again know love in its simple, purest form. A life without love was truly desolate. She clung to Mairi for the child's sake but for her own as well.

It was all she had to lighten the despair of her days.

Love was all Mairi would have to save her from the same aching loneliness and isolation.

"Where have you wandered, Lady Lindsay?"

His Scottish burr was rich but not as thick and nearly incomprehensible as that of many of those around her, and Judith's eyes jerked to Glenlyon's face at the gentle query.

"Home," she said before she thought, then flushed at the sympathy in his eyes. "This time of year is particularly lovely in England."

"So I'm told. Where is Wakefield?"

"Below Weardale, near the River Tees." She paused. "Why do you ask?"

" 'Tis not so very far from here," he said. "You could spend May Day there if you chose."

"I hardly think that possible. May Day is a fortnight."

"Less than that." He shifted position, leaned closer to her so that she caught the fresh, clean scent of him, a masculine aroma of leather and washed linen. Dark wool trews fit him snugly, his tunic of unbleached linen open at the neck and belted at the waist. He wore no plaide in the warm weather, and his knee-high boots were much cleaner than her own shoes. There was something appealing about him, despite his obvious desire to be rid of her.

He reached out, tugged at the tail of hair she'd worked into a neat plait before leaving her chamber that morning, smiling slightly at her uplifted brow. "It sounds as if I wish to be rid of you, and perhaps I do, though not for the reason you may think. Lochawe is no place for you, milady. You're as a blooded mare among the sheep. You do not belong here."

"No," she said sharply, jerking her hair from his grasp, "I belong few places, it seems! I never belonged at Caddel Castle, I do not belong here, and it seems that I do not even have a warm welcome at Wakefield. I very much fear that you are burdened with me, sir, and you will have to make of that what you will."

Heat scoured her neck and face as she turned away from him, chagrined that she had revealed so much with her outburst. Tugging at the rope handle of the water bucket, she only succeeded in sloshing it over her thin slippers and wetting the front of her léine as it tipped.

"Give that to me," he said, and despite her efforts to avoid his help, he took the heavy bucket from the edge of the well, hefting it easily. "I assume you want this in the kitchens."

Before she could reply, he strode toward the kitchens, his long legs quickly crossing the muddy yard. Even with his stride betraying a slight limp, Judith barely kept up.

Curse him for interfering and making her recall things she'd just as soon forget!

Inside the kitchen, she moved quickly to put the newly scrubbed table between them. The warmth of a fire glowing on the hearth reflected in burnished pots that hung neatly from proper hooks. Baskets of vegetables lined one wall, and iron utensils were arranged in tidy efficiency on wooden shelves. Even Catriona was fairly clean, with her short tunic belted now at the waist and proper shoes upon her feet. Her hair had been pulled back into a knot on the nape of her neck with only a few wayward strands escaping.

Glenlyon stopped short, looking around. "Where am I? Surely not in the kitchens of Lochawe's keep; it cannot be the same as I saw only a day or two past."

He meant it as a jest, she knew, but she couldn't help a flash of irritation.

"It would not have been so difficult to do yourself, if you had any pride."

Smoky eyes shifted to her face, and he slowly set down the full bucket on hearthstones blackened by usage. Rosy firelight briefly touched his face, glittered in his eyes as he stared at her.

"Do you sharpen your tongue on flint, Lady Lindsay?"

"Betimes, I do." Her chin lifted slightly at his close regard, though her heart rate escalated alarmingly when he moved closer to her. He had behaved decently, she scolded herself, and she repaid him with sharp words, but could she trust him? He was the Red Devil's son and the next laird of Lochawe, a man who made it clear he wanted her far away from Mairi and Lochawe. Trust was a fragile thing, and it was so hard to know what to do with this man, a mysterious stranger for all that he had his moments of courtesy and nobility.

Nor could she forget that afternoon in the tower room

when he had kissed her near senseless, leaving her more
shaken than ever she had been in her life. It was a moment
she'd relived in dreams and scalding memory since, and
she didn't know what to make of her reaction to him.

Or what to make of his steely-eyed regard now.

"You tread dangerously," he said softly and put a hand
on her shoulder.

It was disconcerting, his touch warm, burning into her
even through the thick wool plaide over her shoulder, a
heavy weight that reminded her once again of her position.

Swallowing the spurt of nervous fear that threatened to
render her into quivering jelly, Judith affected a careless
shrug of her shoulder that dislodged his hand. She put
space between them by leaning back against the scrubbed
oak table.

"Do you threaten me, sir?"

"No. Betimes I promise, but I rarely threaten. It's a
useless motion, I've found. Far better to act than waste
words."

It was a warning; she felt it to her marrow, and a
strange lump formed in her throat. She wanted to reply,
to say something clever and devastating, but no words
came. A heavy blankness invaded her mind, so that she
could only stand and stare at him in the dim, moist kitchen
shadows.

He moved closer, a hand lifted as if to touch her again,
but stopped suddenly, his head jerking toward the door.
Tension vibrated in his lean frame, and he swore softly
as he spun on his heel away from her.

Judith blinked in confusion. Then she heard it, a thin
wail of pure terror and the deep-throated baying of a
hound. Fear nipped her with sharp teeth as she recognized
the childish treble.

"Mairi!"

He was out the door before she was halfway across the kitchen, shoving past Catriona. Sunlight and chaos met her eyes when Judith burst into the byre. Sheer horror filled her as she saw the old wolfhound barking ferociously and Mairi clinging frantically to the spokes of a cart wheel.

"The dog has run mad," she shouted as Glenlyon sprinted across the yard, then saw her error.

It was not the dog who had Mairi and Tam scrambling for safety but a vicious boar. Yellow tusks slashed at Mairi's little legs, and she screamed again as she tried to gain purchase on the wheel and Tam tugged at her from the bed of the cart.

Lifting the trailing ends of her léine, Judith ran across the mud, feeling as if she was moving far too slowly, legs churning like leaden weights as fear coursed through her body. *Mairi,* she thought she screamed, but knew she'd made no sound. All she could hear was the savage barking of the wolfhound and the piercing screams of the child.

The hound lunged forward, nipping the boar's hind legs. The hairy beast whirled, lunged, and the old hound barely escaped being ripped open with a tusk. Snarling, Caesar circled the boar, snapping at it, presenting a new target that distracted the animal from the children.

Small reddish eyes focused on the hound; white froth dripped from snout and tusks as the beast aimed a vicious blow at this new danger. It was muscled and powerful, fully capable of killing a man. Dogs were frequently killed on the hunts for boar, and Caesar was old—but successful in offering a distraction.

For the moment, Mairi was safe as Tam succeeded in tugging her into the bed of the cart; she tumbled over the side in a flurry of wool and kicking legs.

Yet the danger was not lessened for those still in the byre yard. Men scattered, shouting, seeking safety behind stone walls. The boar was wounded and crazed, breathing fury like a smithy's bellows as it lunged at the old hound again.

Judith paused now that Mairi was out of immediate danger, trembling knees threatening to deposit her in a heap on the ground as she grabbed at a stone wall of the granary for support. Glenlyon alone approached the beast, heedless of the peril, a stout cudgel in one hand. He wore no sword, had no weapon for defense, only the length of oak.

"For the love of all that's holy," Judith cried, "let the dog keep the beast at bay until aid arrives!"

But she saw, even as she said it, that the old hound was flagging badly. It had sustained a wound from one of the tusks, a long gash along the left rib cage that only seemed to inflame the boar as it smelled blood and victory. Squeals of hate rent the air as the beast lunged at Caesar again, hooking a tusk in the dog's leg. There was a loud yelp, and Caesar went down as the boar lowered its head to finish the dog by gutting him.

But Glenlyon had reached the combatants and aimed a mighty blow at the boar's head with the oaken staff. The blow fell between the boar's eyes and momentarily stunned it. It staggered slightly, shook its massive head, then turned toward this latest threat. A snort blew froth, dripped from evil tusks, slathering from the hairy muzzle as it charged toward this human tormentor.

Judith watched in frozen horror as Glenlyon took a step back, gripping the cudgel with both hands as he swung it in an almost horizontal swipe that caught the charging boar across the poll of its head. To her amazement, the beast went down like a dropped stone, a heavy thud the only sound it made.

Quickly, Glenlyon knelt beside it; there was the flash of steel, a quick slice, and the boar was finished.

His dirk dripped blood, and he calmly wiped it on the hairy body before rising to his feet. By this time, more men had come running, wielding pitchforks and staves. He surveyed them coolly, his steady gaze an accusation and a reminder of their cowardly delay.

"I will learn later who allowed this beast loose in here," Glenlyon said harshly, "but first will see to the only one brave enough to offer challenge."

He moved to Caesar, who'd lifted to his haunches, his tongue lolling out as he panted heavily. A soft whine drifted from the old hound as his master knelt beside him, a gentle hand on the faithful head.

"Old fellow, you are truer than most," he said softly, and Judith jerked from her trance and moved toward them.

"I have some small knowledge of healing," she offered, and Glenlyon glanced up at her. "My mother was adept with herbs and salves. 'Tis a shallow wound but should be swiftly tended before corruption sets in."

He hesitated only briefly, then gave a grim nod of his head. "This creature is a favorite of mine. You will earn my gratitude if you can save him, Lady Lindsay."

"Any creature courageous enough to confront such a vicious beast to save Mairi deserves whatever my skills can accomplish. Have him brought into the kitchens whilst I fetch some herbs."

Access to the larders had provided her with a scant supply of necessary healing herbs. Apparently, those who sought the aid of the healing arts visited an old woman in the village for their ailments. But, still, there were some useful herbs tucked into forgotten baskets that she'd discovered in her explorations, and she'd carefully hoarded them.

Glenlyon himself brought in the hound, cradling the tan and black body as tenderly as if he held an infant. Mairi and Tam were anxious attendants, silent and solicitous as they scurried to plump straw into a comfortable mat near the hearth.

Judith set to work with cleansing cloths dipped in old wine, and poultices steeped in herbs and rendered fat. She spared a moment's lament for the more familiar herbs of England, and a longer moment of gratitude that she knew the herbs she'd found.

"Chickweed," she said in explanation when Glenlyon gave her a quizzical glance. Her hands worked swiftly, but the old hound was quiet as if he knew she meant only to help. "It aids in the healing. Here. Help me bind him with this strip of linen to hold the dressing on the wound."

Obediently, he took the end of linen she thrust into his hand, lifted the hound gently as it was wound around his body over his ribs. Judith's movements were swift and sure, done without thought, the times when she had helped her mother bind the hurts of Wakefield coming back as if it had been only yesterday.

"Will he live?"

His question came when the deed was done, when the old hound lay dozing on the straw mattress near the fire's warmth. Judith glanced up. His face was creased with emotion that startled her, eyes nearly black beneath the brush of his dark lashes. She'd expected to see concern in Glenlyon's face but not this sorrow. It took her back.

He looked away again, said shortly, "I have experience with the wounds of men, not dogs."

"Yea, he will yet live a while longer, I think. He's a hardy creature. Rather like his master, it seems."

A faint smile was her reward for the comfort she offered. He cleared his throat.

"Unlike his master, he is deserving." Before she could form a reply he stood, his voice brusque as if to deny any betrayal of emotion. "Do whatever is needed for his recovery, for he has behaved with a bravery none other exhibited."

She rose to her feet, wiping her greasy hands on a strip of linen. "Untrue, sir, for 'twas you who slew the beast and kept the children from harm."

"If not for the carelessness in the byre, none would have needed saving. There are some here who will have time to reflect upon their want of courage once I've convinced them of the error of their ways."

Bemused, she stared at him. "You mean to chastise the gillies for being frightened?"

"Nay, lady, I mean to chastise men for being negligent. They near caused the deaths of two bairns and a faithful hound. I do not countenance such lack with my own tenants, and will not suffer it here with my father's."

"You are a hard man, Robert Campbell of Glenlyon."

He stared at her. Rosy light from the kitchen fire lent his features a softness that was a lie. His jaw was set so hard that white lines bracketed his mouth. Points of light were a glitter in his eyes, and his lips flattened grimly.

"Aye, when I must be."

It sounded very much like a warning.

Chapter 9

🗡

Sunk into his chair near the fire, Angus nursed another cup of whisky while Fergal hovered nearby, anxious as always like a mother hen with only one chick left. The Red Devil of name and legend seemed more sodden than fiery.

"Ye need tae eat," Fergal persisted, pushing forward a trencher of roasted boar and peas. " 'Tis tasty, I vow."

Ignoring him, Angus continued to sit in sulky silence. Rob watched his father through hooded eyes, sitting in the far shadows of the hall, his aching leg propped upon a block of wood to ease it some. He'd spent the morning seeing to tenants' complaints, a task his father should perform, and it grated on his temper that Angus refused to shake off the grief and guilt he'd brought upon his own head.

"If 'tis tasty," Angus muttered, raking a hand through his unwashed hair so that red gold tufts stood up like a cock's comb, "then Auld Maggie must have died. She's never been a decent cook."

"Auld Maggie thrives well enough." Fergal smiled with relief at Angus. "Eat now, and yer belly will be grateful."

"My belly roils, Fergal." Angus looked up at the old gillie with something like entreaty in his red-rimmed eyes.

"Aye, 'tis certain it does, wi' naught in it but whisky of late." A finger nudged the wooden trencher closer to the laird. "Put good roast boar in it tae soak up th' spirits." His hand shook as Angus dipped it down to lift a chunk of meat with his fingers. A savory gravy dripped, redolent with spices. The shelf of brow over his eyes lifted slightly as he regarded the trencher.

"New peas. Bannocks. Sweet Mary, Auld Maggie has done well this day."

Fergal waited until Angus had devoured the portions on his trencher, sopping up gravy with a chunk of bannock, then said, "Auld Maggie willna step foot in the kitchen now. 'Tis a blessing, it seems."

"No?" Angus shook his head, wiped a hand over his grizzled jaw, and leaned back. "A blessing indeed. Then who is running loose amongst the pots?"

Rob tensed, expecting the worst as Fergal said, "The Sassenach. Glenlyon hae set her to work."

"Has he now?" Dragging a sleeve across his mouth, the red-rimmed eyes narrowed as Angus contemplated this news. "Is't Glenlyon the laird of Lochawe? Has no one seen fit to tell me?"

Before Fergal could form a reply, Rob lurched to his feet and stepped from the shadows, gaining his father's instant attention.

"Glenlyon would not need to set gillies and ladies to work if you would see to it yourself," he said shortly, and his father's eyes narrowed even more.

"Is that right? Ye have set yerself to be laird here as well as yer own? Yer brother's body isn't cold yet in the grave and ye step into his boots—"

Anger whipped through Rob like the crack of a whip. He moved swiftly forward to face Angus, hands descending palms down on the table with a loud smack as he leaned close.

"If you think to lay that blame upon any head but your own, be warned that I will not tolerate it!"

"Ye will not tolerate it?" Angus snarled. He shook off the restraining hand Fergal dared lay on his shoulder and lunged to his feet, not quite eye level with his taller son as Rob straightened. "Sweet Christ, ye have no rights here!"

"So you leave stewardship of lands and tenants to the gillies? Set Fergal to hearing the tenants' claims, then, and I will gladly go back to Glenlyon."

"Go back and be damned!"

Tension crackled between them, while outside the peel tower could be heard the distant growl of thunder. A storm approached, no less savage than the one inside the hall. The air reeked of dissension.

Into that charged atmosphere, Lady Lindsay unwittingly walked, stopping short just inside the hall.

Angus seized upon her appearance, turned his anger to her, charging like a rampant bull.

"Curse ye for a bloody witch. Ye'll not be allowed to run free in my hall like a tame fox!"

He bore down on her with all the furious speed of a runaway wagon, but Lady Lindsay stood her ground. Rob took a moment to admire her courage if not her wisdom, before he moved to intercept his father.

Angus reached her first, his meaty hand closing in the thick folds of plaide swathing her shoulder and breast. His arm flexed, dragging her up to her toes while he snarled,

"I should not have brought ye with us! I should have slit yer throat as I wanted, and not brought such shame and sorrow into my own keep. . . ."

"Aye," she said steadily, her hands moving to grip his thick wrist and hold his fist away from her, "but if you had, who would you have to blame but yourself? It's easier for you this way, it seems, with so many others to take the blame rightfully yours."

Drawing back his other arm, Angus meant to strike her, but Rob reached him then, grabbing his arm and holding it in a tight grip.

"You will not lay hands on this woman," he said softly. "She is hostage here of your will, not hers, and will not be misused. Leave her be."

Angus released her abruptly and turned his fury upon his son as he raged, "Ye'll not tell me what I may do here! 'Tis my keep, and my hostage—"

" 'Tis your keep, but Argyll's hostage." Rob lifted his brow and added sardonically, "Or have you forgotten the earl charged you with her care as well as the bairn's?"

"Argyll gave me leave to do what needs be done with her. A ransom, he said."

"A worthless ransom, should you harm the lady."

Lady Lindsay stood still, her face white with strain and her eyes huge as she watched them. Rob saw her beyond Angus, recognized the wary fear that vibrated in her slender body and radiated from her eyes. She looked ridiculous, he thought suddenly, in the bulky Scots garments, ill-fitting and unflattering as they were on her. She should be garbed in silks and velvets, with rich embroidery at her throat and a jeweled circlet to hold a veil upon her head.

His gaze shifted back to his father, who stood glaring at him, his chest heaving like a smithy's bellows. There were lines of strain around his mouth and eyes, his matted hair evidence of indifference; his tunic was stained, legs bare and dirty, feet encased in scuffed leather shoon.

Some of Rob's anger faded, replaced by a detached pity for his father's state. The deaths had near laid Angus low, and he struggled yet to rise above his grief. It was an emotion Rob understood, angry though he was at such waste of life. Placing blame would not bring back his brothers. The deed was done.

Angus stepped close, the smell of whisky strong on him, his hands bunched into fists. "D'ye take her part against yer own blood?"

"I take the part of fairness."

A sneer curled the laird's mouth; his head curved back to look up at his son, taller by half a head than he, dark where he was fair.

"Ye take the part of a Sassenach."

Rob's mouth flattened. He recognized that stubborn tilt of his father's head, the set of his jaw. There was to be no reasoning with him now.

"You will not abuse her, Sassenach or Scot."

There. He'd set the boundaries, drawn the line Angus was not to cross, and the laird knew it. Grooves cut deep on each side of his father's mouth, eyes narrowed slightly, and Rob braced himself for the expected reaction. It had been this way since he was but a bairn in leading strings. No one defied Angus Campbell and escaped unscathed.

The fist came swiftly, and Rob did not try to avoid it. Let Angus do what he would; it may defuse the worst.

The blow rocked him back a step, a harsh jab on his jaw that made lights explode in front of his eyes. He didn't see the next blow until it felt as if the roof had collapsed on his head; his ears rang loudly, and the taste of blood was on his mouth. Staggering, he remained upright.

Vaguely, he was aware of Fergal behind the laird, and

the lady so still and white, her hands pressed over her mouth and her eyes wide with horror. He made no effort to defend himself, allowed Angus one more blow, then shook his head to clear his vision.

"Enough," he said softly, and he saw his father pause. A light haze obscured the hall, blurred around the edges, as if he peered through water.

Angus stood still, panting with effort, and the rage in his eyes slowly faded. His fist opened, and he wiped his hand, bleeding on the knuckles, down the front of his tunic. He gave a jerk of his head.

"Aye, 'tis enough."

Glenlyon waited until Angus had quit the hall, then lifted a hand to gingerly wipe away the blood from his mouth and jaw. Aware that Fergal watched, and the lady, he turned slowly to keep from going to his knees, and traversed the length of the hall with slow, deliberate steps. Rushes snapped beneath his boots, evidence of recent cleaning, and a faint, sweet smell as of fresh herbs drifted upward with each step. Whatever else the lady may be, no one could argue with her housewifery skills.

Scuffling sounds behind him betrayed the lady's pursuit, and he stifled a sound of annoyance when she said, "Pray, let me tend your hurts, sir."

"I need no tending."

His curt reply was no deterrent to stubbornness, it seemed.

"You bleed for my cause. I must see to your hurts."

Turning, flinching slightly at the spurt of pain in his thigh, he eyed her narrowly. "I bleed for my own cause, and for the laird's. He has hurts that are unseen. If it eased him to inflict pain on me, then I owe him that as my sire. I can tend my own hurts."

Her brow rose, a delicate sketch of disbelief. "I think not. You limp yet with the wound given a month or more ago. It should be nearly healed by now. With your care, it may still turn green and corrupt."

"It heals slowly."

"It does not heal at all. No, before you offer more argument, I'll tell you that there is a stench about it that I can detect even from here. If you survive, it will be with only one leg, I fear."

The suspicion that she was right formed slowly; he'd been concerned with the leg, had allowed even Auld Maggie to tend it with noxious grease and chants against evil.

"Have you seen Caesar?" she asked, and when he nodded, smiled. "He's as he was before the boar, not even a sennight past. I'll do you no hurt. Allow me to tend you as best I can. If I succeed, you will be whole. If I do not, you have lost nothing."

"Saints above, you're a stubborn lady."

"Yea, so it has been said. Do you prefer the kitchens or a more private chamber?"

"I hardly need all of Lochawe knowing my hurts. Come to the solar on the third floor. It should be empty this time of day."

Without waiting for her reply, he moved on to the spiral of stairs that wound upward, climbing slowly. Niches in the wall held burning lamps; arrow loops allowed in light and wind that reeked of the coming storm. Thunder was closer now, bearing down on Lochawe like an enemy horde, the rumble a reminder of English cavalry and the din of battle.

Even the air felt charged with danger and destruction, a familiar sensation that invaded Lochawe even in peace. But it had rarely been peaceful here, nor in Scotland, not since he could recall. He'd been born into conflict, coming into the world when William Wallace rode free and roughshod over the English, when Robert Bruce was not yet recognized as king by even his own, when raids and

death and burning lands were as common as sunrise. Little
had changed in his thirty years.

A sword had been familiar in his hands since he was
but a lad of six, barely able to wield even a small sword
yet determined to fight. It was a matter of pride to the
Red Devil that all his sons were warriors, a matter of
necessity to Scotland.

Wounds were an expected hazard of battle, common
enough to most. It was shameful to make anything of
them. Pain was to be borne, bloodshed to be vaunted as
a natural consequence.

And now, to be tended by an English hostage was not
to be made common knowledge. If not for the very real
concern that he would, indeed, be a one-legged warrior,
he would refuse the lady.

In the solar, straw pallets littered the floor on each side
of a wide bed. A table and stool stood near the stone
hearth, cold ashes a reminder of the incompetence of Lochawe domestics. Rob sat on the three-legged stool with
a grunt of discomfort. A cursed inconvenience, an unhealed wound, courtesy of an English sword in the skirmish at Norham on the day Edward III was crowned king
in the place of his abdicated father. Over two months now,
and it still broke open when he exercised unwisely.

If Lady Lindsay had healing skills, as certainly made
evident by Caesar's recovery, perhaps it would soon be
whole again. Men had died of battle fever, or at the least,
lost limbs to the surgeon's knife. He didn't want to be
one of them.

A slight tap at the door heralded Lady Lindsay's arrival.
She held a basket on one arm and a length of linen tucked
beneath her other arm as she entered with a brisk smile
and appraising glance.

"This should not take long. It will go more swiftly if
you remove your trews, however."

Accustomed to wearing only a tunic regardless of the cold, Glenlyon belatedly recalled the trews he'd begun wearing to conceal his injury. Shrugging, he stood, quickly untied the tapes that held them around his waist, and let them slide downward.

The lady unpacked the basket and arranged items on the table; herbs, salves, a jug, and pots of mysterious potion. She stood still for a moment to assess her work, then nodded with satisfaction. Unfastening the simple brooch that held the brèid over her shoulder, she carefully removed the bulky garment and laid it aside. Clad now in only the long léine, she hitched the hem up to tuck into the belt at her waist, giving her freedom of movement and him a glimpse of bare leg beneath linen.

"Your dirk, please," she said, and held out her hand as she surveyed the table, "for 'tis better than using kitchen knives."

After only the briefest of hesitations, he unsheathed his dirk from his belt and put it in her hand. The hilt was of polished bone, carved with a thistle, a token of his new estate and rank.

She knelt, slid the blade beneath the linen wrapped around his thigh, and expertly sliced the bandage in two. It did not fall away but clung to the wound, a prickling grip that made him grit his teeth. She glanced up at him.

"Sit down, if you will, for I see that hot water will be needed in order to remove that bandage." She glanced at the cold hearth. "It seems the inefficiency of your staff extends even to your own quarters."

"Shared quarters. There is hardly room for a private chamber." He added grudgingly, "A fire is needed. Summon Fergal."

"Easier and more swift to fetch hot water from the kitchen. Sit down, I said, for your face has gone white. I do not need such a braw man stretched his length upon the floor, though it would probably be more comfortable for you."

A faint smile curved his mouth and he sat stiffly on the stool. "Your command is obeyed, my lady."

"Would that you obeyed all my commands so swiftly and so willingly," she said with a soft laugh. "Now stay until I return. Do not try to remove the bandage, or it may tear good flesh."

She needn't have bothered with that last admonition, for he had no intention of pulling at the linen stuck to the wound. Already, the stench made his belly roll, he who was well used to the fetor of the battlefield.

When she returned with a pail of hot water, she brought also a jug of wine and a cup.

"It will ease your discomfort," she said and filled the cup to the brim. "Drink it now, while I prepare."

"Do I seem so frail that I cannot bear the least pain?" Irritated, he set the full cup on the table, wine sloshing over the rim as he did. "I'm no wee bairnie, my lady."

"No," she said with a thoughtful glance at him, her hands still shredding herbs into the hot water, "I see that you are not. Do as you wish, but you must be very still and not jerk away when I set to work."

It was a task easier imagined than achieved, he realized when she lay hot cloths atop the bandage on his leg. Heat seared into him, moist and encompassing, expected yet startling in intensity. To take his mind off the leg, he stared at the lady, studied her as she worked intently.

A faint frown furrowed her brow, pale skin like English cream flawless and looking as soft as a summer breeze. There was the faintest hint of rose on her cheeks, a deeper rose on her lips, downcast lashes smudges of shadow beneath her eyes. She wore no cap upon her head as did most, but kept her hair in neat plaits wound atop her crown and tied with a piece of string. He thought again of her adorned in jewels and silks. A woman such as this seemed out of place in crofter's garb. There was an elegance in the way she held her head, in the long, slender fingers that moved with gentle expertise upon his aching leg.

"This will hurt," she murmured, and before he had time to react, pulled the old bandage away in a swift motion that sent a jolt of pain through him.

He revised his opinion of her as gentle, regarded her with baleful eyes. "You said the bandage should not be torn away."

"No, it should not have been until it was ready. The wound needs to be opened again, it seems, to release the poisons. Drink your wine."

This time he did not argue.

A brisk wind swept into the room through an open solar window; a wooden shutter banged loudly. Outside, the storm pressed closer, snarling thunder attended by sharp cracks of lightning. The air was damp, smelling of rain, cleansing as it penetrated to the far side of the chamber.

It left him strangely restless. The touch of the lady's hand on his bare thigh was unnerving, the throb of his wound a reminder of how close a careless lance had come to unmanning him. Every sense seemed heightened, the brush of her hand against his fevered skin, the sharp scent of herbs, even the faint fragrance of heather beneath it all, combined with the rolling sound of thunder and the view she presented of the vulnerable nape of her neck where her head was bent over her work . . . the taste of wine was heady on his tongue. He took another sip from the cup, breathed in the fumes, turned his thoughts in another direction from the lady.

War . . . the Bruce's determination to exterminate the last of English resistance to acknowledging him king. . . .

She was too close, too close . . . a temptation despite

the circumstances, and he recalled the day in the north
tower when she had untied her laces in a blatant invitation.

What if he had accepted? Would she have continued?
It had been a daring ploy, he'd recognized it even then,
and it had angered him that a such a lady would offer
herself to him like a three-penny whore.

But what if he had accepted?

It teased him, the conjecture of what lay beneath her
linen shift, the glimpse he'd had that day of snowy skin
and quivering flesh, the wild pulse beating in the hollow
of her throat, and the swift, aching erection that had come
upon him so strongly he'd near staggered with it. He'd
wanted her then, but not like that. Not like any common
woman of the streets lying down for gain.

Now he doubted his decision, for the need for her grew
stronger with each day, each meeting. She should not be
here like this with him, alone and closeted in an empty
chamber, for he wasn't at all certain he could trust himself
with her alone.

A gust of wind brought rain in through the open window. Light dimmed nearly to dark, though it was yet early
in the day. A lamp on the far wall flickered, danced, sputtered as if dying.

Looking up, her hands stilled on his thigh. "I need more
light to finish. Do not move."

He watched, silent, as she rose and moved to the lamp
in its holder on the wall, took it down, and brought it
back to the table, where she lit a rack of candles carefully.
A glow spread through the room, erratic beneath the press
of wind.

Light caught in her hair as she bent back to her task,
picked out silvery strands among the fair, darker in places,
a woven tapestry of beauty that beckoned him to touch
the neat plaits she'd bound atop her head. One hand curled

into a fist in his lap, his other gripped tight the cup of wine.

Her hands moved against him, heedless of the tunic that was pushed higher on his thighs. He thought of those elegant hands on him, moving beneath the tunic to tend stronger needs with a prurient intent rather than medical.

It was arousing.

Heat scoured him that had nothing to do with the wine he drank or the rack of candles. The wind through the open window was chill, carrying rain, the shutter banging a loud, relentless theme against stone, and still the heat engulfed him in ruthless embrace.

He wanted her, a fierce need that had nothing to do with who she was, or who he was, or their circumstance, but instead had everything to do with the sweet smell of her and her courage—that brave defiance of her own life and liberty for the sake of loyalty. It was as arousing as her face and form, yea, even more so.

That first day, he'd seen it in her, though so trapped in his own misery and grief he hadn't dwelled on it then. It was only later, when the initial sharp pain of loss had begun to fade a little that he'd remembered her generosity in offering compassion despite the gravity of her situation.

It was an awkward realization, this wanting of her when she was hostage, when he'd opposed his father for her sake.

When the easing would only bring more wanting. . . .

"Lift your leg, sir," she said, and he raised his leg to allow her to slip a linen bandage beneath it, wrapping it around his thigh with efficient hands. She tied strips of linen to keep it in place, then sat back, wiping her hands on the tail of a cloth. "It should heal quickly enough now. It was corrupted. The dressings need be changed every day, with more herbs to speed the healing. If you prefer, I'll instruct Fergal, and he can tend you."

He regarded her over the rim of his cup. "Fergal is ham-handed. And he's the laird's gillie, not mine."

Her brow lifted; candlelight sprayed over her face. "Is he? I thought him to be the steward here."

"He has been my father's gillie and companion since they were both lads."

"A rare thing, such familiarity with servants."

"Things are done very differently in Scotland than in England." He watched her face, the way the light gleamed gold and rose on her features, the quick lift of her lips in a faint smile. A tiny dimple flashed in one cheek, and he was fascinated. Why had he not noticed that before?

"Your speech is more English than your father's. Even your Scots is different." She began to gather scattered herbs, carefully collecting the tiny stems and dried buds in her palm. "Why is that?"

"I've spent more time in England, perhaps."

Collected herbs were carefully replaced in a leather pouch. When she concentrated, her mouth pursed and created two more dimples at each corner of her lips. It was most intriguing. Beguiling, as was the husky timbre of her voice.

"Have you? I can only imagine how that time was spent."

"Not all of it was war." He shifted and sipped his wine as he stretched out his injured leg to ease a cramp. He wore only his belted tunic, his discarded trews abandoned beneath the table. So little barrier to hide the rising proof of his need. There was no way to hide his reaction to her without her taking note. Tented linen in his lap would betray him for a certainty.

A dull ache sharpened to acute need when she finished gathering the herbs and organizing the basket and looked up at him with an assessing gaze.

"You still have blood upon your mouth, sir. Here . . . it will take just a moment to wipe it away."

Rising to her knees, she pressed a damp edge of cloth to his mouth, a gentle touch on his tender flesh. The act brought her closer to him, her body between his spread knees as she tended his mouth and jaw, dabbing gingerly at the hurts with the cloth and surveying him with a critical eye.

Sharp and sweet, the scent of heather emanated from her body as if she lay in a field of it. He closed his eyes for an instant, heard her clucking compassion.

"Tch, tch, you'll be bruised for a few days, but the cuts are not deep."

His eyes opened to find her face inches away. He wanted to warn her but couldn't find the words. *It must be the wine.* Blood surged through his veins in a rapid tide, pounded to his groin so fiercely that he had to curl his hands into tight fists to keep from crushing her to his chest. The cup of wine was gone, but he didn't recall setting it aside. He couldn't think, tried to follow the thread of her conversation, saw her lips move and knew she'd asked a question. He blinked, then made sense of what she'd said and cleared his throat.

"My time in England . . . I became familiar with the land and language." Why tell her his time was spent mostly in an English prison? Or in raiding villages and laying waste to English fields?

"No doubt, you spent much time in decent company and not in low," she said.

"Not so. The taverns in York are delightfully depraved. The Scots do not have complete jurisdiction over immorality, it seems."

" 'Tis not what King Edward claims." She laughed softly. "Yet I'm inclined to agree with you, being familiar with both countries as I am."

She slid the tip of her tongue over her bottom lip, an instant lure that brought him to full, aching erection. He wanted her with a ferocity that was startling and untimely. "And with depravity, milady?" He leaned forward when she drew back, fixing her with a steady gaze. "Are you well acquainted with the lustier natures of men?" Her smile faded. She looked flustered and wary. "I am a widow, sir. I'm not ignorant of a man's more bestial side."

"There is a vast difference between brutality and seduction, Lady Lindsay."

Stiffly, she said, "I have little experience with that, sir."

"Perhaps it's time you did." He had the satisfaction of seeing hectic color rise to stain her cheeks. Why burn alone? Light caught in her eyes, twin flames mirrored as she stared at him. He leaned forward, cupped her chin in his palm, marveled at the velvety softness of her skin, like the furring of a rose petal.

"Yea," he murmured, "perhaps 'tis time I accepted your offer."

"My—offer?"

His thumb rubbed gently along the curve of her lower lip. "You offered a trade, milady. Seduction for the promise of freedom."

"And you accept?"

"The seduction is mine to accept, the freedom is not my choice. If it were . . ." He dragged his thumb over her lip in a slow, teasing glide, spreading moisture. "If it were, I would give you all you ask."

"So you offer nothing." Her voice was strained, eyes wide and searching, a compelling gaze.

He wanted to lie, to offer freedom, the sun, moon, and stars to her if she would only yield. Fiercely, he wanted to say anything that would gain the luxury of her sweet body, but the words would not form on his tongue.

Bitter regret, that he could not lie—*would* not lie. Honesty required him to shake his head. "Nay, nothing."

"Yet you expect compliance!"

"Nay, lady, I hope for it."

Chapter 10

✝

A STEADY THUD slowly penetrated Judith's senses, and she recognized her own heartbeat, loud in her ears. Ruin lay in any response but a refusal, and yet . . . and yet there was a strange temptation to accede to his demand, to yield to the heat that coiled inside her at his touch, blossoming like a summer flower. Never had she known passion, only the duty of a wife to her husband.

But she had heard of it, whispers from those who were fortunate enough to claim love, songs sung by the minstrels that told of soaring passion. A myth, she'd always thought, for if 'twas true, why had she never found a swain who inspired such emotion?

Years ago, when she was not yet betrothed to Kenneth Lindsay, she had thought herself enamored of a young squire visiting Wakefield with his lord. There had been innocent flirtation, yearning glances, brief touches of hands during a dance, but not so much as an exchanged kiss between them. Her father had interfered, and the young squire was sent away before there could be fodder for the gossips.

She had not wept, had felt only a vague sadness at the loss. And when Kenneth died, she had not felt even that. An arranged marriage left no doubts as to suitability, but it lent no reason for wooing. There was no tenderness in the wedding night, only business quickly done and relief for both when it was over. Her husband had made plain his resentment of an English wife, and she had missed England too much at first to attempt to change his mind. Later, it was too late, for they both felt trapped.

But now . . . but now, there was this man, this bruised warrior of legendary ferocity, and his touch was gentle for all that he pursued his goal with determination.

Lunacy, to even consider surrender, yet the storm that raged outside paled in comparison to the turbulence she felt at that moment.

His hand drifted downward, fingers dragging along the arch of her throat, a leisurely glide that made her shiver with reaction. He smiled, a darkly dangerous smile.

"Yield, lady. . . ."

Powerful persuasion, his husky voice, the wanting so plain in his eyes, and she wavered, some primal force inside her answering the lure despite common sense, despite the remembered warnings of the priests about lust and hellfires.

A crack of thunder rattled stone roof tiles, and lightning lent a sharp acrid smell to the air, made her gasp with sudden fright. A divine warning of retribution for wickedness?

Glenlyon's hand stilled, a heated weight against her breast. The air was thick, reeking of herbs and potions and possibilities, and she gathered strength in the waiting, in the hesitation.

"I cannot. . . . It would not be right. . . ."

"No," he agreed, the truth in his eyes, the devil in his clever hands as he caressed her breast, "it would not be right."

"No . . ." She drew in a soft breath when he scraped his thumb over the hill of her breast, thin linen of her léine the only barrier between them. Erotic shivers arced through her at the caress, sparked a flame that burned deep in her belly and lower. She shuddered, unable to move.

Thunder rumbled, shook the tower, rain a howling beat against stone, spraying the chamber with fine mist through the open window, making candle flames dance wildly. Shadows cavorted over walls like gleeful demons, light played over Glenlyon's face, and resistance faded beneath the temptation of his smile.

Her breath was shallow, labored, a moan trembled on her lips as he tugged loose the single string that held closed the neck of her tunic. A loose garment, severe in its simplicity, easy to don and discard.

Cool air washed over her breasts, summoning another shiver, and he leaned forward, a finger hooked beneath her chin to lift her face for his kiss.

Almost desperately, she submersed herself in the kiss, as the restless heat inside climbed higher and higher. Hot inside, cold outside, the kiss was a reassurance as his lips moved over her mouth with remembered familiarity; he had kissed her before, an intrusion but not an invasion, the fine line uncrossed between yielding and force.

He'd pulled her closer so that her body lay between his open thighs, still on her knees before him, his bandaged leg beneath the light hand she used to brace herself. Somehow, the neck of her tunic slipped from her shoulders, leaving them bare, and she fumbled at it clumsily before he caught her hands in his, held them firmly as he deepened the kiss.

It was so hard to think, so hard to resist when the tip

of his tongue teased entry into her mouth, a seductive play that left her breathless and oddly aching. Sharp sensation flared, spread like molten fire through her veins as his hand shifted beneath linen, cupping the bare skin of her breast. No man had ever touched her like this, not even her husband, and it was as novel as it was agitating.

He lifted his head at last, freeing her mouth, and a moan escaped her in a soft exhalation. Her fingers dug into her palms, her wrists still held in his grasp. She leaned back and away from him, but the movement only brought her breasts closer to him.

Through glazed eyes, she saw his head lower, and then his mouth was on her, his tongue a hot, wet brand over her shivering flesh. The world tilted, blurred, and the thunder and rain and wind seemed to envelop her in a hectic embrace that swept her away. It was so hard to breathe, the air so thick and heavy . . . heat engulfed her, a consuming blaze that seemed as if it would devour her entirely.

She couldn't think, could only *feel,* as the world dissolved into acute sensitivity, his hands and mouth on her an agony of pleasure. He drew her nipple into his mouth, and a spiral of heat plummeted to her belly, exploded there, and plunged between her thighs. She writhed with it, uncertain and floundering, not knowing what she should do or what he would do. . . . Her body responded without her consent, eager for his touch, quivering at the exquisite sensations he lured from her traitorous flesh.

He'd released her hands. She curled her fingers into his tunic to keep from collapsing. Someone cried out, and she recognized it as her own voice, a wordless cry that echoed in the storm-rent room.

When had they stood? He was holding her hard against him now, her bare breasts scraping against his tunic. Their bodies melded together, and she burned with relentless need. The pulse between her thighs beat with deep, heavy strokes. His hands moved to mold her closer to him, cupping her hips against him so that she felt the rigid shape of his erection pressing urgently into her belly.

It shocked her.

This proof of his intent was like a douse of cold water that brought her back sharply to the implications of the moment, and when he scooped her into his arms and moved to the wide bed, she gathered the remnants of resistance.

"No . . . you cannot—do not!"

He'd reached the bed and lowered her to the mattress. Bed ropes squeaked a protest as he leaned over her, a hand on each side of her pressing into the coverings. He kissed her again, smothering her protests, until she almost ignored the warning peals in her head . . . dark laird, the devil's own with clever hands and enticing mouth . . . damnation lay in the act if not the wanting of it, in lying with him without the blessing of the priests . . . in yielding to the sweet, wild need he coaxed from her with such ease. . . .

"Give over, bonny lass," he muttered, his voice a low rasp against her ear, wine-sweet breath feathering across her cheek in potent promise as his mouth moved over her parted lips, the broad Scots accent as much a lure as his kiss. Emotion ran rampant through her, the betrayal of his need evident in that lapse, that fraying of his taut control a sign that this laird of Glenlyon was as affected as she.

Resistance unraveled, spun away in scattered shreds when he tucked his hands behind her head, tilted up her chin with his thumbs, his mouth trailing wet heat over the arch of her throat, then her lips. Surrender beckoned. Unseasoned passion trammeled her senses, left her wavering.

Thunder growled a warning, and a bolt of lightning lit the darkened chamber to the strength of the midday sun, a brief flash that snatched her from the brink of surrender. It would change everything if she yielded.

"No!" It came out on a wheezy gasp, her head jerking back as she wrenched her mouth free, the palms of her hands pushing at him, immovable as a stone, and his face so close to hers, so close. . . . "No, 'tis not right . . . I cannot. . . ."

He halted, eyes half closed, a hard glitter between his lashes; his expression was taut, strained. She put a hand to her mouth, scrubbed the back of it over her lips so hard her teeth grazed her knuckles, fingers shaky as she stared up at him.

Braced on his elbows, his body fit to hers so that she was far too aware of his need, stiff and unyielding against her. She tried to draw in a deep breath but couldn't, could do nothing but look up at him.

He lifted a hand, stuck his finger into the curl of her half-closed fist, drew her hand down and away from her mouth.

"Your lips say one thing, your body another, sweet lady mine," he murmured, his voice husky, thick with desire.

She tried to think, but the world was a heated haze, so difficult with him so close, with his body notched to hers in the age-old way of men and women, his arrant sex pushing at her through the tunic . . . and she knew it wasn't Glenlyon who frightened her nearly as much as her own need, the hunger he'd awakened inside her almost overwhelming, making her forget everything but the moment.

"I do mean it . . . I do. . . ." She sounded unconvincing even to her own ears, breathless, and her voice all wrong, so high and quavering.

Silver gray eyes, translucent and backlit with fiery need, tracked her face with a steady gaze, his very silence a mockery of her denials. Lean-muscled arms braced on each side of her body, his hands pushing into the mattress, his weight still heavy on her. Ah, saints help her, she felt the throb of him *there,* in the cleft between her legs, a scrape of linen against linen as he shifted.

She drew in a sharp breath, saw his eyes narrow, his bruised mouth flatten into a grimace. There was a taut clip to his words:

"You now deny what you first began, lady."

"Yea, so I do." There was no denying that she had first initiated intimacy, but the reasons were far different, that intent more noble than mere pleasure. She should admit her fault, the serious flaw in her character that had led her to desperation, but her lips could not form the words.

His gaze smoldered, burned, accusation evident in the deliberate mockery: "I could still take what you so freely offered."

"Aye, there are none here who could stop you."

He sat back, raked a hand through his hair, silky black strands skimming through his spread fingers. A curse rode his sharply expelled breath, his brows dipped low over his eyes in a scowl. He bent a harsh gaze on her.

"Christ above, woman, you undo me."

Her lashes lowered; she couldn't bear to look at him longer. Shame heated her cheeks. An awkward moment, made worse by her inability to deny her obvious surrender.

Glenlyon seemed to have no trouble. "I do not take unwilling women," he said softly, "but I do not think you are unwilling."

Her heart pounded in her chest, her breath a rapid drag of air into her lungs, the heat in her face scalding. She rose to her elbows, fumbled at the untied strings to cover herself, unable to look at him. After a moment, he pushed her hands away, his fingers deft as he pulled the léine up to her chin and tied the string. To her horror, tears welled in her eyes.

He saw them, touched her dewed lashes with a fingertip; his brow lifted, and she felt the tension in him easing.

"Be at ease, lady, your secret is safe for the moment."

An indignant reply died unborn on her lips at the swift glance he gave her, a challenge that she dared not answer.

And then it was too late to comment. He withdrew, his face impassive as he turned away from the bed.

Sitting up, she drew up her legs, hugging her knees to her chest as she watched him cross the room. Thunder still rattled outside, louder now, the rain flailing walls and roof. He retrieved his trews from the floor and stepped into them, his back to her as he tied the laces; then he turned.

"There will be another time, my lady."

It sounded very much like a promise.

THE CANDLES HAD guttered. Judith stirred at last, the sound of rain still a drumming patter on the stone ledge of the window as she rose from the bed. Gloom filled the solar, though the storm had passed.

Would that the storm inside her had eased as well.

She fretted, repacked the basket twice, but still the herbs and pots would not fit as before. Her mind was not on the basket nor on the tasks that awaited her below but on the man who had turned her world backwards but a short time ago.

It was true enough that she had opened that door on her first encounter with him, and she'd always been aware that men were more susceptible to certain female wiles, but she'd not thought herself so vulnerable. A laugh strangled in her throat, turned to a sound like a sob.

How foolish she had been!

Robert Campbell of Lochawe and Glenlyon had given the lie to that naive assumption quickly enough. For nearly a month she'd been hostage at Lochawe, yet she was more of a prisoner now to her own heedless deeds and emotions.

The corridors outside the solar were empty, musty, and dim-lit by foul-smelling lamps. Her footsteps echoed eerily on the steps. Even the hall was vacant of the usual chaos, a few men clustered by the fire, but no sign of the laird or Glenlyon, a blessed relief when she was still so unsettled. Rushes squelched beneath her feet, water seeping through the doorway to saturate the floor. No one seemed to notice, men hunched against the chill, jugs in hand and the storm ignored. Her mouth flattened. It was obvious no one would think to sweep away the water or sodden rushes unless she set them to it.

She entered the kitchens, where the only light came from the open door and a faint glow on the hearth. Catriona was there, tucked into a knot of misery by the fire, her eyes wide and round with fear and apprehension.

"What ails thee?" Judith murmured distractedly as she put the basket on the table. "The storm passes. Where is Mairi?"

"Gone wi' Tam and th' lady Saraid."

Judith's brow lifted. Saraid—Kenneth Campbell's widow. "For what purpose? You were charged with her care," she said sharply, fret raking at her for the child.

"Aye, yet the lady ha' wee bairns tha' romp wi' Mairi. It didna seem harmful."

"No," Judith said after a moment, "no, 'tis not harmful for her to play with other bairns. Why do you crouch there by the fire? Were you hurt in the storm?"

"Did ye conjure tha' storm, m'lady?"

Catriona's quavering voice came from behind hands she'd clasped over her mouth.

"Of course not." Judith's reply was brisk. "Why would I do such a thing?"

"Auld Maggie said 'twas tae prove tae the laird tha' ye are more powerful than he. . . ."

"What nonsense." She turned, put her hands on her hips, frowning at the girl. "If I wish to perform magic, it will be to my advantage, not to frighten the simple."

Catriona hesitated, then rose from the hearth and held out a knotted rag. Her hand shook. "She said 'twas yer hand tha' saw this done."

Three knots were tied in the cloth, and Judith knew at once that the old woman must have put them there. " 'Tis a trick, Catriona," she said, "but not of my doing."

"Three knots and a thrashing stone bring fierce storms tae Lochawe."

"Perhaps, but not for my sake. Here. Put aside fears of curses and storms and lend a hand. Water soaks the rushes in the hall. Fetch some others."

She filled the time with mindless work, concentrating on anything but Robert Campbell, anything but the memory of his hands on her. . . .

Anything but the memory of that wild, sweet yearning he'd made her feel, the mystery of the minstrels' songs solved at last.

Chapter 11

✝

IT WAS QUIET in the bailey now, the storm having passed
over. Sticky mud sucked at hooves and boots, abducting
loose shoes with careless ease.

"Och, 'tis foul as a wee bairnie's napkin," Fergal said
in disgust, knocking his shoe against the barnekin wall to
dislodge clogged mud. "A yard more an' the marsh would
be in our hall."

"It delays my return to Glenlyon," Rob said, squinting
at the impassable road beyond the keep. "The road is covered with water."

"As usual this time o' year." Fergal grunted, gave his
shoe another slap against the wall, then shoved his foot
into it with a grimace. "Cauld an' wet, by hell."

"Is the only damage to the stable roof?"

"Aye." Fergal jabbed his hand toward the littered yard.
"An' a door bashed in by yer wicked beastie. He doesna
like the noise, it seems."

"So it seems." Splintered wood lay scattered in the mud

near the stable. Debris was being cleared by several men: shingles and tree limbs, the usual result of a fierce storm, some a good size. "The storm was fierce," he said, more to himself than Fergal, for he barely recalled it. The storm in the solar had been more intense, the aftermath unpleasant.

"Aye, tha' it was," Fergal agreed. His old eyes thinned a bit. "The lady tended yer hurts well, did she."

"Well enough." He had no intention of allowing Fergal to bait him over Lady Lindsay and turned abruptly away from the barnekin wall and his view of the swollen marsh. "Whether the water goes down or no, I'll return to Glenlyon. Now the laird is recovered, I need to see to my own lands."

Fergal rubbed a hand over his grizzled jaw; the gesture made a faint scraping sound. "Aye. Ye left 'em in good hands, hey?"

"In good hands." That was true enough. Simon MacCallum was cousin and loyal companion, an able steward. He had sent Simon word of his brothers' fates, unwilling to tell of it when he returned. It was hard enough to think of it now, without having to relive it in the telling.

Restless, Rob descended the short flight of steps to the bailey grounds, sidestepping sodden drifts of straw. A displaced rooster squawked irritably, wings flapping as it avoided efforts to catch it.

Puddles reflected clouds and sunlight, tiny rainbows gleaming in some; he splashed through one that was deceptively deep, cursed softly at the mud on his boots, stomped his feet when he reached the hall. The rushes were soiled, soggy from the rain and wet feet, lying in clumps on the stones while several girls worked with brooms to remove them. New rushes waited in a barrow, sharp-scented and fresh from the storeroom.

Pausing as his eyes adjusted to the dimness, he knew she was across the hall without seeing her. Perhaps it was the faint fragrance of heather that had nothing to do with the herbs strewn in the rushes, or just knowing she would be there to oversee the work.

A taut awareness shimmered in the air, crystalline and palpable, so that he wasn't surprised when she looked up to meet his eyes. The hall seemed changed somehow, as if with a new perception that sharpened sight and sound, ardent memory shared between them now a barrier.

"I told ye the marsh near came inta the hall," Fergal said behind him, grunting irritably at the mess. "A spout needs repair o'er the door, it seems, or we'll need tae grow gills and fins tae live here. The lintel is cracked."

Rob barely listened, his response curt: "Tell the laird and not me, Fergal."

He felt the old gillie's recoil, knew that he had offended him, but it needed to be said. It was time Lochawe tended to Lochawe. He had naught to do with this keep, as he had been forcibly reminded that morning.

"Lochawe business needs be tended by the laird of Lochawe, not by Glenlyon," he reminded Fergal tersely.

While the sharp words rose ready to his lips, his focus was on the lady. Amber and gold light from torch and candles glinted in her hair, lit her face with soft color. She wore the brèid again, the length of wool fastened upon her breast with a rough brooch. On her, it draped in graceful folds for all its bulk, a dark swatch of color over the rounded contours of her breasts.

For what seemed an eternity he watched her, remembered the silken feel of her skin beneath his hands, soft as down and fragrant with heather. If he touched her again, he would not stop.

Pivoting on his heel, he was vaguely aware of Fergal following after him, of the lady's gaze as he moved to the circular stairs and took two at a time, the burn in his leg displacing the burn in his groin. He had to leave Lochawe before he disgraced them both. Hostages were treated with respect, not as prisoners—a fact of which the laird of Lochawe needed to be reminded before he left for Glenlyon.

The morrow would see him quit of Lochawe, away from sire and lady before he went against all he knew, all that was right and familiar in his life. Cursed day, when the earl of Argyll had sent the Red Devil to steal a hostage.

For now it seemed as if he was held hostage as well as the lady, tethered to her by a need that only grew worse with each glimpse of her face or form. She'd ignited a ferocious itch in him to have her, and if he lingered here, he would ignore caution and integrity to gain his desire.

Better to leave than to stay and burn for it.

"Ye canna leave her here, Glenlyon."

Rob turned sharply on Fergal. The corridor was empty, torches giving off yellow light that was reflected in the gillie's black eyes. It gave him the appearance of an owl, wide-eyed and wise.

"When I leave here, I take my horse and my gear. That is all I brought and all I will take with me."

Shaking his head, Fergal smiled slightly. "There's been no ransom. Will ye leave her tae reckon wi' the laird on her own now?"

"Little choice. She won't leave the bairn, and Lochawe will never let the bairn leave."

"Then bide a while yet, hey."

Unspoken was what he really meant, that Angus Campbell had not yet resolved the deaths of his sons, that resentment of Lady Lindsay may be dangerous to her. Perhaps he wouldn't kill her, but left to his own, Angus may well do her harm.

Bitter resignation settled in Rob's soul. He would have to deal with his demons on his own, and he wasn't certain that he was not more dangerous to the lady than was the Red Devil. It was hardly a situation that he could admit, though Fergal was more canny than he pretended.

"Aye," he growled, "for a time. But only until the lady is ransomed or Lochawe allows her to go free."

"Work toward tha' end, laddie. 'Tis no' her fault she is here, but she's a thorn in Lochawe's side an' he willna let it rest until she is gone."

No point in telling him that the lady unsettled him far more than she did his father, but for a much different reason.

†

BELTANE FIRES FOR May Day celebrations were to be lit on the slopes beyond the marshlands. Shepherds had already cut a circular trench and gathered sacred wood to build the fires. A thin skin of water still covered the road from the keep to the mainland, shallow enough to easily traverse, deep enough to wet ankles and fetlocks of men and beasts, a minor inconvenience for the day's festivities.

Angus came down to oversee the cleansing of the kine and sheep. His eyes were clear again, his half-grown beard shaved away, and his garments clean. There was purpose in his stride, though the marks of grief still lay deep upon his craggy features.

From a distance, Rob watched Angus, admiration for his resilience tainted with resentment for his actions.

The laird had once more banished the lady to the tower room, no doubt one of his subtle cruelties that reeked of vengeance. For what, Rob had yet to discover. It could be anything, but most likely, it was just because she existed. The laird of Lochawe was not without his petty faults, his capricious retaliations.

It was well he'd stayed, Rob knew, for he had abundant experience with the Red Devil's justice. A harsh man, an able laird, a vicious warrior when needed, Angus Campbell had earned his epithet honestly. Men like him were the very backbone of Scotland, fighting alongside the Bruce for long years of struggle, suffering deprivation and losses and yet never yielding.

Tribute for Angus Campbell was always earned, but there were those who would see him fall. Petty squabbles never ceased between clans, raids on keeps and villages a constant possibility. Not even the war with England had ended those feuds, just given them rest for a time.

Relative peace saw the resumption of old feuds.

"Few men are left to guard the flock this year," Fergal said, a reminder of their loss. "Widows and bairns make poor warriors ag'in reivers."

A cool wind blew over the marsh and barnekin walls and dispersed the cloud of midges that harried Rob relentlessly. He leaned on the parapet stones to observe the festivities.

"War still threatens. The raids may abate."

"Aye." Fergal's tone conveyed his doubts. "Ye ha' Simon set to guard yer beasties, hey."

"What kine I have are few. The king granted me lands and position, not the means with which to support them." His mouth twisted in a wry grimace. "If I am to increase my herds, I'll take to reiving with the MacGregors."

A soft laugh curled in the air between them, and the old gillie eyed him with a lifted brow. "Yer mam wa' all MacGregor betimes, from the day the laird brought her here. A handfast, it wa', a year an' a day o' total war, wi' the lady winning out."

It was hard to imagine the mother he vaguely remembered as besting the laird, and Rob smiled. "He took her to stop the feud, and it near started a war."

"Aye, tha' it did." Fergal scratched his chest idly, gnarled fingers work-worn and twisted, still competent for all that they pained him at times. "MacGregors dinna let insults pass by unavenged."

Another complex memory, the early days of flights and feuds, the nights when men rode against the keep, still half-built then, roofs constructed of wood that burned far too easily—a sign to Angus Campbell that stone tiles would best suit. It had been an education for Campbell sons, that bitter enmity, a training ground for warriors that had seen them all well seasoned before tall enough to be called men.

Rob eased into a relaxed position against the wall. "Do you seek to remind me of old loyalties?"

"If ye find a lesson in th' past, 'tis always wise tae heed it, hey."

"True enough." He straightened, stretched, glanced over the barnekin wall again. Fires had been lit, smoke rising in thin curls at first, then spreading out. Cattle and sheep were coaxed into leaps over the trench, passing through the smoke, an ancient ritual to cleanse them. Later, the flocks would be taken to the shielings for the summer, guarded by the men left, and held against raiders if they were fortunate.

Familiar rites to confirm that the world went on as it always had, despite the actions of men, despite losses. It should have been comforting. Instead, it was disturbing that nothing seemed to have changed.

"Godalmighty," Fergal said, slapping at returning midges, "curst creatures! Och, a bane they be. D'ye join the Beltane festivities?" He jerked his head toward the greening slopes and milling beasts and tenants. "Argyll ha' sent a fat purse wi' his regards, an' the laird means tae disperse it between the widows and bairns."

"No." He bent a narrow stare on the old gillie. "Are you set to guard me, Fergal? Is that why you dog my heels of late, to keep me from speaking my mind before tenants and laird?"

A light shrug was answer enough. Bitter amusement rose, and Rob shook his head.

"You waste your time. I've said all I intend. Lochawe will do as he pleases. Just as I will when the time comes for me to act."

Taut silence fell. Fergal shifted, looked away, seemed about to speak, then shook his head.

"Do as ye will, Glenlyon."

It was a concession and a denial in the same breath, the words saying one thing, his use of Rob's title saying another.

"What is it, Fergal?" he asked softly. "I know you have much on your mind of late."

Fergal's jaw set; his mouth worked for a moment, as if the words fought to be set free. He blew out a heavy breath and shook his head again.

Unconvinced, Rob stared hard at the old man. Turmoil was too obvious in his grizzled face, fret in the jerky motions of his hands as he hitched up his belt, stomped a foot free of mud, turned his eyes toward the Beltane fires.

"Whatever it is," Rob said, "you can tell me when 'tis time."

Fergal's dark gaze snapped back, studied him for a long moment. "Charms ha' strong powers on the Beltane night. 'Tis said the milk ha' been bewitched of late. A deliberate curse tha' needs be released."

Impatient, Rob waved a hand to indicate that he wasn't interested in the usual tales of witchery and curses. He'd seen enough of life to consider the possibility that curses were usually man-made and not of witches or demons, save those that lived in men's souls. It was an unpopular opinion to have, and he knew that well enough, but to give credence to faith in witches was to give them power. He'd seen abuse of power in too many forms, was not ready to believe in the power of the unseen.

Stepping close, Fergal put a hand on Rob's arm, his grip conveying a sense of urgency.

"Since I was born I ha' been th' laird's sworn man, at his side in all, an' I willna betray him. Yet I say tae ye tha' there are forces at work in Lochawe tha' may well see him destroyed." His grip tightened. "An accusation ha' been made. Suspect witches must suffer pain to recant spells."

Comprehension bore down on him then in swift horror. "Lady Lindsay has been accused," he said, and Fergal dipped his head in agreement.

Rob's gaze whipped to Angus Campbell. As if expecting it, the laird looked up to the wall where they stood. Light glittered in his eyes, a determined reflection, and Rob knew what his father planned.

"May the devil take him!" he swore softly and pushed away from the wall, descending the stone steps three at a time, anger and disbelief spurring him sharply. He ignored Fergal's shout, ignored everything but the drumming rage that flared higher and hotter, blotting out caution.

His horse had been brought and Angus was mounted, his heels drummed hard against the sleek sides to urge the beast forward. Rob caught up with him at the gates, grabbed the bridle to halt his progress.

"Do you flee my anger or your own reckless actions?" he demanded when Angus swore at him. "You blame innocence for your own guilt!"

"Release my horse," Angus snarled. " 'Twas not my doing that the witch cursed the dairy."

"You know that's not true." Rob held tight to the reins while the horse danced and sidled nervously, eyes rolling and nostrils wide with fret. He put a hand on the muzzle to quiet the beast. "You accuse her unjustly."

"The woman will be allowed to prove her innocence."

"By sewing her into a sack and tossing her in the loch to see if she drowns? That's not a test, that's murder."

Angus glared at him. "D'ye refute the law? Witches must be tested." He leaned forward, lowered his voice, a growling sound like low thunder as he said, "The hot iron is to be used first. If she holds it without crying out, she is not a witch and may go free."

Another diabolical test. Rob swallowed the sudden bile that rose to his throat.

"I will not let you do this to the lady."

"No? Ye have no say here, Robert of Glenlyon. Ye have made plain yer choice; ye are free to leave Lochawe."

"Aye, and so I shall. Christ above, you are not the man I thought you. Is the sacrifice of your sons worth nothing to you? What if the child dies, too? Is it all for naught?"

The Campbell's mouth twisted into a grimace. "She canna die, not as long as a red-haired lassie can be found on either side of Loch Awe. Now move, or I'll run ye down!"

There was no hope of changing his mind. Rob recognized that fact and released his father's horse. He stepped back, and Angus spurred the beast forward, through the open gates and splashing through the water.

Fergal reached Rob's side, panting from the swift pace he'd set in pursuit, his voice anxious. "Wha' will ye do? He has the devil in him now, and willna listen. I fear Argyll's rage when he learns the hostage has been killed."

"Where is she?"

"Ye willna be allowed to see her, ye must know. A guard ha' been set to watch her."

"Is she in the tower or the pit?" He rounded on Fergal when there was no reply, eyes narrowed. *"Where is she?"*

†

THIS CHAMBER WAS smaller even than the first. Judith sat upon a narrow cot, staring out the window that looked over the loch. Water nibbled at the sloping banks that fell away from the keep, stretched as far as she could see, hills rising up on each side, thick with trees. A small island floated in the midst of the loch like a becalmed ship. In the hazy distance lay the Pass of Brander, a narrow and perilous track slashed to only a few yards in width by the sheer flank of Ben Cruachan on the right and a dizzying drop into the cold gray waters of Loch Awe on the left.

Prisoner again, rudely thrust into this small, cold cell and locked away, this time without Mairi for comfort. Misery gnawed at her composure; she felt like weeping. But of what good would that be? Little enough, she knew. And she was not a woman prone to tears, for she'd learned early how futile an act it was to yield to such emotions.

There had been no tears when she'd left Wakefield, alone and apprehensive about her future, no tears when she had wed a man who made it plain he disliked her, no tears when he had died and her hopes to return home were dashed, and none when she was so brutally wrenched away from even that home.

And yet, on a stormy morn with Glenlyon, unaccountable tears had sprung into her eyes. Shame, she had thought then, for her thoughtless surrender. Only later, alone in her bed in the dark of night, had she pondered the true cause.

It had not been shame for yielding to the magic of his hands and mouth; it had been bitter regret for years lost, for the absence of love in her life—of love for her sake, not for lands or heirs or passing lust. Was there no one in this world who craved her presence for the mere sake of idle conversation, of lazy hours on a riverbank, or sharing tales before the fire of a night? Did she not have more to offer than manor houses or her body?

Even here, in this rough keep so ill-tended by laird and gillies, she was unwanted. The old woman resented and feared her, the laird blamed her for the results of his own deeds.

And now she was accused of witchcraft.

Her own fault—she should never have baited Auld Maggie as she had. It only made it worse, had only lent credence to the old woman's accusations.

Did Glenlyon know of her fate? Had he heard what had befallen her?

Would it concern him?

Resting her chin on the backs of her folded hands, she watched sunlight chip on the surface of the loch. Robert Campbell had defied his father for her once, but that was before she had lain in his arms and then pushed him away. He was less likely to help her now, when she had refused him.

In the hall later, he had stared at her as if he wished her across the breadth of Scotland instead of in Lochawe. It had left her breathless, that intense stare, and she had known the moment he'd walked into the hall. She'd not needed to even glance toward him for she'd *felt* his presence, a tingle down her spine, as if she stood in a storm and the air was crackling with lightning; it had left her unsettled and awkward.

God. She had ruined all with her willful recklessness. If she had remained remote . . . but she had not.

Poor Mairi would suffer most, alone in the keep now, save for Catriona and Tam. During the past days, they had found one another pleasant company, a surprise to Judith, and a bit disturbing that Mairi's main companions were a stable lad and a kitchen wench. Now she was grateful for it, for Mairi would not feel so alone.

A soft wind blew in the unshuttered window, smelling of the loch and faintly of smoke. The Beltane fires . . .

There would be celebrations, wine and ale and oat-cakes, and a caudle of eggs, butter, oatmeal, and milk to spill upon the ground to ensure the safety of the flock. She had helped to gather the eggs for it just that morning—before disaster struck in the form of sour milk and Auld Maggie's shrieks of doom.

The misfortune of the laird within hearing had sealed her fate. He had seized upon the accusation at once, and in a trice, she was hustled up the steep stairs to this chamber that had once held a loom. Remnants still lay scattered upon the floor, bits of wool, a cracked distaff that was beyond repair—a terrible waste, as it looked to have once been a fine tool. Had the former lady of Lochawe used it, she wondered, or was it left there by a careless servant?

A muffled noise caught her attention, and she turned from the window. Four inches of solid oak separated her from the corridor, but she recognized the angry male voice: *Glenlyon.*

She was standing when the door swung open, though she could not recall the conscious decision to do so, her hands knotted into the folds of linen tunic as if to still their trembling. Beyond Glenlyon, she glimpsed the outraged face of her guard, and her eyes widened.

"Are you unharmed, Lady Lindsay?"

His curt question summoned a nod from her, but still

no words came to her lips. She could only gaze at him, blood rushing to her face, her heart a pounding drum in her chest.

"You have a bruise." He moved forward, leaving the door ajar, to touch her lightly on the cheek. His hand was warm, and she suppressed the insane urge to grasp it and hold it to her face, to draw strength from him.

He obviously expected her to explain, and she groped for the memory of how she had received the blow. It came to her suddenly, and she lifted her eyes to look into his face.

"It . . . is nothing. An accident."

"Did he strike you? Christ above, answer me—"

"As you pointed out, I have a hasty tongue. I speak unwisely at times, and when I was accused of witchery, of cursing the milk, I said only a fool would believe that."

Something dangerous flared in his eyes, and his mouth thinned. "He will not strike you again, lady. I give you my oath on it."

She believed him. She looked into his eyes and believed he meant his oath. It was a novel thing, this trust in a man who had given her no reason to trust him.

Lifting her hand, she curled her fingers around his wrist and nodded. "Yea, I believe you, Robert of Glenlyon."

Chapter 12

†

IT WAS QUIET in the hall; a low fire burned, warming
those who slept near it, curled in blankets and on straw
pallets. Candles had guttered, and only a single torch gave
off light.

Rob moved quietly, and only the old hound lifted a
head to track his progress. He had anticipated Caesar's
interest and brought a strip of meat to distract him. The
dog snapped it eagerly from his hand, noisily chomping,
hardly noticing the farewell stroke of his soft ears.

Lamps in the wall niches burned fitfully if at all as he
climbed the stairs. Stones were damp as he ran his hand
over the walls, moving by memory more than sight. He
meant to take the lady from the tower before his father
could do what he intended.

It was vengeance against the lady, an innocent pawn,
but even more vengeance against his own son for chal-
lenging him as he had. He'd not see the lady harmed for
his sins, Rob thought grimly. He would return her to her

family once his father came to his senses, but until then, he'd see her safe and away from Lochawe.

As expected, a single guard stood watch outside the locked door of Lady Lindsay's prison, the weaving room where as a lad he'd watched his mother work the loom, her hands deft and sure with the woof and warp of the cloth, the distaff disgorging skeins of twisted wool, and her laughter with the other ladies as they worked. The room held pleasant memories for him, and he thought of Ailis MacGregor often. A shame her image was so vague, when he could recall well the sweet scent of lavender she'd worn, the gentle touch of her hand on his cheek, her lilting laugh . . . gone now, as were so many he'd loved.

Ailis MacGregor had been a hostage bride, remarkably had come to love her husband despite the rough wooing. There had been another side to Angus Campbell once, vanquished now beneath the weight of loss and sorrow. But the memory of the other man his father had been kept Rob from overt violence.

He waited in the shadows at the head of the stairwell. A single torch spread yellow light over the door and the guard nodding sleepily. The jug of wine at the man's feet testified to the power of wine and sleeping draught—and an aching head on the morrow. Easy enough to slip the herb into the jug, yet much harder to wait while it took effect. Time was his enemy. The watch on the walls would be performing their duty as usual, even with the Beltane fires smoldering still on the hill. If good fortune was with him, they would have drunk some new ale and be less efficient.

Finally, the guard slumped against the wall; his pike swayed, fell, clattered against the stones, and he did not wake. Rob moved forward swiftly now, his hands searching for and finding the key on the guard's belt. He fit it

into the lock and turned it in a rusty grating of metal on
metal, swung open the door, and stepped inside.

Light from the torch in the corridor slithered into the
room, the only illumination. He stepped into it, moved to
the cot where Lady Lindsay slept. She lay on her side,
one hand flung up to rest beside her head, her hair unbound and streaming over the wool coverlet beneath her.
The window was shuttered against night air, the chamber
dark beyond the hazy light. He heard a slight scuffling
sound, cursed softly under his breath as he realized someone else slept in the chamber.

Wily old laird . . . his visit earlier had no doubt been
duly reported and precautions taken. Unforeseen compli-
cation perhaps, but not a deterrent. He moved quickly to
the guard lying on a straw pallet, bent to clap a hand over
his mouth, and discovered Auld Maggie. He hesitated just
long enough for her to rouse, then overcame reticence to
clip her on the jaw before she could scream a warning.
The blow rendered her immobile, a grunt of pain her only
sound. It took only a moment to bind her wrists with her
discarded belt, and stuff her own stocking into Maggie's
mouth for good measure.

It would buy them more time if her escape was not
found till morning. Swiftly, he moved back to the cot, put
a hand over the lady's mouth to stifle any cry she might
make, and in the gloom saw her eyes fly open.

"Make no sound," he said against her ear, and when
she nodded, he removed his hand. "We must hurry, lady,
so do not dally. Are you fully clothed?"

"Nay," she whispered, sitting up and snatching at the
length of plaide that lay upon the foot of the cot. The
tunic billowed around her, unbound at the waist, and he
stood up to move to the door again, peered out into the
empty hall while she dressed.

She was at his side quickly, the plaide slung over her

shoulder and unfastened, shoes clutched in one hand. A woman of decisive action, he noted with a faint smile, and he took her by the hand.

At the rear of the keep a postern door opened onto the loch side, fringed by a small green slope, accessible only by boat. He had already unlocked the door, and he pushed it open now.

She shivered beside him, greeted with the lap of water against the curve of land. Her fingers dug into his arm.

"Mairi," she whispered. "We must—"

"Nay. She will be safe here." He grabbed her fiercely by the hand when she protested. "You will do her no good if you are dead, milady! The charge of witchcraft is a serious one. Even your father's ransom could not save you."

She wavered; he saw it in the faint gleam of her eyes barely visible in the murky light. Soon the moon would be out of the clouds. The sense of urgency grew sharp. He gave her arm a rough shake.

"Trust me, my lady, there is little time to spare if you wish to live beyond the day's end. It pains me to say it, but my father is intent upon seeing your destruction. He is unbalanced since my brothers' deaths, and I know of no other way save this one to keep you safe from harm."

"But the child . . . Mairi. What will become of her if I am not here?"

"Dead or gone, the child will not know the difference, but you will."

There was no time for more debate. He swung her into his arms, ignored her gasp and stiff resistance, swore he would drown her himself if she continued her struggle. It seemed to overcome her, and she sagged against him, her arms moving around his neck to hold tightly as he stepped into the water.

"I cannot swim," she moaned, clutching at him as water

lapped around his boot tops, then his waist, drenching the dragging hem of her tunic.

He laughed softly. "Then you are no witch, it seems. You would have passed the council's test well enough and be exonerated in your grave."

Her reply was a soft mewling sound of fright. Her warm weight was a sharp contrast to the cold loch; she smelled faintly of heather.

Beyond the loch on the mainland side, a rim of tall grass marked the banks. He made for there, the water rising higher and higher, covering him to his chest, so that he had to sling the lady to one side, letting her float like a hide punt beside him, soothing her with a constant murmur, aware of her fear. She looked like a water sprite, pale hair a mat of delicate seaweed such as mermaids wore, her tunic a dome of bloated linen atop the water.

"Easy lass, easy," he murmured, " 'tis not so very far now, just ahead of us lie the banks, and off we'll be, safe enough once we're clear of Lochawe.... Easy, bonny kelpie, be easy now while I swim a bit.... Hold my arm.... That's it, let me bring you safe alongside me now...."

Solid ground bumped beneath his boots at last, and he pulled her with him, held her in front of him until her feet found purchase on the grainy bottom of the loch. Marsh grasses waved gently, and a clump of brush defined the edge.

Once aground, he looked back. The black towers outlined against a paler sky blinked with bobs of erratic light. The watch prowled the mainland side. He pushed the lady down to the soggy ground beside the clump of bush, stretched beside her, and waited, motionless, his fingers on her arm a warning for her to remain still. Bog grass danced, swished around them in a whisper of sound. A heron coughed, a shrill *shrrakke!* of annoyance at being disturbed.

At last the watch lights disappeared, and he urged her to her feet, holding her arm when she stumbled. It was still dangerous, the chance of discovery high, for there were those who might be about yet, the celebrations of the day lingering. But most had gone to bed for the night, the flocks moved to the shielings, the slopes of Ben Cruachan dotted with shieling huts and sheep.

Saturated earth of the marsh oozed beneath their feet, and the wind was sharp on wet clothes and skin. He felt her shiver beside him, but she made no complaint. She'd tucked the hem of her léine into the belt at her waist, leaving her lower legs unhindered by sodden linen. A glance rewarded him with a glimpse of gracefully curved leg, slender calves, and fine-boned bare feet, her shoes clasped in one hand. Just that brief glimpse sent heat flashing into his belly.

It was a miserable trek across the marshlands, urgency biting at his heels, clouds overhead parting to let a thin curve of moon shed light enough to see but not be seen, and he hoped the horses he'd left in a wooded copse would still be there.

The willows gave way to pines and oaks, thicker now, offering shelter from the elements and unfriendly eyes. His feet made squelching sounds inside his boots as he broke into a faster pace, letting her trail behind. Just ahead lay the natural copse beneath dense pines, several yards from a lay-by for weary travelers on the Tyndrum road. A risk, but dared for the sake of time.

Relief warmed him when he found the horses there, with none disturbed. He beckoned her to hasten, wanting to be well away from Lochawe before she was discovered gone. When she faltered, he moved swiftly to her and lifted her in his arms, swinging her atop the smaller of

the steeds. Her hands flew out to grasp him on his fore-
arms, clutching tightly.

"Put this around you," he said, and wrapped the wool
brèid around her body. She still shivered, uncontrollable
tremors that racked her, and he snatched a plaide off his
horse to wind about her head and shoulders. "No, take
it," he said when she protested that he was just as wet
and cold. "I brought several with me. 'Twill do until we
are far away enough to find a warm fireside."

Through clattering teeth she said, "G-Glenlyon is near
thirty leagues f-from here."

"Do you think I cannot find a welcoming fire between
here and Glenlyon? Lady, you misjudge me. I have kin
the length and breadth of Scotland that will receive us at
their hearth and make no mention of why we are in such
sad state."

That was true enough. Their safety depended, however,
upon which branch of MacGregors or MacNeishes he
chanced to meet first.

They rode below the south ridge of Glen Lochy, coming abreast of Ben Lui by daybreak, the humped peak and
folded ridges a sluice of shadow and light. Tyndrum lay
just north, a crossroads they must avoid. By now her absence was surely discovered, and while he knew the Red
Devil would guess his destination, he did not intend to be
overtaken.

Cutting south again, he pushed the horses and the lady
relentlessly as the day wore on. Not even a league past
Tyndrum lay Kirkton, where they would seek shelter for
the night. He glanced over his shoulder; she hadn't
flagged, had accepted the quick meal of oatcake and swig
of water he'd given her without a murmur, but it was
obvious the lady was exhausted.

Faint bluish shadows ringed her eyes, and the hands
holding tight to her saddle were white-knuckled. They had

paused only once, a discreet halt for necessity, and she had mounted the rouncy again herself, not waiting for him to lend aid. There was strength in her, a tenacity that he had not suspected.

" 'Tis true about English stubbornness," he teased her, and was rewarded with a faint smile though she did not lift her eyes.

"Don't grieve for the bairnie, lass," he said, moved by her sorrow. "Auld Maggie has a soft spot for bairns and will tend her well."

She looked up at that. Her eyes searched his face for signs of a lie, and then she nodded. "Aye, perhaps she will. There is no cruelty in her toward her grandson. Tam seems a contented lad."

"He is a scoundrel, always up to mischief, is our Tam. I fear your Mairi will be enticed to evil ways."

That wrung a true smile from her, a swift sideways curve of her lips that unexpectedly hit him in the gut. In his desire to see her safely away from Lochawe, he'd not considered how difficult it would be to have her so close. It made him feel awkward.

Late afternoon shadows dipped between the snow-mantled crags of Ben Lui and Ben Oss, crept over the willows and grasslands in a swoop toward dusk. A cold wind blew down the mountain trough. It stirred her loose hair, set it in a pale drift across her face; the hand she put up to drag it away was fine-boned, graceful, a reminder of more than he wanted to recall.

He looked toward the blue-hazed slopes that fringed the road. Kirkton would lend them shelter this night in the ruins of an ancient priory. Saint Fillan's Priory was a shrine now, holding the bones of the seventh-century saint, gentle ghost with which to rest. None would search for them here.

It was quiet at the abandoned priory, ivy and sedge and

scrub willows growing up where once had stood monastery walls. A tumble of fallen stones formed a moss-covered cavern in what had once been the chapel nave, providing a barrier against the wind. It was nearly dark now, cold with the absence of the sun to warm them. While he tended the horses, Lady Judith took flint and dry tinder and started a fire in what had once been a font for holy water.

"It seems a sacrilege," she said when he joined her, and she looked up at him with a frown. "It would have been best to light a fire elsewhere."

"And have it be a beacon in the night? Nay, lady, this is the only place, lest we be discovered."

She was silent for a moment, using dry grass to make the fire blaze. "Do you think Lochawe will pursue us?"

He didn't tell her that it was not Lochawe he worried about most, but Argyll. The earl would hear of it, and he would not hesitate in pursuit. Lochawe was just an unwitting instrument, though he'd never believe it if Rob told him. He thought the earl above such dishonorable deeds. What would Angus say if he knew the truth? If he knew the full extent of Argyll's treachery?

"You do not answer," she said, her voice strained, and he looked from the struggling flames to her face.

"Lochawe is bound by duty to bring you back, if not for his own purpose, but because he swore to keep you hostage for the earl."

"Argyll."

"Yes." He tossed a small stick into the fire. "Argyll."

She fell silent again. He rose, moved to the small sack he'd brought, and then returned.

"Our evening meal will not be as savory as those you are used to," he said, "but it will fill empty bellies."

Growing dismay was obvious in her face as she saw

the pouch of oats and the small iron plate, loathing in her flat tone when she said, "Oatcakes."

"Yea, the staple of the soldier. Hot and filling." He mixed oats and water, patted them onto the round of iron plate, then held it over the fire. "There were times I would have been glad enough for such tasty fare, so that it would seem like a banquet."

"I cannot imagine being that hungry."

"Believe me when I tell you that such times are far more frequent than I would like to remember. Ah, for you, my bonny lass, the first one is always the best."

He held it out, and she gingerly removed the hot oatcake from the plate, hissing between her teeth when she burned her fingers, then juggling the cake from one palm to the other until it cooled. Watching her, he smiled at her expression of concentration. She seemed more resigned now to her circumstances.

"So you take me to Glenlyon," she said when she'd eaten two oatcakes and washed them down with water from a leather pouch. Holding her hands out to the warmth of the small blaze, she looked at him over the flames, the rosy light painting color in her cheeks.

"Yes."

"And you think they will not look for us there?"

"It will hardly matter. Glenlyon is mine."

Her brows drew together. "You have a mighty fortress, then."

"Nay, lady, I have a hall not much larger than a crofter's hut, and when I saw it last, the walls around all were still incomplete." He wiped off the cooled iron plate and returned it to his sack. "Sheep graze on my roof. If I know Simon, there are cows in the hall."

"Simon?"

"My cousin." He paused. "And trusted steward. He

holds my lands in my absence. A cursed useless absence, as he warned me it would be."

She pulled the wool plaide more snugly around her, draping it over her head and shoulders. "You went to Lochawe to stop the Campbell from riding to Caddel Castle after Mairi."

"Aye, so I did. Foolish of me. The ride near killed me, and my brothers still died."

Sparks rose from the fire; a twig snapped, burned through the middle. Bitterness swamped him. Heat washed over his face, but the wind at his back was cold and dark.

"If you had not gone," she said, drawing his eyes to her face, "I may not be alive."

It was true enough. Lochawe would have blamed her still and found a way to punish her for his own misdeeds. He blew out a harsh breath, shook his head.

"Pray, lady, that you will be alive long enough to reach Glenlyon."

"I will." She smiled. "I ride with the Devil's Cub."

On her lips, the epithet sounded very much like praise, and he nodded. "Aye, so you do."

Chapter 13

 ✝

PURSUING HORSEMEN THUNDERED down the road and woke her sharply, the ground shaking from the force of hooves. She sat up, fright spearing through her as the rumble grew loud, and she heard Glenlyon say, " 'Tis only a storm that threatens."

Relief flooded her. A dream. It had been a dream. In the distance beyond the priory, the dark shape of Ben Lui loomed like the hump of a dragon against the horizon. A fitful moon still scattered light over the priory, picked out a curl of ivy tumbling over a broken wall, lit grazing horses on cushioned grass that had once been a chapel floor. She lay back down.

Ben Lui—Calf Mountain. It looked to her more like an ancient beast poised for assault. She closed her eyes, tucked her chin more deeply into the warmth of plaide wound around her, thought of Robert Campbell an arm's length away.

She had wondered what he might suggest when night

fell, but he'd only tossed her an extra plaide and told her she could sleep first. He would watch, and wake her when it was her turn.

But he had not woken her. Her eyes opened. She saw from the low position of the moon's cloudy curve that it would be light soon. Had he remained awake all the night?

Stalwart warrior—he was intent upon her safety. It was a miracle of sorts that he risked so much to keep her safe from horrors she didn't want to contemplate. Witchcraft summoned its own brand of torments, designed not to absolve but to destroy those accused. She knew well enough what might have happened, reserved gratitude for this Highland laird who dared defiance of his father for her sake.

He would not appreciate her telling of it, that much she had gleaned from their previous conversations. Any word of praise earned her a scowling glance or mocking reply. It seemed to embarrass him or perhaps remind him of his father's part in their flight from Lochawe.

Would he welcome her shared pain at the spurning of a parent? Her own father had made it clear he valued more the lands he held than her return. She fully understood how sharp a sorrow it was to be so maligned.

Glenlyon rubbed idly at his leg, a reminder of the wound he had suffered. She watched him, wondered if it healed properly. It had been a week since she'd tended it, time enough for the healing to ease him.

The wind brought the smell of rain, and in the distance, thunder rumbled ominously. Glenlyon rose, his stride loose and competent as he moved to the horses, a sign her care had been effective. She smothered a smile in wool. The arts her mother had taught her had not been forgotten in the years of stagnation at Caddel Castle.

With daylight near and the rain threatening, she would

rise and tend her needs before Glenlyon returned. She watched him with her head bent, so he would not see should he chance to look up.

Save for his words of comfort about Mairi, they had spoken little on the swift, arduous ride. He seemed closed in on himself. Since that stormy day in the solar, she'd thought about him too much, tried to reconcile her actions with her emotions—and his reactions. She'd thought he hated her. Now she wondered.

Rising, she folded the plaides and sought privacy in a stand of brush some distance away from the priory walls.

When Glenlyon returned from tending the beasts and making them ready for their journey, Judith had stirred the fire and prepared oatcakes. They sizzled on hot iron.

"Rain threatens," she said by way of explanation when he gave her a surprised smile, and he nodded.

"Aye. We'd best be on our way."

The rain held off until they were well away from Kirkton Glen. Greening slopes boasted strange rock formations, gray boulders thrust up in the middle of meadows of harebells and meadow grass as if carelessly left behind by giant hands. Bell heather ranged on lower slopes, pinkish purple blossoms spicing the air. In the mist beyond, a bluish haze signaled more crags, while a dark curtain of rain behind drew closer, as if in pursuit.

"Glen Dochart lies not far ahead," he said when they paused beneath a craggy outcrop of rock to wait as the rain broke overhead, "where I've kin to see us sheltered for the night."

"Campbell kin?"

He grinned through the dark beard stubble on his jaw. Gloomy light danced in his eyes. "MacGregor kin."

"MacGregor!" She stared at him, aghast. "All have heard of the MacGregor clan, a wild, thieving bunch, 'tis said, with no regard for the devil himself; staunch enemies to the Campbells."

"True, all true. A wild lot they are, but kin to me by my mother's blood. Enemies of the Campbells as well, though they hold no favorites when it comes to reiving beasts where they will. Lochawe took Ailis MacGregor to bind them to him, and it eased the reiving if not the enmity when he wed my mother." He shrugged, ran a hand over his face to wipe away rivulets of rain that found a way into the rock hollow. "Tonight we take shelter with the MacNeish of Glen Dochart, a cousin to the Mac-Gregor. They have pride in hospitality to kin, and in their incivility to all else. My MacGregor blood is why the king granted me Glenlyon. I am less likely to be burned out than most."

It was a reminder to her of the close ties between the clans of Scotland, of the feuds they shared and the quarrels ignored when united against a common enemy: England. A strange people, she mused, hunching her shoulders against the bite of the wind that whipped against them with growing frenzy. It seemed the rain would never lessen.

Footing was uncertain, the horses sliding on wet mud, when at last they rode onto a thickly wooded track that closed out the view of the crags and lent shelter from the rain. The air smelled of bracken and decaying leaves, of eons of deadfall, pungent and familiar. It was hilly here as well, new leaves sprouting on tree branches intertwined over rushing burns, clear water tumbling in lacy white over rocks and fallen limbs.

Glenlyon refilled their water pouches at a burn while she sat her mount beneath a stout oak, still huddled in her plaide.

"By night's fall," he said when he handed her the full pouch, "we will be warm and dry."

Her expression must have been disbelieving, for he gave a laugh, his hand briefly touching her wool-clad arm. "I tell you no tales, Lady Kelpie."

"I'm no kelpie," she muttered ungraciously, feeling as wet and bedraggled as a muddy hen, "to drown men in the sea."

"Aye." His glance lingered, the laugh fading to a bemused smile, "Yet there are times you steal my breath just as completely."

Rain pattered on limbs and leaves, filtered through the canopy to wet her hands and the plaide over her head, yet she felt only a spurt of warmth at the heat in his eyes before he turned away. Unexpected gallantry from a man unused to such things, she thought as they rode on, for Glenlyon did not have the courtly manners of men more used to light words with the ladies. He was intense, as dark and brooding as the Highland crags at times, and as stormy.

Yet there had been sincerity in his eyes along with the heat, as if perhaps he cared for more than her safety. It left her silent and pondering.

Pondering, too, the unfamiliar wash of emotions that came when she thought of him, when she contemplated what he had done. She was well aware of what he risked for her sake, and it awed her. No one had ever risked so much. The aching void inside that had been her constant companion for so long eased, and in its place a spark ignited, wondrous and yet so terrifying. What if she loved him and he did not love her?

†

AS GLENLYON SAID, the MacNeish welcomed them with open smiles and cups of ale, with savory roast meats and bowls of porridge, his table set with pride and generosity. "I knew a visitor would come," Dugald MacNeish boomed, "for the cock crowed three times and put its head into the door." He waved an arm toward the table. "Bide a while, Glenlyon, wi' your lady."

Judith shot a glance toward Glenlyon, but he did not refute his kinsman's assumption, putting a hand upon her arm as he led her toward the chaotic hall. It was not as large a hall as Lochawe. She had glimpsed through heavy mist wattle walls encompassing wood and thatch structures, but it was warm and dry, which she was not.

A woman appeared at her side, clucking softly. "Puir wee thing, ye're wet as a salmon. Come along wi' me."

When she hesitated, Glenlyon gave her over to the woman with a faint smile. "Kyla will see to your comfort."

Kyla led her down a short, dark corridor to a thick door lit by a single lamp set into the wall. She expected cheerless comfort awaited her but was pleasantly surprised when the woman swung open a creaking door into a warm, well-lit chamber, small but cheery.

" 'Tis better here," she said, bustling over to a huge chest against the far wall. "Warm yerself at the fire. Ye need a dry léine, for ye're soaked to the bone."

Cold, fumbling fingers tugged at the knotted wool that held the brèid on her shoulders; there had been no time to search for the brooch, dented as it was and nearly useless. She succeeded in loosening the knot and let the length of wet wool settle to the floor. Shivering in the linen tunic that clung to her body like a second skin, she curled her toes inside the thin shoes, wishing for warm wool stockings and leather boots in their place.

Kyla made a sound of satisfaction and straightened from where she bent over the chest, a length of linen draped in her hands. "Here it be, nearly at the bottom o' the thing. It belonged to my lady, God rest her. And we ha' some good bits o' plaide left to put around ye, too, aye, for it gets airy in tha' hall. Tch, and there ye stand wi' no stockings, and shoon like wet leaves on yer puir wee feet. Dry yerself wi' this cloth, while I fetch ye some proper gear."

Feeling very much as if she'd stepped into a whirlwind, Judith allowed herself to be fussed and petted, dried off with a thick towel, then garbed in fine linen. This léine was not as the other, but close-woven, a saffron color with finely stitched embroidery at the throat and wrists. A belt of linked brass fit around her hips, and the soft woolen brèid was secured on her breast with a pin of pretty stones set in silver.

Kyla put a hairbrush in her hand, her tone brisk as she said she had a lovely bit of ribbon for her hair. "Scarlet," she added, "to keep awa' the witch's curse."

Judith faltered, the brush stilling on its downward stroke through her hair, but there was no guile in the woman that she could see, only a chance remark.

"Och, let me," Kyla said when Judith began to plait her hair, "and I will work in th' ribbon for ya."

Content to be fussed over, Judith sat quietly on a stool by the fire while Kyla arranged her hair, her voice a cheerful chatter as she worked.

" 'Tis good to see Glenlyon here," she said as she divided Judith's hair into plaits, "for we thought he may not come again for a while. It's been a year or more since he was held in that English prison. Tch, and a shame it was, too, that there was none of his own kin to lend him aid during that terrible time."

"Prison . . ."

"He was always a brave lad, fierce they say, on the battlefield. But ye know all tha'. Saints keep them, not one o' his brothers was the warrior he is, though the young ones may well hae grown into it. 'Tis the Mac-Gregor blood tha' makes them so savage, though 'tis not wha' Lochawe would say, of course."

Judith murmured agreement, shocked by the revelation that Glenlyon had been in an English prison. Of all she'd heard, never had it been mentioned that he was held in a prison. A prisoner—hostage to the English, for of course he would not be freed unless ransom was paid.

The fact that he knew full well the impotence of her position as hostage explained much. He would know how helpless it felt to be used as a pawn.

When she returned to the hall, Glenlyon sat on a long bench at the table, an ale cup in his hand.

He looked up when she entered, a potent glance that seared her to the bone. There was appreciation in his eyes, a slow regard that took her in from head to foot.

"A bonny lass ye have there, Glenlyon," MacNeish boomed with a wide grin, "bonny indeed."

"Aye," Glenlyon said with emphasis, his dark brow cocked upward as he watched her approach, "bonny indeed."

She felt a rush of emotion when he rose to take her hand and lead her to a place beside him, flushing a little at the warmth in his eyes. It was novel, this feeling of having value, of being wanted.

"This is the MacNeish," he said to her, grinning as he added, "known in some quarters as the De'il's Dugald."

"Aye, that I am!" A broad hand smacked loudly onto the table's surface. "A name I own to proudly, by God!"

Glenlyon leaned close to her, his voice soft and rich with laughter. "One of the peculiarities of Scottish manners is the prevalence of descriptive names, you ken. Over there, we have Lang Will and Dark Donald, easy enough to see the reason for their names, but at the far end of the table, there beyond the jug of ale, sits Hen-Harrow next to Cat Lick, their Christian names long forgotten."

A bubble of laughter rose in her throat, and she tried not to look in their direction when Glenlyon named Three-Fingered Davy and Nebless Geordie. "They come from the Middle Marches, near the Tweed," he said in explanation.

Understandable explanation it was, as the Marches were too frequently ravaged by English and Scots armies alike.

"Glenlyon," the MacNeish bellowed, "what of Simon MacCallum? Does he still tend yer beasties, or are they all in MacCallum bellies by now?"

There was general laughter at the question. "My beasts are safe enough with Simon," he replied, "but there's rumors said that a score of MacNeish hooves tread the Rannoch Moor of late."

Hoots followed this sally, and MacNeish gave a good-natured shrug. "Aye, lad, twenty good beasties they were, gone in a trice to Davy MacCallum, may the de'il take him."

"Your walls need building."

"Aye, as do yours, I hear. I've a mind to build a stone peel, much as Lochawe has done."

Judith felt him tense and a muscle in his jaw betrayed him to any who noticed, but Glenlyon's tone was easy enough when he said, "He's still building. It wants finishing the dyke to be done. Lochawe is too close to the mainland, cut off only when the marsh floods."

Scratching his jaw, MacNeish nodded thoughtfully. " 'Tis time to build of stone, I think. I have lived in turf long enough." He gazed around at the hall with an expression of dissatisfaction. "This is sturdy enough but willna withstand a determined siege."

As the men spoke of war engines and sieges long past, Judith dipped porridge and meat into her trencher. Her stomach growled. She was near faint with hunger. Dreams of soft white bread were tantalizing illusions, the nearest she'd come to such luxury of late were the bannocks baked at Lochawe.

Satiated at last, with quantity if not quality, Judith was lulled by the ebb and flow of conversations around her, the warmth of so many bodies in an enclosed area, the fire that blazed on the hearth exuding smoke that stung her eyes. She closed them, only for a moment to ease the sting, and gave in to weariness.

Her muscles slowly relaxed so that she sagged against Glenlyon, his solid frame ample support, and she jerked upright, eyes snapping open. He hadn't seemed to notice but continued his discussion of proper defenses for towers and free-ranging beasts. Her eyes burned, prickled with the need for sleep. She fought it—and lost.

The tension of the past weeks slid away, and in this cocoon of warmth and security, Judith felt herself easing into lethargy. It stole over her, crept beneath the barrier she'd erected, left her vulnerable and drowsy.

It was so extravagant, to rest without disaster looming over her head, with relief from constant strain.

This is what it's like to be content, she thought hazily as she drifted on the tide of conversation that floated over her head, laughter and teasing bouncing from one to the other, *how lovely.*

┼

SOFT HEAT LEANED against his shoulder, her weight as slight as a bairn's. Rob was far too aware of her, of the press of her thigh alongside his on the bench, a heated pressure that drew his mind to things other than wattle walls or stone. He tried to keep his mind on MacNeish's talk of dirt mounds and rocks, but the lure to put an arm around the lady leaning into him was too strong.

He moved an arm, slid it behind her to circle her waist, and felt her ease into the embrace like a sleeping child.

A distraction, this lady Judith, scented and soft and far too alluring. He saw the sidelong glances at her, the speculation in men's eyes, the way their gaze skittered away when they caught his attention instead.

"Yer lady finds our company tiresome," MacNeish jested when Rob looked back at him.

"We have traveled hard today."

"No sleeping posset for her tonight, hey. There are extra pallets by yon wall, Glenlyon. Ye are welcome to them, or to a dry stall with the beasties, as ye like."

Rob stood, pulling her up with him, his arm bearing her weight. She immediately tensed, then pulled away.

"It seems I have been rude," she said in Gaelic to her host and flashed him an apologetic smile that had the chief shaking his head in denial.

The husky timbre of her voice was lower than usual, and MacNeish struggled to his feet in belated gallantry, swaying slightly from effects of too much ale.

"A rough wooing is it, to make ye so tired," he said with a laugh. "Dinna fash, lady, for no Campbell dares come to Glen Dochart wi'out risking a meal of good steel. If no' for his mam, not even Glenlyon would dare."

Faintly, she said, "God's mercy to you for your welcome this night."

"Aye, a good night to ye, lady," MacNeish said, lifting his cup high, "and good health! May all yer bairns be strong as a MacNeish and wily as a Campbell!" His salute earned laughter from the men at the table and a wry smile from Rob.

It wasn't likely he would forget Lady Lindsay, Rob knew well, nor would most present in the hall tonight. It was a blessing and a curse, for though her Gaelic was smooth and perfect, the English tinge was unmistakable. Several at the table lifted a brow, but none would be rude enough to speak out in MacNeish's hall. The strict rules of hospitality were understood.

He found them pallets in a shadowed alcove; the hall was crowded yet, the alcove down a corridor and relatively quiet. They would leave early on the morrow, for there was another day's ride before they would reach Glenlyon.

"Where shall I lie?" she asked, and he plumped a pile of straw into an inviting mound covered with a plaide.

"You'll be safe next to me."

Wrapped in plaides atop the straw pallets tucked into deep shadows, he lay down beside her, her back to his front, fitting against him from chest to thigh. She lay with her cheek resting on her curved hand. Long, slow breaths measured time, and the torchlight down the corridor grew dim, the revelry in the hall fading into silence at last. He should sleep, for he'd slept little the night before.

Yet it was near impossible with the lady so soft beside him, so close, her hair a light rope neatly plaited with red ribbon. A breathy sigh escaped her; she snuggled closer, half turning so that he saw the pale moon of her face in the murky light. A soft cushion indeed, this Lady Lindsay, this contradiction that slept in his arms.

So fragile, small bones as delicate as a bird's, yet strong enough to resist raiders abducting a child, strong enough to face down the Red Devil in a rage, strong enough to endure a breakneck journey across rugged crags and moors. There was steel beneath this silk, a strength he hadn't imagined.

He watched the contours of her face, the gentle slope of cheek and brow, the soft, parted lips and the dark wings of her lashes against creamy skin. The knot inside him began to loosen, unravel, giving him ease.

A drift of glossy hair escaped the braid, slipped onto her shoulder. He lifted it gently in his palm, tested it between his fingers, and fell asleep at last with it clasped in his hand.

Chapter 14

BRIGHT SUNLIGHT GLEAMED on the waters of Loch Tay, a glittering jewel set between creased slopes of Ben Lawers and Meall Greigh, towering crags that thrust proud peaks so high into the sky it seemed they nearly reached heaven. The air was clean and fresh, brisk as it blew over the loch, a promise of warmer days riding the current.

Lifting her head, Judith let the plaide settle about her shoulders, its warmth not needed. The léine and brèid she had borrowed for a night were hers, a gift from Kyla, who had insisted she keep them. The generosity was unexpected and welcome. More welcome were the stockings and shoes on her feet, warm wool and boots to her ankles, most welcome indeed.

Glenlyon had forsaken his trews, garbed now in only his short tunic and plaide, sunlight gleaming on his hair. He looked the very image of a Highland laird, with his proud bearing and noble profile. Her heart lurched oddly when he happened to turn and glance at her, a silvery flash of his eyes in her direction, the ghost of a smile touching his mouth before he looked away again.

She had woken that morning with his hand tangled in her hair, his body so close to hers a broomstraw would not fit between them. And known at once the urges of his body, for they were not hidden. Immobile, not daring to move, she'd felt his breath against her neck, knew that he slept yet, while his body made known his dreams.

The MacNeish's salute the night before still echoed in her mind, and the thought of bearing children for Glenlyon left her unsettled. A hundred times she had wanted to ask his intent, for if she'd guessed his reason for taking her from Lochawe, she had no idea of his objective. There was no mention from him of marriage or even handfasting, yet there was no mention either of ransom. What did he intend?

Uncertainty gnawed at her, a relentless malady. She ached with it at times—ached, too, with questions about the laird of Glenlyon. There was something intrinsically good in him, that much she'd seen.

Robert Campbell had ignited flames of hope in her heart that day in the solar, as well as fires of need. She had been certain he felt more than just desire. But his silence now made her wonder if she was wrong. The barriers she'd erected had been breached, and now she tried to build them even higher. It was too much to risk.

They rode along the banks of the loch, weaving in and out of trees, the hills rising thick and forested on one side of the track they followed. This night they would sleep in Glenlyon, he'd told her, a hard day's ride. Six leagues or more away lay the lands he'd been granted by the king.

It was easier now, the threat of pursuit faded with the passage of time and distance. Full pouches of oatcakes and salted fish hung from saddle loops, meals eaten on the hoof as they pressed on. Days were longer, dusk stretching into a purple haze that lingered with enough light to see the road.

When they crossed the old Roman bridge that spanned the River Lyon at last, Glenlyon's horse snorted eagerly, ears pricked forward in anticipation of rest and fodder.

"He knows the way," was the laughing observation, and Judith rode closer.

It was still day, a misty glow that delved into shadow in places, but lent light enough to see the cluster of thatch-roofed huts and stone walls under construction as they rode down a hill into a vale of emerald green. It was not as rough as she had thought from his description; a peel was well under way, two stories high, piles of stones lying in wait for workmen's hands, scaffolds clinging to walls like ivy. Beyond, blue green humps were clothed in mist.

"Glenlyon," he said, and turned to look at her. "It has not seen a woman's hand, so do not expect overmuch."

Her heart lurched. "I expect only a warm fire and dry bed, no more."

"It has that, or did last time I slept here."

Their horses broke into a trot with the promise of the journey's end, and the sound of hooves brought a man to the entrance of the tower, naked sword in one hand, then a wide smile when he recognized the front rider.

"Glenlyon, alive still, by God!"

"Did you really doubt me, Simon?"

"Aye, as well you know," came the quick retort, and hazel eyes shifted to Judith. Sandy hair fringed his face, a handsome man, with an open regard as he surveyed her. "Will you give a name to such a bonny lady, Glenlyon?"

"Lady Lindsay of Caddel Castle." Glenlyon dismounted, came to where she still sat her horse, reached up to put his hands around her waist. "Late of Lochawe.

This rogue is Simon MacCallum, my lady, reiver and kin."

Over his shoulder as he swung her down, Judith saw the speculation in Simon's eyes and understood it. He must wonder about her place here, though not as much as she did.

Cramped from the long day atop a horse, her legs gave way suddenly and she sagged. Glenlyon caught her, a smooth curve of his arm scooping her against his side.

"Clear the way, Simon," he said, "before the lady swoons."

"I'm not swooning," she protested, but he ignored her, gave a whistle that brought a man running toward them to take the horses. His arm around her tightened as he walked her toward the tower.

Against a far wall that looked nearly finished, stables had been built, roofed in thatch, with the smell of new wood and rushes rife in the air. Stacks of unhewn logs lay near.

"There is no roof of turf," Judith said, and his laugh stirred loose hair over her ear and made her shiver.

"The sheep must have eaten it. Can you walk?"

"Of course." She paused. "Though I am grateful for your arm."

Inside the tower, Judith was greeted with the sharp scent of a peat fire, burning brightly on the hearthstones. It was not a large hall but comfortable enough, with flagged stones bare of rushes and a new table dominating one side. Long benches leaned against a wall. Light seeped in through high windows, and beams of new oak spanned the ceiling.

"Simon is my builder," Glenlyon said, "and slow at it, from what I see—or don't see."

"Och, to be so maligned," Simon sighed. Humor curved his mouth. Hazel eyes danced in the gaze he turned to

Judith, and she couldn't help an answering smile. "You
are well come to the family, Lady Lindsay."

"The lady," said Glenlyon with a dark glance in
Simon's direction, "is a visitor."

His distinction was plain, and Simon's sandy brows
rose even higher. "Is she now? Not a bride but a guest?
Good news for me, cousin."

Glenlyon turned abruptly from inspecting wall beams,
and the threat in his gaze was obvious even to Judith.

"Leave off your play at gallantry, Simon."

Amusement flickered on MacCallum's face as, unabashed, he shrugged away the warning. "Och, your glower
can frighten wee bairns and sheep, but I'm made of hard-
ier stuff."

Judith wanted to laugh at the expression on Glenlyon's
face but didn't dare.

"She is Argyll's hostage," he said then, and she heard
the interest sharpen in Simon MacCallum's tone.

"Even better. I've always wanted to tweak that old bas-
tard's nose. Grant pardon, lady, for my bold speech. So
you are important to Argyll, are you? Interesting."

"At the moment, Simon," said Glenlyon, "she is more
important to me. What chambers are serviceable?"

"A dour lad . . . the hall is complete, the second floor
near done, the third floor has the sky for a roof. Wet when
it rains, but other than that, quite serviceable. There is
straw for beds."

"Daft rogue. You have made more progress than I
thought possible. How did you manage it?"

"Bribed the stonemasons and got the carpenters drunk."
A smile belied his words. "And paid them double wages."

"Devil take you! You didn't."

"Of course not." Simon slid his gaze back to Judith,
who listened with fascination. "Double of nothing is still
nothing. Do you cook, perchance, my lady?"

"I have been known to be a fair hand at it." Despite his obviously roguish ways, she found herself liking Simon MacCallum.

"Ah, lovely. I fancy something other than oats, though God knows, 'tis better than what I've eaten lately."

"A Scot who doesn't like oats?" She tilted her head, a smile widening.

"I've had my share these thirty-six years past. I fancy beef these days."

"Christ above, whose beef?" Glenlyon didn't hide his amusement. "Have you been lifting MacGregor cattle?"

"You grieve me, cousin. Would I go reiving my own kin? No, these beasts were gifts from John MacDougall."

Glenlyon snorted disbelief. "It would interest me to hear if MacDougall knows that. Never mind that now. The lady looks ready to collapse. I'll show her to a chamber, and we can discuss accounts later."

How had he known? Thoughts of a straw pallet held more allure for her at this moment than anything else. Her legs threatened to fold, and she feared she would crumple to the bare stone floor at any moment.

A curved staircase led upward, lit by a single torch but with niches where lamps would go. The smell of new wood mingled with that of fresh mortar. Glenlyon's arm was warm, his step sure. She cast about for an ordinary topic, decided to choose the obvious.

"How large do you intend to build?"

"For now, this is as large as I can afford." He guided her up the steps to a corridor on the second floor. "Not so large, as you can see, but t'will withstand storms of nature and of men, I think."

"Do you expect storms of men?"

"Always."

Long shadows lay thick in the corridor, and he bade her wait while he fetched a lamp. His steps echoed loudly in the empty hallway and on the stairs. Light from the torch below flowed across the floor in a faint square. It was silent in the shadows, and as she stood there alone, she thought how it would be to belong here in this keep of new wood and stone, built of dreams and determination.

It awoke a fierce yearning in her.

Light grew stronger, chasing shadows to far corners, and she turned as Glenlyon breached the top step. He held a small lamp in one hand, and it cast a rosy glow over his face.

"There is no bed, but I'll have one of the workmen find one for you on the morrow," he said, and he led the way to the only chamber with a door already hung. It swung open in mute efficiency, solid oak with huge brass hinges.

She wanted to ask if he intended to ransom her. Did he? Had he already written her father to demand payment for her return? And what would he say, she wondered, if she told him she would rather stay here?

"Simon is fetching a servant to lay a fire and bring up more straw and a plaide for your bed," he said as he crossed to set the lamp down near the hearth, "and a girl will bring you food. Simon was telling the truth about the beef. One of the carpenter's wives sees to the cooking."

"Where will you sleep?" she asked, a question weighted with implications. She wanted to ask what lay ahead for her, if she was to be set aside yet again.

He turned to look at her. "In the hall."

Judith walked to the narrow bed of straw against the far wall. A jug sat near it, empty now but with the residue of wine a faint fragrance still. A length of wool lay atop the straw. The window was wider than most, with a deep ledge around it and odd-looking strips of iron set into the stone instead of wood shutters.

"Window glazing," he said, coming up behind her

where she stood at the window. "The glazier will set it soon. He cost me more than a week's work for the master mason, but I remember my mother always wanted a window of glass."

"Did she ever get one?" She leaned against the ledge, watching him as he gazed out the window. A light breeze pushed his hair back, lifted it slightly where it lay against his neck in dark shadow.

"You've seen Lochawe. It was not important to my father to have a glass window. 'Wasteful,' he said, and he's right about that. It is a waste, when there are so many other necessary supplies to buy, carpenters to pay, smiths and woodcutters, the carters—" He paused, pressed knuckles to his brow, and said with a rueful smile, "I begin to think I should have been content with the turf and wattle hut."

"When it's done, you'll be glad."

"Aye, and penniless, unless the Whitsun rents are paid." He scraped a hand over his jaw, shrugged, and slid her another faint smile. "I'll not bore you longer with the accounts. Sleep well, lady, and the morrow will be easier."

It was difficult not to tell him that sleep would be much easier if she knew her fate. Still, when he had gone and she was alone, she reasoned that if he meant to ransom her, he would have said so. As yet, he treated her with only courtesy and regard, even with swift intervention of another man's interest. What else could she think but that he would keep her here?

That, she learned shortly, was a misconception.

A tray of beef and the eternal porridge was brought to the chamber a short time after Glenlyon left, the woman who carried it cheerful and talkative.

" 'Tis no' so very hot, m'lady," she said, "but 'twill fill

yer belly for the while. There's new ale in the jug. Is there aught else I can bring ye?"

"No—yes, if you will. I thought tomorrow I would lend my hand to setting all a'right in the kitchens. I'll need a kerchief for my hair. Those who are used to the cooking and cleaning will meet me before first light."

Hesitating, the older woman bobbed her head, then said, "As ye please, m'lady."

"What is your position and your name?"

"Me husband is Simkin, the tinker, and I am called Morag."

"Well, Morag, we shall deal well enough, I think, and set the laird's household to good running order."

"Aye, m'lady, as ye say. But—" She paused again, then said in a rush, "But what shall I say should the laird take me tae task?"

"Why should he, if we are efficient in our work?"

"Grant pardon, lady, if I offend ye, but I was told tha' ye are hostage, first tae the Red De'il, and naow the De'il's Cub. Is't naught o' it true, then?"

A cold bleakness gripped her, but Judith managed to ask her, "Did the laird tell you that?"

"Nay, m'lady, he didna."

"Then until he does, I shall see to his household."

When Morag had gone, Judith sat quietly on the cot. The trencher of beef and porridge slowly congealed into a cold, unappetizing mess as time crawled by. Uncertainty was worse than certitude of disaster.

After a while, as the lamp burned low and shadows crept from corners to claim more territory, she straightened, grim determination replacing her indecision.

Tomorrow. By all that was holy, tomorrow Robert Campbell would tell her yea or nay!

Chapter 15

✝

DAYLIGHT PICKED OUT details in the construction that evening shadows had hidden. Rob went over the accounts with Simon, then supervised the workmen's labor, watching as the masons carefully placed stones on the third floor. Ramps and scaffolds clung to the sides of the tower, and the steady tap of carpenters' hammers on joists and floorboards sang a melody of progress.

"Much of the materials are local," Simon said as he squinted up at the workmen on the scaffolds, "and that has saved you money. The master mason costs you four shillings a week, while the cheapest worker still costs six-pence."

"What of the barnekin walls?" Rob said. "Will they be finished by summer's end?"

"Och, aye, with only a little more to go." Simon shot him a frowning glance. "Do you expect trouble?"

"When has there not been?"

"Peace these four years past—what do you know?"

"The Red Earl of Ulster is dead, and the king is in
Ireland. Trouble is afoot, and men are gathering."

"The regents stir up war."

"Aye, and hired mercenaries are converging in York.
If Edward moves north, the Bruce will meet him."

"What of you?" Simon asked.

"Word will come when I'm needed."

"And the lady?"

Turning to face him, Rob said, "She will remain here
until I decide."

"Will you return her to Argyll?"

He had wondered that himself. Loath as he was to admit it, he knew that to relinquish the lady to a cruel fate
was impossible. He would never do it willingly. Argyll
would have to come to his gates with an army to recover
his hostage, and he didn't think him fool enough for that.
There was the matter of treason that hung in the bal-
ance. . . .

"Or to her family?" Simon asked when Rob did not
reply at once. "You could ask a hefty ransom of Wakefield."

He swore softly.

"Christ, Simon, you have more questions than an oak
has leaves."

"And you are in a devil of a temper." Simon leaned on
a carpenter's frame, eyeing his cousin. "You never told
me why there is such bad blood between you and Argyll.
Oh, I know of his treachery that saw you arrested by the
English, but there is more to it, I think, than you have
told."

"Aye, so there is." It was a thing he'd not told anyone,
for to reveal too much would be to share the danger. Argyll was ruthless and wouldn't hesitate to use any means
to find the proof of his treason. But that was hidden well,

where no man could find it until he was ready. The time would come. He had only to wait.

There was a shout, and both men turned to see one end of the scaffold slide and a stonemason leap free just before it came crashing down. The man was unhurt but shaken, and large blocks of stone lay broken on the ground.

"Grant pardon," he kept muttering, shaking his head, his leather apron covered in stone dust, "grant pardon."

"Take him to the shade," Rob said, "and give him some ale."

The master mason gave directions for new stone to be cut, while the shaken worker was given a jug of ale. Rob surveyed the damage with Simon, his cousin's attention diverted at last to the waste of coin the accident caused. Once, Simon had been steward to Nigel Bruce, but since that man's death at the hands of the English, he had remained in Glenlyon with no desire to leave. A brutal death, the same as suffered by William Wallace years before, and it had done for Simon. He'd loved the king's brother, for all of Nigel Bruce's reckless foolishness at times, and he grieved for him still.

It was a grief Rob understood well.

So many lost, comrades in arms as well as kin. And it was not over, not with Queen Isabella and her lover Roger Mortimer the real power behind the boy king on the throne. It was whispered they had murdered Edward II, a foul crime unproven—yet. Now they turned to the Scottish king, with the blood of their own king still on their hands.

If peace was to last, Robert Bruce must drive home his point with ruthless finality. Edward III was young yet and would likely never be the warrior king Longshanks had been. King Edward I had died fighting Scotland, not of wounds received but of age and rage for battles lost.

But God, Glenlyon was weary of war, of the smell of

blood and sound of battle. There always seemed to be another battle to fight. Another death to grieve.

He thought of Lady Lindsay in the second-floor chamber, his own chamber, where he would have glass in the window for his mother's memory. It seemed oddly fitting for the lady to be there.

Hostage to Argyll, she was hostage still in Glenlyon, of a different sort, perhaps. To negotiate her release to her family, he risked losing all.

And in truth, his thoughts of her had changed direction from what once they had been, diverted somehow from terms of her importance as a hostage to memories of grass-green eyes and a tempting smile, of the soft cushion of scented skin beneath his hand. And she knew it.

That stormy day in the solar had altered more than perceptions. He'd seen that in her eyes, in the heated awareness of him, though no words had passed that gave him reason to think she thought of him as more than captor.

Restless, he strode into the hall. Soft gloom closed around him, a marked difference from the bright light that was so welcome outside. His eyes adjusted slowly to the change. It was quiet here, the clamor of building a muted sound within these thick stone walls.

So much yet to do, and the burdens of the days dragged into his nights, leaving him unsettled and sleepless. How did he reconcile his duty with his desires? Abducting the lady from Lochawe and Argyll's custody ignited trouble, he knew that well enough, yet there had been little choice.

Gone was the man he knew as Angus Campbell, and in his place was a stranger, a brutal man intent upon his own destruction, it seemed, any fairness vanquished by grief and a misplaced sense of honor. To leave Lady Lindsay there would have meant her death.

And to bring her here may well mean his own.

In terms of practical defense, he could count on the

MacGregors, MacCallums, and MacNeishes to rally to his cause, should it be required, but Argyll commanded many more men. Rob had not yet been laird of Glenlyon long enough to assess the mood of those who now swore to him, was not certain of their loyalty.

Christ above, he was not now certain of anything, the order of the world set awry by his own hand. He'd set himself against his father and against Argyll—overlord, for all that he was so treacherous. All for the sake of a woman, an act he once would have sworn he would never commit.

Not for him the gallant rescues plied by chivalric knights of the minstrels' lays, idle amusements that had no bearing on truth. Rare was the lady who would inspire men to such foolhardy risks.

And yet . . . and yet the Lady Lindsay had induced him to her cause without a tender word from her, without the sweet reward of her surrender. He wondered at his own recklessness in taking her from Lochawe. Other means may well have seen her safe, a message to Argyll, perhaps, or even to the king, as the earl of Wakefield was a powerful adversary to anger.

Yet he had brought her here, to a keep not yet strong enough to tolerate assault or even a siege. He must have been moon mad. She wanted to go home. He should send her.

"Give you good day, sir," the soft, familiar voice of his dreams said behind him, and he turned, the knot in his belly drawing tight as Lady Lindsay glided across the hall. Her saffron léine was belted around slender hips, falling to her ankles, and she wore a kerchief over her hair.

"There is ale in the jug," he said after a moment, with a wave of his hand toward the table, and she smiled.

"Aye, so there is. I placed it there myself this morn."

"Did you?" An answering smile dragged at his mouth.

"I should have known you would resort to housewifery."

"Idle hands belong to the devil, I was taught as a child. My mother always insisted my sister and I learn all to know about tending a household. It is easier to instruct if one has experience with the task."

"Do you black boots as well?"

"Ah, no, but I have mixed the concoctions for it." Her smile lingered as she crossed to the hearth, where a fire burned steadily and without smoke. "There is art to even laying a proper fire, but the drawing of it depends upon the stonemasons. If they do not know their task, smoke will fill the hall."

Despite her smile and apparent composure, she betrayed tension with the restless motions of her hands, the self-aware touch of her fingers to her brow, to the white kerchief folded over her hair, then the flutter of her hand as she gave a swift stroke along the table's surface. She prowled like a nervous feline, moving from hearth to table to the stack of benches against the wall.

"I will not send you to Argyll, my lady," he said, and she grew still, half turned from him, one hand lying upon the edge of a bench.

"Will you not?"

"You are more useful to me here."

She turned then, eyes wide. *"Useful?"*

"Aye, there are few here who know how to black boots and lay fires."

He'd expected a smile at his jest, but she did not. A strange expression marked her face, and hot color rose in her cheeks.

"Is that all you think of me, laird of Glenlyon, that I am *useful?*"

Unexpected anger flashed in her eyes, and he frowned. "What would you have me say? That I will not release you to Argyll or Lochawe because I would rather send you to your father?"

"Is that the reason?"

"It has occurred to me. Do you not want to go home? Is that not what you said to me in the tower of Lochawe? Christ above, woman, you are as changeable as the wind!"

"I have not changed in what I want, Glenlyon," she said as she came toward him, halting within a hand breadth to stare up at him with surprising ferocity. "I want now what I wanted then, what I wanted six years ago."

At a loss in the face of her fierce emotion, he shook his head. "It is not my duty to know what you want nor your privilege to demand it."

"Oh aye, it has never been my privilege to demand the courtesy of consideration for my desires, but only that of men to dictate my actions, what I do or say, or even what I think or feel! I weary of it, by God, weary of being a pawn for the idle amusement or convoluted schemes of men. It seems I misjudged you, Robert Campbell, for you did not take me from Lochawe to save me but for reasons of your own that have little to do with my welfare."

It was so inherently unjust that he did not reply for a moment, only stared at her with his temper rising.

"Aye, lady," he said softly after a moment, and saw her take a step back, "you have certainly misjudged me if you think I will tolerate unfounded accusations."

"How are they unfounded?"

He'd mistaken her backward step for a retreat, it seemed, for she launched another assault.

"Was I consulted before I was dragged the breadth of all Scotland to appease the greed of a baron? Nay, nor was I asked if I had a defense against an accusation of witchcraft by an old woman given to practicing her own spells—"

"That has nothing to do with me."

"No, but I do not recall your asking if I wished to leave Mairi behind and come with you."

"You prefer drowning or burning?" He set his jaw and said through clenched teeth, "By hell, lady, if you prefer death to my company, tell me now, and I'll oblige you quick enough!"

There was an instant of silence before she said softly, "Were I given the choice, I would have chosen to be with you over any other, Campbell of Glenlyon."

It shocked him. The implications of her words sank into him like a stone, and he stared at her with narrowed eyes. A hush descended upon the hall. He was aware of workmen on the far side, trapped by the battle, caught between escape and notice. It was the time but not the place to continue this discussion, and he had no intention of abandoning it.

His arm flashed out, his hand curling around her wrist to pull her with him across the hall. There was a soft gasp from her, and behind him he heard Simon's startled curse.

"Sweet Christ! There is mischief afoot!"

"Nay, Simon, no mischief," he said as he drew the lady with him to the staircase that spiraled upward, "only a pleasant conversation we wish to continue in privacy instead of within hearing of half of Glenlyon."

Resistance trembled in the tensed muscles of her arm as he pulled her up the steps, but she made no sound. It was just as well. He would not have heeded any protests she made now.

Torches batted shadows into the corners, the second-floor corridor dim and cool. The oaken door to his chamber was ajar; it was much brighter there, the window embracing soft breezes and sunshine. Dust motes rode hazy bars of light that picked out details on the stone mantel over the hearth. Carved lions, fleeing hinds, woodsmen captured for all eternity in stone were the only witnesses when he closed the door behind them. Rare privacy.

He released her arm. Dignity marred by anger stared back at him, the window light a relentless inquisitor.

"What did you mean, Lady Lindsay?"

Her chin lifted, a gesture he had come to recognize. "I meant that you need not have imposed your desires on me without my permission."

"Nay, lady, that is not what you said."

She looked away, the flush on her cheeks an eloquent admission. Her lips flattened, and her husky voice was so low he had to lean close when she said, "I said I would be with you over any other by my own choice."

"Yea," he said, "so you did." He drew in a deep breath. An unfamiliar warmth that had nothing to do with lust and everything to do with softer emotion eased into him to leave him uncertain. He had wanted verification, and now he had it. But he was at a loss about how to respond.

He wanted to touch her, to put his hand against her cheek and feel her warmth; he wanted to take off her ugly kerchief and unbind her hair so that it spread over her shoulders in a gleaming cape like silk. He wanted, he thought fiercely, to hold her through as many long nights as the world would grant them.

God, life was inherently precarious and uncertain, and this lady who stood before him in eloquent and vulnerable dignity was an unexpected gift.

He was not the man to refuse such bounty.

When he put out his hand, she hesitated only an instant before placing her slim white fingers into his palm, and he had to curb the impulse to move too swiftly. Slowly, he drew her closer, turned her hand over, lifted it to his lips. He heard the soft inhalation of her breath when his mouth moved from the hill of her palm to her wrist, his tongue flicking out to tease the delicate blue tracery of veins visible beneath her pale skin. The faint scent of heather drifted toward him, struck him with all the potency of a blow, and he held tightly to restraint.

"You smell," he murmured against the cushion of her wrist, "like a Highland heath."

Faintly, " 'Tis heather—" Her voice caught when his lips worked up her arm, the loose sleeve of her garment offering scant barrier—"put into chests to keep—" another catch in her voice when his tongue washed over the bend in her arm and moved higher—"moths away . . . oh my. . . ."

He glanced up, burning with growing desire. Her lips were parted, eyes a shadowed green, and the pulse in the hollow of her throat was a faint throb beneath soft skin.

Jesu! His need grew apace with the delay, and he fought the urge to take her standing against the wall. This was a lady, not some village trull, and he was no greenling unable to master his need.

He put his hand beneath her chin, pressed his forehead against hers, breathing her in as he gave her the chance to refuse him.

"Lady, should you yield, you are compromised. There may be no ransom of you if your father learns you have lain in my bed."

"What of you?" she whispered. "Is the ransom what you wish most?"

"Ah, no. It is not." He spread his fingers under the kerchief atop her head, pulling it free and loosening the pins that held her hair. "What I hold in my arms is treasure enough for me."

Chapter 16

†

TIME SPUN, SHIMMERED with the echoes of his words. No man had ever thought of her as a treasure. Emotion closed her throat so that she could not speak, could only pause for what seemed an eternity. So many doubts, fears, and longings coursed through her, and overriding all was the dawning of hope, sparked by the simple words of this Highland laird.

A shiver swirled through her. He looked so intense, the light from the window bright on his shadowed jaw, gleaming in the smoky gray of his eyes.

"Ah lass," he murmured when the silence stretched so long she ached from it, "you do not have to answer me now if it is not what you want."

Her hand lifted to cup over his, over the strong brown sinews and corded muscle, holding his palm still against her cheek. Blood pounded loudly in her ears, and the breath was scant in her lungs.

"How . . ." She paused, licked lips that were dry and

trembling, tried again, "How will I know what I want? You have made no vows, and I have not asked for any."

Would he pledge to her? Would he say that he wanted her to stay with him for love and not reward?

"I brought you here." His finger circled her ear, a light touch that ignited heat. "That is pledge enough that I mean to see you safe."

A knot formed in the pit of her stomach; tension pulled it tight as she shook her head.

"Nay, I would have the words." She looked away, tried to stifle the rising surge of disappointment and distress, but she knew that she could never yield until she heard them. It was more than honor that stayed her. It was the knowledge that she required allegiance before she could give her heart, and that is what it would be with this man. To yield her body alone was not enough.

He blew out a soft sigh of exasperation. "Sweet lady, I can vow to protect you, to keep you safe from your enemies and mine to the best of my skill and intention, but I warn you that your family will not approve any binding vows."

"It is not their approval that concerns me." She looked back at him, studied his face, the handsome features that she saw even in her dreams, so dear to her.

His brow shot up. "You want the blessing of the church? All of Scotland is under an interdict by the pope that bans priests from performing marriages or even prayers for the dead—"

" 'Tis not the blessing of my family nor the priests, nor even God, that I ask now, Robert Campbell, but of your own intent!"

Warm window light caught in his hair, gleamed in the sudden spark in his eyes. She recognized a struggle in him, in the shadows that rose to drown the light. He did not love her. He may want her, but he did not love her. . . . How foolish she had been to think he might, to think that she would find love in this Highland laird.

His silence lengthened. She watched window light shift while the bleak shadows of old grief swooped to claim her. He would say he could not, would say that her value as a treasure lay in her worth to earls and kings.

It was not unexpected.

Yet, for a brief span of time, a bright hope had flared inside her that had turned her days to light instead of dark. It was difficult to extinguish it.

"Lady mine," he said softly, "I have little enough to offer. All I have is this tower and a few tenants, and even that coveted by Argyll. I can promise you nothing but great toil ahead and the possibility of total ruin always lurking outside my gates."

"And you believe that I wish your lands instead of your vow?" She stared at him, shook her head slowly. "How little you know of me, Glenlyon. It is not that which lures me to you, for I have lands enough of my own, albeit English and not Scots." She put her hand on his arm, felt his muscles tense beneath her touch, saw the gathering frown on his brow, and knew he did not understand. "Lands matter, yea, and 'tis all I have had to count my worth these past years. But it is lately come to me that there are things far greater in value than fields and cattle."

"Easy enough to say when one owns fields and cattle," he said with a wry twist of his mouth. "Far less easy to say when it is a fight to gain and hold even a sprig of heather to call your own."

"Yet you have done so. By the strength of your courage and your heart, you have gained this glen. I trust in your ability to hold what you have earned."

His bitter laugh bruised the air between them. "Aye, but what will you say should I lose it all? If we must take to the caves and live on boiled nettles?"

A risk . . . a risk to say what was in her heart when she didn't know his, but how else did she answer him?

"I will say," she whispered, "that I am the richest in the world to love such a man."

His gaze was shadowed by the black brush of his lashes over his eyes, but she saw the quick spark of light in them. He put his hands on each side of her head, fingers tangled in her hair, his thumbs light beneath her chin to tilt up her face. "Brave lady . . ." He brushed his mouth over hers, "Foolish lady . . ." His hands tightened, and a tremor shot through her at his intensity. "Sweet lady mine, God help us both."

Then he released her, stepped back, and drew in a deep breath. "There is no priest near, nor could he say us vows, were he sitting in my hall. But there are vows we can say to one another by Scots law, just as binding though none but the birds of the air hear them. Do you ken my meaning?"

She nodded. "A consent-made marriage."

"Yea." He reached out, dragged a hand along the slope of her cheek, his voice low and husky as he said, "A handfast is legal, but once we lie together, 'tis as binding as a marriage made in front of priest and kirk. It will need only vows made on the kirk steps to be irrefutable."

Handfast . . . a betrothal ceremony that usually entailed the giving away of the wife for a bride price. And she had nothing to give, save her heart.

A faint smile rode his lips when he said, "I give you this chance only to say me nay, for once we are handfasted, I intend to consummate our vows."

It took only an instant for her decision.

Later, few things stood out in her memory; the rest was like a blur, but those memories were sharp and precious.

The laird of Glenlyon, tall and straight, his hand holding hers and his eyes never leaving her face as they stood

before the fire in the hall with Simon MacCallum and
Morag the tinker's wife to witness their vows. "I, Robert
Campbell, will take thee, Judith Lindsay, to my spouse
wife as the law of the Holy Kirk allows and thereto I will
plight thee my troth."

Her response was made in a trembling voice, aware that
he had left no room for possible repudiation with vows
taken before witnesses, and that in itself was a confir-
mation.

Simon's face, unaccustomed to solemnity, aware of the
importance of his presence, eased at last into a grin as he
called for wine and cakes, and Morag bustled about, tears
glinting in her eyes, while those without the keep were
invited in to celebrate.

"Och," Morag said, shaking her head, " 'tis not lucky
to have a May wedding."

"The wedding proper will come on All Hallow's Day,"
Rob said, "this is just the handfast ceremony, binding as
it is."

"Not binding until the bedding," Morag said without a
hint of a blush as she waggled her finger at him.

"It will be binding before the morrow comes," was his
answer, and Judith felt the heat rise to her cheeks.

✝

OUTSIDE, LIGHT HAD faded, but the revelry in the hall
below had not, when at last they stood alone in the chamber where shadows blurred the corners and the only light
was from the hearth and a single lamp. An awkward silence fell between them, strange and clumsy. Judith was
aware of him watching her, too aware, and her heart beat
so fast and hard that she marveled he did not remark upon
it.

"You did not ask for a bride price," she said to break the silence.

He smiled, a dark curve of his mouth in a face half shadowed. "There was no need. Even if you had aught to give, I would not ask."

"No?" She moved to the table, poured them both some wine from a jug into cups, though her hands shook slightly. Foolish, to be so nervous, for she was not an untried maid! She knew well enough what came on the bridal night and after, though with this man it would be different. Yea, it would be far different, for he kindled desires in her that she'd never thought to feel.

She turned, pressed a cup of wine into his hands, said, "Yet I should give you something—"

"Oh," he said, taking the wine and pressing his hand over hers, "you will, sweet lady."

A hot flush burned her face, and it was difficult to draw in an easy breath. Flustered, she set down her cup.

"I meant—"

"I know what you meant, lady mine."

She watched him, waiting, her heart a thunder in her ears as he sipped his spiced wine, his eyes regarding her over the rim of the cup.

"This all . . . happened so swiftly," she said after a moment, and he nodded.

"Aye, so it did. More swiftly than I thought it could." He paused, took another sip of wine. "I have never abducted a bride before."

"No," she said, laughing softly, "I did not think you had. Nor do I think you meant to do it this time."

"Oh aye, I meant it," he said, and his gaze was potent as it rested on her face, "I meant it full well."

Something hovered in the air between them, and then he set down his wine, took two long strides to her side, and she was in his arms. His mouth found hers, and the heat in his kiss sparked fire in her, as if a lightning bolt struck. The world tilted, ablaze, and when she moaned, he slid his hands into her loose hair, combing his fingers through it.

Her hands spread on his chest, soft wool cushioning the steady thud of his heart beneath her palm. His tongue slid between her lips, opening her with a sweet ferocity, tasting of heady wine and need. She breathed him in, and the slow, steady pulse between her legs grew sharper, more insistent.

"Lady fair," he muttered finally, dragging in a breath that sounded frayed and uneven, "I see that there is now a proper bed."

"Yea." A laugh trembled on the air between them. "It was brought up early today, as you commanded. The mattress is newly stuffed. . . ."

"It would be a shame to waste it."

Silent now, she quivered as he untied the laces to her léine, unfastened the clasp that held the plaide around her, and slid them free. She closed her eyes, shivering in the cool air. Morag had helped her bathe earlier, had entwined blossoms in the circlet around her head, sweet-smelling and her only adornment now.

Still clothed, he slid his hands along the arch of her throat and lower, his touch light, caressing. Her knees were weak, and she put out her hands to grasp his arms to keep from collapsing. The bed loomed at her back, draped in green curtains like a bower in the greenwood. She felt light-headed suddenly, awash with cool air and heat and anticipation and the pounding need that throbbed relentlessly inside.

Skimming one hand down her back, he tested the curves he found there, then slid to the front, his hand between them as he cupped her breast in his palm. Fire shot through her, searing and rampant, and she gasped. He raked a thumb across the beaded nipple, provoking another spear of heat, and the pounding beat between her thighs increased.

He shifted slightly, lifted her in his arms, and sank with her onto the yielding mattress beyond the curtains. A sweet fragrance surrounded them. He tucked her body next to his so that she fit full against him, breast to thighs, the slightly abrasive scrape of wool against her bare skin oddly arousing. Murmuring softly, he stroked his hands over her, his fingers playing along her ribs, the flat surface of her belly, then up again, cupping her breast in his palm. Her breath caught in her throat, and an excited shiver swept through her.

Again his mouth found her, tongue washing a path from her mouth to her throat and lower, until he came at last to the taut, aching pebble of her breast. Agitation fluttered as he drew it into his mouth, a steady pull that sent heat plunging to her belly.

"Glenlyon," she heard herself moan, a sigh and a plea at the same time, asking for something that hovered just out of her reach.

"Rob," he said against her breast, and he lifted a gaze to her that was hot and smoldering. "Use my given name. . . ."

Her hands tangled in his hair and her hips arched when he nibbled lightly on her breast, tongue teasing her until she could hardly bear it, until the steady, pounding pressure threatened to explode into some bright, unknown force that waited just beyond. There was a primitive need to hear the sound of his name on her lips, a familiarity that signaled that he belonged to her now.

She must have cried out his name, for he was whispering her own name in her ear, his breath hot and making her shudder, as his hand slid lower to the aching fire that blazed between her thighs. When his hand slipped inside, she cried out softly again.

Plucking fretfully at the wool tunic he still wore, she tried to slide her hands beneath, needing to feel his skin, wanting to touch him. He took his hand away, and she looked up at him, green-hazed with the light streaming through the thin curtains, the fire behind him a rosy glow, and his face in shadow. But she could see his eyes, the silvery light that gleamed down at her as he sat up.

She started to protest, but he stood to remove his tunic and boots, and she watched, shameless and brazen, wanting to see him as he saw her. Outlined against the scant light, Rob stood at last with only his pride to clothe him. Her breath caught a little.

A bonny laird, indeed, with powerful shoulders and sculpted bands of muscle on his chest and belly, dark skin only lightly furred with hair on his chest and lower, marked with badges of courage from sword and life. Potent strength in every line, his fluid grace and sleek beauty summoned images of primeval warriors.

The thudding of her heartbeat was loud in her ears when he returned to the bed and leaned over her, intent hot in his eyes, and she arched up for him, arms wide and welcome, with love in her eyes and heart.

He settled between her thighs, braced on his arms, his hands gently pushing the hair from her eyes. With his body so close, his hard length a throb of heat at her entrance, he pressed his forehead against hers and slowly eased inside. A moan escaped her, and his mouth found hers, tasting of wine and urgency, until he was fully sheathed within. The heavy fullness pulsed, almost to the point of pain, but he stayed still for a moment until the discomfort eased, and she relaxed beneath him.

Sliding her hands over the sleek contours of his muscled back, she felt him shudder. A sensual haze that she had never experienced enclosed her, erotic and shutting out everything but Rob, the feel of his skin beneath her hands, his weight atop her, the sweet scent of wine, and the elusive fragrance of heather from the mattress. The world narrowed to just this moment, just this bed, shut off from the past and the future, where nothing existed but this moment in time.

And she wished it would never end. . . .

Then he whispered her name, a husky sound like a sigh as they shared a rhythm of body and desire, sweeping faster and faster toward the same end, toward the unknown that still awaited her, haunting and sweet and powerful.

And when she found it, that melting wave of soaring ecstasy flowed over her like heated honey, until she drifted at last, weightless, on wings that brought her gently back to earth.

✝

"DRUNKEN LOUTS," ROB said, but his tone was amused as they passed through the hall the next morning, stepping over the sprawled forms of the revelers.

Judith laughed softly. "Even Simon snores." She pointed to the steward where he lay draped over a table, an empty wine bottle clutched beneath one arm.

"Aye, well, give them their rest. One day cannot matter much. The work will still be here on the morrow for them."

It was quiet in the bailey, and Rob saddled two horses, a smaller one for Judith, and his own black steed. They rode through the open space where the gates would be and into the soft morning light beyond the tower keep. Judith let the hood of her léine fall back and the sun warm her as they rode down the narrow, rutted track that led toward the loch.

It was rocky and hilly in places, leveling to a wide stretch of field that bore a single standing stone. Beyond, a huge ancient yew spread its branches wide, casting deep shade.

They paused beneath it, and the sharp, spicy scent filled the air. Rob reached up, pulled loose a needle, crushed it between his fingers. His mount snorted, danced, and finally lowered a sleek head to graze on tufts of grass.

" 'Tis said that Pontius Pilate was born beneath this tree," Rob said, frowning at the ruined yew needle in his hand, "of a local woman and a Roman soldier. The Romans once ranged free here. They conquered all in their path, but now they are gone."

Slightly puzzled, she nodded. "Yea, so they are."

"Now Glenlyon is mine, granted me by the Bruce, to hold as I can." He tossed away the yew needle and looked up to meet her eyes. "I mean to do what I must to hold it."

"Yea, I have no doubt of that. You will hold it against all who might try to take it from you."

He nudged his mount closer, until it sidled next to her smaller pony, and leaned down to cup her chin in his palm. In a low, fierce voice he said, "I keep what is mine, sweet lady."

Her throat tightened at the possessive emotion in his tone and eyes, and she nodded. "Aye, so keep me well and long, laird of Glenlyon. I belong to you."

While there had been no words of love from him, there had been vows of fidelity, and that would be enough for now. One day, he would say the words she longed to hear from him, more than sweet words of passion, but those of love.

His mouth brushed over her lips, first lightly, then with growing need, and she had no doubt that the day would come, whether he knew it or not.

Part II

Chapter 17

✝

WARM DAYS CRADLED Glenlyon, when fields grew tall and green beneath a summer sky. Sheep and cattle grazed on the hills and grew fat, and the barnekin walls were almost completed around the tower. Work stopped only when it rained, as it was now, a steady beat that turned the ground to mud and sent all indoors.

"Whitsun rents paid for some," Simon said, frowning as he studied ledgers spread on the table. A rack of candles shed light on the pages. "If all goes well, Lammas rents will see us through."

"Thank God for quarter days." Rob rubbed idly at his leg, almost completely healed now, paining him only when it rained, as now. "What else?"

"Two new plow oxen for the fields at a cost of ten pounds, offset some by the rents, since they are used by tenants as well. Eight pounds for iron for nails, but the wood for beams came from last quarter's accounts. Stone as well—though the cost for stonecutters increased to four shillings a week."

"Each?"

"Christ, no. Total. Most of the stone has been cut. All said, the rents are in now, in coin or kind. I have totals."

Rob's attention drifted from the neat figures Simon had so painstakingly copied to the hearth across the hall. Lady Judith sat before the fire, mending in her lap, a look of fierce and utter concentration on her face. Rain rattled the shutters, but the incessant sound of hammers and awls was absent. He thought of the bed upstairs and an afternoon spent beneath the green canopy with Judith.

She fascinated him. Tawny firelight caught in her hair, an amber gleam, and turned her cheeks a rosy pink. A ribbon was entwined in her thick plait, draped over one shoulder as she worked, squinting slightly at the stocking she plied with needle and wool.

Simon continued his talk of rents and expenses, of the costs of wine and spices and cloth, and the number of sheep at the last count, but Rob had ceased listening.

Much more pleasant to think of hours whiled away on a mattress stuffed with heather, of the lady in his arms and the sweet mysteries of her body discovered anew. He would loosen her hair so that it spread beneath her and carefully remove her garments, kissing her as each layer was peeled away, until she was as ready for him as he was her. The soft scent of heather would envelop him, until he drifted away on it—

"Are you listening to me?" Simon asked with his brows tucked into a frown, and unwilling to be caught mooning over the lady like a callow youth, Rob nodded.

"Oh, aye. Sheep."

Simon put down the ledger sheets and glanced toward the hearth. A faint smile pressed at the corners of his mouth.

"No, I was talking about wine casks. Now I find myself in need of some."

He rose from the bench, and with another amused glance at Rob, left the hall. It was quiet, the sound of rain a steady song, the snap of the fire reassuring.

Rob moved across the hall to Judith, sweetly scented rushes rustling beneath his boots. She looked up when he touched her shoulder, green eyes lit with gold from the fire's dance.

"Are you finished with your accounts, sir?"

"Yea, for now." He put out a hand, saw her hesitate a moment, then a slow smile bent her lips. "Come with me, my lady, for there is another account in arrears."

The mending abandoned, she went with him up the curve of stairs. His heartbeat quickened when the door was closed behind them and she turned, diffuse light through the glass window creating a misty halo behind her head. A Madonna, but more lovely than the paintings and statues he had seen in kirk and abbey. Slowly, she reached up, fingers tugging at the ribbon in her hair, freeing it, then loosening the plait so that her hair fell free around her shoulders, a glorious mass that gleamed with a life of its own.

It never failed to stir him, her pristine beauty like a beacon that drew him close enough to burn.

And he burned . . . God above, he burned.

He lifted her chin with a finger, his hand dark against her pale skin, then bent his head to capture her mouth. He sucked in a deep breath, drawing in her breath with his own, and savored the taste of honey and ginger. Potent, powerful, a flash of heat went through him like summer lightning. She undid him, this lovely lady. He wanted to tell her, wanted to put into words how he felt, but it was beyond him. He was no minstrel to say pretty words, but only a man who felt them.

She trembled in his embrace, a delicious shiver. He lifted his head. "Judith . . ." Her name on his lips was near a prayer as he had come in God only knew how long, wicked sinner that he was, but there was reverence in the saying of it, in the way it rolled off his tongue.

Her lashes lifted, dark brown and thick, and she gazed at him with emotion stirring in the depths of her eyes. He kissed her again, fiercely this time, his hand cradling the back of her head, fingers wide and combing through the wealth of her unbound hair, letting cool, silken fibers flow through his hand.

A groan escaped him when her hands slid along his back, fingers digging into linen and muscle as she worked them up to his neck to cup behind his head and hold his mouth more tightly to hers. He teased her lips apart with his tongue, tasted the honeyed flick of her response against him. Heat rose higher, coursed through his body like a wildfire.

Outside the tower, thunder rumbled and rain swept coolly over heaths and crags, but inside this chamber, fires raged.

His fingers skimmed over the arched curve of her throat and down, laces parting with a few tugs, his hand slipping beneath linen to caress velvety skin. Sweet, soft . . . He slid a hand over her breast, felt the nipple bead against his palm. She moaned, a low fluttery sound deep in her throat.

He moved forward, his hand behind her back holding her against him, her step halting as he took them toward the bed against the wall. Green velvet bed hangings parted, swallowed them as he laid her upon the mattress and followed, his body fit to hers with growing urgency.

Heated whispers, soft murmurs, and exploring hands; clothing lay discarded on the floor beside the bed. Shadows claimed them. Need was fierce on him now, the cushion of her body soft and welcoming.

When she reached for him, he groaned as her hand tested his length, fingers curled around him, a slide up and down that made him shudder. He pushed into her hand, slow and luxurious, felt her grip tighten. Sweet torment; tension built, stretched tighter and tighter.

"Enough," he muttered at last and held her wrist. His lungs worked, his breathing labored as he tried to drag air into his starved lungs.

Heart pounding, fire raced through his body as he slid over her, his hand skimming up the curve of her thigh and hip. His fingers splayed over the swell of her belly. Soft flesh quivered beneath his caress, and he dipped lower, dragging his hand down to the cleft at the juncture of her thighs. Her breath came faster now, cheeks a high color and her eyes a green glitter beneath her lowered lashes.

"Bonny lassie . . ." He wanted to say more, but the words would not come. They flitted through his head, disjointed and elusive, but it was impossible to form coherent thought.

He felt her tremble as his hands worked into the damp folds between her legs, slipping over tender flesh in arrant sensuality. The pad of his thumb raked over the tiny bud at the top of her sex, inviting the soft cries and delicate shudders.

Delicious heat . . . beguiling woman . . . seductive and consuming . . . Through the haze of urgent need, he held tight to control, to bring her to fulfillment before he reached his own.

Her body arched into his hand, her breath was swift and harsh, and when she cried out, he smothered the sobbing sound with a hard, fierce kiss. Body throbbing, he slid inside her at last, felt her close around him, velvet heat clenching. She rocked with him as he thrust deeply, losing himself inside her, forgetting everything but this woman and the churning need she ignited.

┼

THE RAIN HAD stopped. Gray light seeped through the window and bed hangings, and Judith stirred to rise to one elbow. Rob slept. She watched him, studied his face as if trying to memorize it. Perhaps she was. There may come a day when she would long for this memory. A shudder tracked her spine.

Why did she have this inescapable sense of finality at times? It was as if she borrowed sorrow, when she prayed daily for life to go on as it had been these last weeks. It was as near as she'd ever come to happiness, and she clung fiercely to each moment.

Oh, there was so much she wanted to say to him, to ask him, yet when the time presented itself, her tongue cleaved to the roof of her mouth as if nailed there.

So little time, so little time . . .

She put a hand upon his rib cage, the sheen of his dark skin a marked contrast to her paleness. Faint ridges marred the smooth flesh in places, puckered scars from old wounds. Her gaze traveled lower. It was nearly healed, the wound on his thigh no longer red but faded to a jagged white line, like a lightning bolt. Downy black hair furred his body, a light pelt on his chest, thicker below his belly.

Heat eased up her throat to her cheeks as her gaze followed the arrowed wedge and ropes of muscle on his abdomen, then traveled lower. A braw man, indeed, powerful even in repose. She looked away, sucked in a sharp breath, and let it out slowly, a chuff of air.

When she looked back at his face again, black-fringed silver looked back at her.

"Dinna stop now, lass," he said, reverting to broad Scots again, "look all ye want."

Embarrassed, she bit her lower lip to still the denial that sprang ready. It would do no good. They both knew she had been brazen enough to stare at him.

"I am done," she said primly after a moment, and his laugh filled the enclosed bed.

He reached up, stuck his open hand into the mass of her loose hair, closed his fingers, and drew her face down slowly to his. His breath warmed her cheek, his other hand lifting to scoop the hair behind her shoulder.

"Sweet lady, I hope you are never done."

Her throat ached with sudden emotion, with the need to hold him fiercely close, to plead with him not to ever leave Glenlyon. Futile, of course, for he would leave when the time came. It was inevitable. She'd listened to the talk of war, of more fighting to the south, along the Marches and over the border into England. It filled her with dread, for him and her and the future.

Resting her forehead against his, she felt the brush of his lashes against her jaw and whispered, "I will never be done until you wish it."

"Then," he said, his hands closing in her hair to hold her head still as his mouth moved to capture hers, "you will never be done."

It was enough for the moment.

Chapter 18

†

ROB WAS WADING in the shallows of the River Lyon
when James Douglas came to Glenlyon. He saw the
riders long before he could tell who they were, climbed
out of the river and back into his boots, and was waiting
by the old Roman bridge for them.

Black eyes, cocky grin, his horse dancing sideways, the
Black Douglas acknowledged Rob with a huff of laughter.

"Eager, are we, to slay the English?"

"Ready, if not eager," Rob replied. He kept an easy
hand on his horse, reined it around as Douglas rode alongside.

"So you've become a fisherman, without battle to keep
you busy."

"Fishing for loose stones under the bridge," Rob said
with a grin. "I was told it was near collapse, but it will
be here long after we are gone."

"A Roman legacy: walls, bridges, and bastards. All

have survived even our efforts. Have you room for us? I
have a plan to discuss."

Rob knew well the plans of James Douglas. They usually involved bloodshed and always involved danger.

"Room enough, if some don't mind sleeping in the stables."

"I've slept in mud and water to my neck; a little straw
and horse dung will not do me harm."

Many of the men with Douglas he knew, some he knew
by reputation, and others were strangers to him, but by
the time the evening repast was eaten and wine had relaxed them, Rob knew that he would know all of them
much better before the week was out. His gaze sought
Judith, who sat on a bench nearby, her expression
strained, her courtesy abundant.

Douglas watched through half-lidded eyes, a faint smile
on his mouth as he lifted his wine. "An excellent meal,
my lady," he said to Judith with his familiar lilting lisp.
"It has been a long time indeed since I have enjoyed better."

A fleeting smile touched her lips, but her eyes were
dark-shadowed as she inclined her head in acknowledgement of his praise. "It has been an honor to serve you,
Sir James."

Douglas slid a speculative glance toward Rob. There
had been no explanation offered for Judith's presence
here, but he would know most of the details already. Argyll had lodged a complaint with the king for the abduction of his hostage, a futile move if he expected her return,
but not the vengeful violence Rob had expected. Had he
found the damning evidence of his treachery? Was that
why Argyll delayed retribution?

"I have gathered forces across Scotland for a foray into
England," Douglas said suddenly, his voice soft. He

leaned forward. "I want Glenlyon to join us."

It was expected since he had seen James Douglas ride onto the Roman bridge, and he nodded. "Aye, so I will."

Satisfaction rode the smile on Douglas's mouth, and he gave a short nod. "If you need time to make arrangements here—"

"No. Simon MacCallum is an able steward, you will recall. He can call up men for defense, should it be needed."

That was true enough. Rob's gaze shifted to Judith, and he recognized the strain that marked her mouth and eyes. The hand that held her wine shook slightly when she lifted the cup to her mouth. Her lips parted, closed on the rim, damp red from the wine.

Douglas returned his attention to the lady, and his dark brow lifted slightly. "It is my understanding that your father is Earl of Wakefield," he said, earning her notice, and she nodded slowly.

"Yea, that is true, Sir James." A drop of wine clung to her lower lip, reflecting light. "I have not seen him in seven years."

"A pity. War separates families at times."

She held his gaze. "It was not war that separated us, Sir James. It was my marriage."

Amusement lit his eyes as Douglas nodded. "Aye, another form of warfare. Yet you are widowed now."

"Yes." The lift of her wine to her lips was an obvious signal that she did not intend to elaborate.

Ever bold, Douglas ignored it. He leaned forward. "Was no ransom offered for your return to England?"

"If you know of my abduction from Caddel Castle, then you must also know that it was not, Sir James. Ask me what you really wish to know. It will save us both much time."

"You are English born, Scots by marriage. Where lie your loyalties?"

Her eyes moved to Rob, and he smiled faintly. "They lie with me," he said before she could reply, "thus with Scotland by default."

Douglas grinned. "I had wanted to hear the words from the lady."

"Then hear me," Judith said softly, though there was an edge to her husky voice that Douglas could not have missed. "My loyalties lie with Robert Campbell of Glenlyon. Should he swear to Scots king or English, I follow his banner."

"That is plain enough, my lady, and answers me quite well."

Distress loomed in her eloquent eyes, and Rob rose to his feet and put out a hand to her. "Come, lady mine, and I will escort you to our chamber."

After the briefest of hesitations, she put her hand in his and bade the company a good night.

"Are you angry with me?" she asked when they reached his chamber, and he shook his head.

"Sir James was being the Black Douglas. He has a reason for persisting, and I will know it soon enough."

"Rob—" Her hands wound into the front of his tunic, held tightly as she said, "I swore to you the night we made our vows, and would do so again. Yet I fear that Douglas has knowledge that may do us harm."

"He's a lot of things, but Sir James isn't treacherous, sweetling." He put his hands over hers, held them tightly for a moment, then gently untangled her from his tunic. "I must return. I'll not wake you when I come to bed."

She leaned forward, bent her head, and pressed her face into his chest. "Nay," she said, the words muffled, "you had better wake me. I want every moment with you before you leave."

He crushed her to him, then reached down to lift her face to his, kissing her fiercely before he set her back and away from him.

"Sleep now. I'll wake you when I come to bed."

Douglas and only a few other men remained in the hall when he returned, the rest having sought their beds in corners or stables. Douglas lifted his wine in a salute.

"I understand the lure, Glenlyon. She is lovely and loyal, two of the best qualities in a woman."

"Wife." When Douglas stared at him, he said, "We are handfasted."

A look of consternation creased Sir James's face. "It's dangerous to thwart Argyll and the king. I cannot think the Bruce will be pleased to hear that you have stolen your overlord's hostage and wed her, backhand though it may be."

"The king is far too concerned with other matters now to worry about my affairs," Rob said, "and when he has the time, I will have resolved Argyll's protests."

"Will you?" Douglas looked amused. "I would be most interested to hear how you plan to do that."

"And I will be most pleased to tell you when the time is right." He lifted his wine in a salute. *"Sléinte."*

Grinning, Douglas lifted his cup. *"Suas e, sios e,"* he said, and did just that, downing his wine in a single gulp.

⸸

SHE WAS STILL awake when Rob slipped into their chamber, though she lay still and quiet so she could watch him for a moment. So precious these hours, so few now with his leaving hanging over her head like doom. Grief rose up in her throat, and she pushed it down. It would solve nothing to let him see her weep, and she didn't want his last memory of her to be with the ravages of tears on her face.

But God, it was almost impossible. . . .

A low fire burned on the hearth to take away the chill of night, putting off scant heat but a rosy light. It played over him as he shrugged out of his tunic and boots, stood before the hearth clad only in splendid male pride. Narrow flanks, well-muscled and burnished with a tawny sheen, flexed as he stretched, his back to her still, the light a pale shadow. Her heart clutched. It was painful to think she might lose him.

Fingers curled around the small sprig she held in her hand, a convulsive movement. She waited until he turned, his step soft on the stone floor, the bed ropes creaking as he eased his weight onto the mattress. Darker now, his profile moved over her, and she reached up to touch his face.

"You're awake, lass."

"Aye. I could not sleep."

He slid down beside her, warm and familiar, a comfort and a blessing after all the empty years.

"What do you have there?" His voice was soft, amused as she pressed the sprig she held into his palm and his fingers closed around it.

"Fraoch ban." Her voice shook a little. "White heather. I want you to carry it with you for luck."

He was quiet for a moment, then said, "I will carry it with me for love. I never smell the heather but what I think of you, sweetling."

She buried her face against his chest, felt the heat of his body like a balm against her cheek, the steady beat of his heart the most lovely melody in the world. She would die if he did not return. How did she tell him that?

Lifting her face, she eased upward to press her lips against the strong column of his throat, felt his indrawn breath as her hand moved over the sculpted planes of his chest and abdomen and lower. Expected reaction, a rising of him to meet her caress, and he turned to push her back into the mattress.

Borrowed time, sweet hours to remember, to hold tight to her in the long days ahead.

Chapter 19

$\dagger$

I T WAS RAINING again, a miserable downpour that soaked
Rob to the skin and made footing difficult for his horse.
It was the middle of June and felt like April, cold and
wet. The track that wound through the Kielder Gap was
rutted and rocky, mud sucking at hooves as they plodded
onward to cross the Tyne at Haydon Bridge. James Douglas rode unheeding of weather or terrain, as always, resolute in purpose.

Once across the English border, the three flying col-
umns led by Douglas, Lord Randolph, and Donald, Earl
of Mar, fanned south into Weardale, laying waste to farms
and villages as they went. Lords Randolph and Mar swept
east and west, while Douglas went south. It was a tactic
designed to prove to Queen Isabella and Sir Roger Mortimer that they would not be diverted, even by the vast
host of mercenaries that were now assembling in an army
in York.

"'Tis said they have a crack contingent of twenty-five

hundred heavily armed Flemish cavalry at their disposal," Douglas told them when they camped in the still-smoldering ruins of a village for the night.

Cattle wandered aimlessly in the field, and Rob heard the ferocious barking of a dog in the distance. He hunched his shoulders forward, munching on hot oatcakes as he mulled over this dismal information.

"What does the king plan?" A MacNeish leaned nearer the campfire; flames illuminated his unshaven face, the weary lines of battle carved into craggy features with grime and soot.

"War," was the succinct reply.

They all looked much the same, Rob thought, with the same grimness in their eyes.

"Is't true the English have a new weapon?" MacNeish asked.

"Aye." The Black Douglas stretched lazily, his posture so unconcerned that the air of tension slightly eased. "It's a gunpowder cannon. Lethal, 'tis certain, but cumbersome to drag along." Black eyes narrowed with amusement. "While they trudge through the bogs, we can watch from a nice dry hill until we have them where we want them. Then we attack before they know we're even close."

"It has merit," MacNeish acknowledged, still frowning, "but reeks of peril."

"All of England reeks of peril." Douglas tossed a stick into the fire, sliced a glance at Rob. "You are quiet this eve, Glenlyon. Are you satisfied with the day's spoils?"

"Yea." He lapsed into silence, unable to summon words that would explain his gloom.

"Tomorrow," said Douglas, "we lay waste to Wake-field's demesne. Your lady will no doubt hear of it."

"Aye."

Leaning forward so that firelight was on his face, he surveyed Rob with a lifted brow. "I have fired my own keep to thwart the English. Do you have doubts now?"

"Nay, not for what we do. Wakefield deserves no less than any English baron. It is not for that I fret but for the safety of the lady left behind." A wry smile curved his mouth. "I am unused to such worries."

Douglas grinned. "Simon MacCallum will see to her good health, as will those devil MacGregors you left behind."

One of the men beyond range of firelight lifted a voice in protest of the epithet, and general laughter eased the tension of moments before.

"Then you've no quarrel with wasting Wakefield's lands and taking what we will," Douglas said when the laughter had died down, and Rob shook his head.

"Nay, for the earl has been no friend to his daughter. I have little use for a man who puts aside his own." There was an unspoken reference to Angus Campbell in his words that he knew James Douglas understood.

Douglas shrugged. "There are many with divided loyalty these days. We shall help them choose, heh?"

"Aye, that we shall."

†

THE RIVER WEAR snaked through moors and sloping hills, plummeted over rocks in places, frothing in deep pools. The rains had ceased at last, but footing was wet and perilous.

They were camped near the river, a rushing torrent that pushed past rugged crags, when a sentry brought news of an approaching force.

Mud-smeared, he swiped a hand over his face and made it worse as he told Douglas, "Three hundred strong or more come from the south. Wakefield's standard flies."

Wakefield. Rob, who had been in counsel with Douglas and several others, felt a spurt of elation. They'd hoped to smoke out the earl. God above, they'd laid waste to near all of his tenants, visiting destruction upon fields and stores with rampant indiscretion, taking coin and goods without regard. It was time the earl came to meet them.

"They outnumber us," said Sir Alec of the Isles, a troubled expression on his face, "by a hundred strong."

The muddied sentry shifted from one foot to the other. He glanced from Sir Alec to Douglas. "Knights ride with the foot, battle-trained, they look, no yeoman soldiers these."

"Aye?" Douglas laughed softly. "What say you, then. Do we wait to offer them cup and cake, or do we ride to greet them on our own terms?"

The decision was unanimous.

Douglas sent a three-pronged column, one at the front and two at their flanks, with orders to harry at will. It was his favorite form of warfare, the harrying and then hiding, swooping down to strike and inflict casualties, and escaping while the enemy rallied for assault.

They gave the English no respite the rest of that day and the night, so that Wakefield's forces spent sleepless hours sitting up in full armor and holding to their horses, ready at a moment's notice to battle the Scots. At first light, the bedraggled troops lent pursuit with determination if not direction.

Rob watched from a high hill, hidden by trees, and saw with satisfaction that the force decided to split in two. It would be easier now to pick off stragglers, demoralizing the enemy with lightning strikes and swift flight.

A party of thirty men, including some his own and those of Sir Alec, rode out to lure the forces into following. They spurred their horses to a grassy hill within sight, and when seen, took flight. A small band of riders broke off from the main force that was already divided and gave chase.

Circling around, they led them straight into the jaws of Douglas and the rest, surrounding them with ease. It was a fierce fight, quickly engaged. Deflecting a sword with his blade, Rob kneed his horse forward, swung his weapon up and around in a wicked slice. Blood spurted over him, thick and hot, and he ignored it, a roaring in his ears like thunder as he worked.

There was no time for anything but the reflexes of his body, the gauging of opponents, and the constant assessment of what lay beyond his blade. An enemy could strike from anywhere, and it was as if another part of him stepped aside to watch and warn. The fight was swift and bloody, with half the enemy slain and the others captured.

"We will accept coin and gear in lieu of prisoners," Douglas said with a grin when he joined them, "and let them reflect upon our kindness on the long walk back home."

One of the knights, bloodied but defiant, swore softly. "May the devil take you back home, Black Douglas! Aye, and may all your damned Scots demons see Hell with you!"

Amused, Douglas spurred his mount close to the un-horsed knight whose dented helmet was tucked under his arm and his blond hair matted with blood. Douglas raked him with a close eye, surveying the crest stitched upon the bloodied tabard. "I know of you. You're Wakefield's whelp."

The young man nodded grimly. "Aye, so I am."

"Then you have family here, young Wakefield. Glen-lyon, come and meet your brother by law."

Giving a start, Wakefield narrowed his eyes. "Glenlyon rides with you?"

"Yea, he does. He stands not a yard's distance from you now."

Curse Douglas for his perverted sense of entertainment. Rob sheathed his bloodied sword, stepped forward to stare coolly at the young man staring back at him with hot green eyes full of murder.

"You have a most droll way with you, Douglas," Rob said tightly and heard him laugh.

"Ah, it was bound to happen one day, Glenlyon. Now is as good as then."

"Give me my sword," Wakefield demanded, "to settle a matter of honor." Rob recognized that upward thrust of chin, square instead of rounded, a man's face for all that he resembled his sister.

"I think not." Douglas leaned from his horse to say, "The familial resemblance is remarkable, do you not agree?" and a thread of laughter rippled through his words.

"Devil take you, James Douglas." Rob said it without rancor, a resigned curse that he knew Douglas would no more heed than he had Wakefield's.

"Give us your Christian name, young Wakefield," Douglas said, "so that we will know whose horse and gear we have."

Flashing him a glance of resentment, he said stiffly, "Sir Payton of Langdon."

"Ah, Sir Payton. Do you not wish news of your fair sister?"

A muscle worked in his jaw, but after a moment, he gave a jerk of his head. "Aye, for the news I have of her must be wrong. 'Tis said she resides with the devil now."

"Do you think 'tis so?" Douglas grinned wider, nudged his blowing horse in a half circle around the young man. "Ah, now I see the resemblance between you."

Weary of the banter, Rob said abruptly, "Your sister is safe, Sir Payton."

"In the hands of a Scot?"

Anger flared. "You are in the hands of a Scot, and you seem well enough, by hell! If you thought it so barbaric a fate, then you should never have sent her to Caddel Castle."

"Had I my way about it, she would still be on English soil," the young man growled. "If you have any honor, you will see her returned to her family."

"Had the earl any honor, he would have paid the ransom for her return," Rob shot back at him. "It seems that Scots manors and estates have more importance for him."

"A lie!" He stepped back, drew off his mail gauntlet, and threw it on the ground between them. The challenge drew instant shouts from his companions, bloodied and beaten as they were, and Rob stepped forward to take up the glove.

"Hold, Glenlyon," Douglas said, serious now, his thin face sober, "we have not the time for such play. It grieves me, but 'twill have to wait until another day." He slid a thoughtful glance back to the captured Englishmen. "Set them all afoot but for this one. I have a special message for the earl that he may carry."

When the dispirited Englishmen were sent away, they had only their braies and bloodied heads to recommend them. It was a fine sight, thought Rob, to see them walk half-naked across the moors, not even boots to save their feet from the rocks and mud.

Sir Payton wore still his tunic and tabard, though his armor and gear had been added to the pile of booty. He sat with hands splayed on his knees, eyes green ice while Black Douglas composed a letter to the earl. It was brief, due as much to lack of proper parchment and ink as to his skill.

"Escort him to the next hill, Glenlyon," he said when he had given the letter to Sir Payton. "I want to know he is guaranteed a safe return."

Flicking his eyes toward Douglas, Sir Payton said stiffly, "I am not a child to need tending."

"Ah no, and that is why I much prefer you far and away while we bear our gifts of horse and armor back across the Tyne."

Interest flickered in Sir Payton's eyes, but he made no comment as Douglas waved him up and on his way. Rob sluiced a frowning glance in Douglas's direction. It was unlike him to betray their plans, but Sir James had only a benign smile on his face as he remounted and directed the dispersion of their spoils.

Limping slightly, Sir Payton began a trek up the steep incline, doing his best to avoid patches of thistles. There were few more sorry sights, Rob thought with a grin, than to see a belted knight afoot.

To add insult to injury, he chose to ride, rather than walk the prisoner to the crest of the grassy knoll beyond, easier than running him down on foot should he decide to flee. It was still early, the sun a bright sheen on field and wood, welcome after days of rain. The light caught in Sir Payton's hair, set agleam the locks of brown-streaked gold.

"You needn't worry I'll go haring off," he said to Rob without looking back, "for Black Douglas has my boots."

"And your horse," Rob reminded.

"Aye. And my horse." He halted, turned, squinted up at Rob. "What of the Lady Judith? Is she well?"

"Very well, when last I saw her."

Silence fell. A magpie flashed by in a blur of black and white and was quickly followed by another. *One is for sorrow, two for joy,* rang in his head, a saying he'd learned as a lad.

Sir Payton continued his walk up the hill, Rob riding behind like a shadow. Near the top he stopped again, turned to face Rob, nearly eye level now with the slope to his advantage. He was older than he'd first looked, evident now under the bright sunlight. His eyes narrowed at the glare.

"It was not the earl's decision alone to leave her with Clan Caddel. The king forbade the forfeiture of dower lands or return of the bride gift."

"And the lady is worth nothing for her own sake?" Rob's brow lifted. "It is well she is now more valued."

He took a step forward but halted abruptly when Rob's hand went to his sword hilt, a warning and no more. It was not likely he would set upon an unarmed man.

Sir Payton's jaw set, teeth clenched. "She is valued, Glenlyon. One day you will learn how well."

"Perhaps that is an assurance you should give the lady. I have no need of it."

"You will." Green eyes clashed with his. "You will."

"Yonder wait your comrades in arms," Rob said, "join them and be glad you have a choice."

He curbed his restive mount with a shorter rein and watched as the young Englishman started down the grassy slope, then wheeled and rode back to join his men.

✝

THE STENCH OF smoke stung his eyes, billowing black clouds of it spiraling into the air, the wind whipping sparks into a frenzy like angry red midges. More blazes sprang up where those landed, until it seemed as if all of England was ablaze, a red and black curtain sweeping across the land.

A woman came weeping and wailing away from her

home as it tumbled into ashes, and she managed to catch
Rob by the foot before he could turn his horse away.

"Please good sir," she pleaded through her tears, "do
not take my beasts! My children will go hungry."

He didn't push her away, but his voice was weary when
he said, " 'Tis not your children that I wish to go hungry,
goodwife."

"I have only the milch cow and her calf left. . . . I beg
of thee, sir. . . ." Tears streaked her gaunt face, and her
head scarf was awry, exposing brown hair heavily laden
with gray.

Fumbling in the pouch at his side, Rob took out a purse
that had been lifted from the English knights and tossed
it to her. "Payment for your kine, goodwife. It will buy
you more than two."

She peered into the pouch, and her jaw sagged as she
gasped, "Godamercy, sir, there's enough here to buy a
new cottage, if I will!"

"Do as you like with it."

Wheeling his horse around, he spurred away from the
ruined village, yet another laid to waste these past weeks.
The English, it had been reported, had left York nearly a
week ago, moving slowly toward Durham. When the
army of Flemish mercenaries arrived, they would find little enough in the way of forage for men or beasts.

"We will lead them a merry chase, lads," Black Douglas had vowed, and so they were.

For two days, the English army slogged across boggy
moors in pursuit, but in vain. Burdened with baggage
trains, they never caught even a glimpse of their quarry.
The Scots were always just ahead.

Then, inexplicably, one of Lord Randolph's scouts reported that the army had abandoned their baggage train
and headed north to Haydon Bridge on the River Tyne to
cut off the Scottish retreat. Douglas was delighted.

"Let them wait, by hell, while we eat their beef and drink their ale! They'll find little enough comfort or food left there."

Lord Randolph shook his head, perplexed. "It may be a trick. Why would they await our retreat when we do not?"

Rob laughed softly. "Because good Sir James let slip to an English knight that we retreated to the Tyne with our new armor and beasts. No doubt, the tale has expanded with the retelling of it."

"No doubt," Douglas agreed affably. "I propose that we await them in comfort. There is a manor house not far away that promises shelter for horses and men. It looks like rain."

For eight days it rained, while the English army waited for a Scottish force that never arrived. The river waters rose, and the camp became a sea of sticky mud. Provisions ran out, and nothing could be salvaged from the wasted lands around them. There was no shelter, and the wood too green and sodden to burn for fires. Saddle leather rotted from the continuous downpour, and men began to talk of mutiny.

When at last the order to recross the river was given, a proclamation was made in the king's name that any man who could locate the Scots would receive a knighthood and a landed estate. Sixteen hopeful squires set off in different directions. One, Thomas Rokeby, had the good fortune to fall into Rob's hands and was promptly taken before Douglas.

After he reported to Douglas of the English misfortunes, Rokeby was given a hearty meal and sent back to tell the king of England that the Scots had been waiting for more than a week to give him battle. The new knight then led the English army to a bank opposite where the

Scots awaited them atop a rocky crag on the south side
of the River Wear.

Flooded, the turbulent water prevented their crossing,
and heralds were sent asking for safe passage across so
the battle could begin. The Scots reply was swift and
scornful:

"We are here in your kingdom and have burnt and
wasted your country. If you do not like it, then come and
dislodge us, for we shall remain here as long as we
please."

The English promptly blockaded the route to the border, and with an impassable marshland behind the Scots,
waited for their surrender. In the days that followed, there
were several skirmishes but no pitched battle. Prisoners
were taken on both sides, but the greatest feat was the
near capture of sixteen-year-old King Edward.

Douglas picked two hundred men and left the main
army to ride a wide circle about the River Wear and come
up behind the English camp. A sentry gave the challenge,
but Douglas soundly dressed him down, and the confused
soldier let them pass into the sleeping camp. It was a near
rout, with two hundred men riding through the lines of
tents, slashing tent lines with their swords, pressing toward the silk pavilion that held the young king. Only the
suicidal gallantry of his loyal household got the king safe
and away, and by that time, resistance was mounted, and
Douglas blew his horn for retreat.

At the winding of the horn, Rob spurred his mount
toward the river to join his men. The night was black, the
range of trees along the steep banks thick and treacherous.
He lost the faint track of the path and found it again, then
became aware of James Douglas riding close behind him
now, his horse blowing.

"By hell, did you see them, Glenlyon?" Douglas called,
his voice heavy with laughter. "Earls bare as the day they

were born, covered with their own tents and swearing like defrocked priests."

Blood pounding, the excitement of the fight on him, Rob leaped his horse over a fallen log, landing heavily on the wooded path, hooves churning out mud and leaves behind him. "Aye, and Randolph will want to best this feat, I wager."

His prediction was proved true, for upon their return, Lord Randolph at once announced his intention to attack the English with a larger force. Douglas managed to dissuade him and proposed a new trick that would see them safely back to Scotland with their spoils.

For the next several days, they remained quiet. Late in the afternoon, they finally began to marshal their troops and create a great racket that attracted the immediate attention of their enemy across the river. The English reacted as expected and stood to arms, anticipating a night attack.

"They wait for us," Rob said as he saddled his horse, and Sir Alec grinned.

"Aye, so they do. 'Twill be a long wait, I trow."

As the campfires burned brightly and trumpeters gave long blasts from their horns, the Scottish forces thinned away into the impassable marsh by the simple expedient of a series of wooden hurdles laid down over the boggy patches, and lifted up when all had passed over them. When morning came, the English would see before them only a bare hillside with not a Scot on it.

By then they would be well on their way to their native soil.

Chapter 20

GLENLYON

CORN WAS HIGH in the fields that lay beyond the keep, ripening for the harvest. Sheep and cows were hazy shapes on distant slopes, and the purple dusk faded slowly into night.

Judith stood on the topmost tower, staring at the sky. It was a soft night. Still and expectant. A full moon shed silvery light that only added to the eerie hush, as if the stars overhead were frozen in place. Nonsense, Judith knew, for the skies wheeled slowly and relentlessly over Scotland, the familiar constellations reliable and reassuring.

What if he doesn't come back? she thought, and she knew that for her, the stars and moon would no longer matter if he didn't return.

It was already August, nearly two months since Rob had gone with James Douglas. Her days were busy with the tasks that must be done, but the short nights were too long, even when she was weary. She dreamed of him and awoke with her hand tangled in the coverlet as if holding him tight.

No word, no word, and God, she was near sick with fret for him, with wondering if he was dead or injured and no one had told her.

"Are you breeding?" Simon had bluntly asked when she'd gone again to the top of the tower to scan the horizon. "I thought you sensible until lately."

"No," she said regretfully, "I am not with child, and your impertinence is intolerable."

Snorting, he had muttered something under his breath but not pursued the subject.

Now the quarter day arrived, and the Lammas rents were due. *Lunasdal,* in Gaelic, the first weeks of August were set aside for the tenants to pay in coin or goods for their huts and fields. Simon was kept busy from early to late with his ledgers and the ongoing construction of the tower and walls.

The barnekin walls were nearly complete. Gates had been hung but needed more work. Carpenters finished the doors and roofs for the granary and storerooms, important for, with the rents due, there had to be room for the grain and goods that would be paid.

"Come inside, lady," Simon said behind her, and she felt him approach on the narrow walk that edged the tower roof. "It grows late."

She pulled the light plaide closer around her shoulders and wound her fists into the wool. "Can you feel it, Simon? It's . . . like a wind. Waiting. Something brewing just beyond the crags."

"Not more rain, I pray. Christ, the crops will wash into Loch Tay."

"No." She smiled slightly. "The night is clear."

"Storms can blow up quickly at times." He leaned on the stone, peered over the edge and down into the bailey. A sound of disgust escaped him. "Fools. They've miscalculated again. The corner of that far wall is uneven."

"You'll set it aright tomorrow."

"It will have to be undone, then done again. Another four shillings gone." He straightened, turned to rest his elbow against the edge. Moonlight silvered his sandy hair, cast his face into sharper shadow as he regarded her. "He will come back."

Her fingers tightened in the edges of the plaide. "Yea, so you tell me every day."

"And I tell you true, lady. Glenlyon is not reckless. A fierce fighter when put to it, but he is smart enough to keep his head."

"Yes." She nodded and turned back to gaze out over the darkened fields. Pale shadows drifted. "Yes, I know."

He blew out a harsh breath. "You say what you do not feel."

"Simon—" She leaned forward, frowning. "Beyond the walls . . ."

His head whipped around and he stared hard into the night. A clump of dark shadow moved down the slope; slivers of light glinted, tiny sparks.

"Is it Glenlyon?" Her heart pounded fiercely, and she leaned forward, straining to distinguish the shapes. "Oh, it must be, Simon . . ."

He took her arm, pulled her back from the ledge, his voice taut. "Seek your chamber. Bar the door, and do not come out until you hear me tell you it is safe."

"But if it's Rob—"

"Lady, do not waste my time with debate!" His hand on her arm was swift, harsh.

They descended the curve of stairs rapidly, Simon cursing under his breath about the sleeping watch, and then he shoved her unceremoniously into her chamber and bade her bar the door. Alarmed, she lowered the heavy bar into place and heard his fading footsteps when it had fallen in a loud clunk. Another raid? Disastrous, with crops nearly ripe.

She crossed to the window, unfastened the leather loop that held the glass closed, and opened it just wide enough to peer out. Nothing moved that she could see, and the only sound was that of Simon below, his familiar voice oddly urgent as he strode across the bailey. Dread made her mouth dry and her hands shake, and she wished she'd thought to leave a jug of wine in the chamber.

Deep shadows hovered, broken only by a small fire on the hearth, and she moved to light a lamp, kneeling on the stones, her fingers trembling as she steadied the wick. It was too long, and she used the tip of her eating knife to trim it, a quick slice.

When it was lit and burned steadily, she set it on the table beside the wide bed. It shed only a small pool of light that would not be easily seen from the bailey.

Uncertainty clawed at her. She moved back to the window again, a hand against the thick, cool glass. The same hush as earlier prevailed, though there was a subtle difference now, the sense of anticipation stronger.

Only once had men come in the night since she'd been here, and Simon had roused his kinsmen sleeping in the stables and convinced the intruders that they should seek elsewhere for beasts and goods. It had been over so quickly she'd not had time to be frightened nor even to hide.

Morag, Sim the tinker's wife, still shuddered at the memory of it, for she had been caught out in the stable yard when they swooped through the opening where the gates should be. They'd only terrified her, for the MacCallum kin had met them swiftly.

The next day, the gates had been completed and hung. And now they would be tested, it seemed, for she heard the rolling Gaelic of the MacCallums as they spilled into the bailey. There was the muted clink of weapons, the lethal rasp of swords mingling with the heavier hiss of axes being tested on empty air.

Yet no assault was launched, no intruders against the gates. A trick of light and shadow, perhaps, that had lent a threat to what was not there. Silence lay thickly, stretched into what seemed eternity, and she began to relax. Taut muscles in her neck and back eased, and she moved away from the window to the bed, smoothed the coverlet that lay over it, her hand drifting over the soft wool in a caress.

She missed him. There were times when it was a sharp ache, taking away her breath. It seemed as if he had been gone for years instead of months.

A dull thud lifted her head, and her hand stilled atop the coverlet. The tension was back, crawling up her spine to prickle her scalp, and she shuddered. Then the thud sounded again, louder this time, and heavy.

Caution bade her douse the lamp, and when the chamber was lit by only the low fire on the hearth, she moved again to the window and eased it a little wider. Her heartbeat pushed the blood through her veins so swiftly she could almost hear it. The sense of anticipation had sharpened into danger, and she heard below a bellow of wrath.

Raiders.

Several thuds shook the gates, and the bailey was suddenly a swarm of activity as men rushed to and fro and bobs of light from torches sped like angry fireflies over the grounds. She recognized Simon and his brother Archie, a mountain of a man and as different from Simon as day from night. Others were still strangers to her, names known but little else, just vaguely familiar faces.

A scattering of huts lay in a wide scythe beyond the tower, crofter's huts, mostly, though of late tradesmen had begun to settle on the flatter land that edged the loch. The workmen building the tower brought with them their own kind of followers.

Now she saw a thatched roof flare, fire licking up the roof so quickly that it must be like dry tinder. She sagged against the wall, fear and dread swooping over her. These raiders would not be dissuaded. They meant to destroy all.

Helpless, she watched, heard the shouts of men and the screams of women as they scurried for safety. The gates were bombarded, shuddered, and there was a loud creaking sound, but they did not yield. Judith's fingers curled into stone, a painful scrape against her skin. Blindly, she stared onto the eerie scene below, the moonlit figures occasionally illuminated by the glow of a torch, flashing splinters of silver that she now recognized as steel reflections.

Simon had bade her stay safe in this chamber, but she could not bear to watch and wait while those below were in danger. And what would it matter, for if they breached these walls, the oak door to this chamber would hardly keep them out.

She glanced around the chamber, moved to the table with the doused lamp, and retrieved her eating knife. She slid it into the small sheath on her belt, smoothed her hands down the folds of her tunic, and crossed to unbar the door.

The bar slid back with a heavy whisk and thudded into place in the metal brackets. She paused, staring at the closed door, the last barrier between her and danger. Fear trickled down her back, pooled in her belly, made her legs quiver. Breathing was difficult; the air seemed thick and hot, yet she was shivering as if cold. She drew in a deep breath, lifted her chin, and swung open the door.

A single torch flickered in the corridor, and she lifted it from the bracket with some difficulty; it spat and sputtered, showered sparks onto her clothes and hand. It needed trimming, an oversight she would rectify if the tower still stood on the morrow. She took it with her, unwilling to leave light for intruders to find their way easily, and made her way down the curve of stairs to the door leading to the hall. This door was the last defense, a thick barrier to invaders when occupants barricaded themselves on the second floor if necessary.

It was open.

She stood, uncertain, listening to the tumult in the bailey, and turned to make her way to the door that led down to the stores. It was close, narrow, a passage carved into the dirt of the mound on which the tower stood, and it led to a musty cavern beneath that held the casks of wine and a few other supplies.

Even with the torch, the darkness closed around her like a fist, smothering and damp and cold. She pushed up the latch, swung open the door, and stepped into the cavern that swept the width and breadth of the tower. Beyond the wine casks, a rack had been affixed to the wall. A dull gleam reflected the torchlight as she went to the rack, and she studied the swords and pikes that hung from it. It was a foolish place to leave such things, she'd thought, in the dampness where they may rust, but there was no sign of rust on these lethal weapons.

She set the torch into a bracket and reached for a pike tipped with a steel head and vicious-looking hook. The shaft was sturdy, and not too thick, but when she tried to lift it, it tilted dangerously to one side, banging against the wall. Dirt drifted to the floor, gouged from the wall by the hook. Too cumbersome; she'd never manage it.

Unmanageable, too, was the broadsword she tried next,

the hilt so big around she had to grasp it with both hands. The blade dragged the stones at her feet, and it took great effort to lift it into a poor imitation of the ease with which she'd seen Rob wield a sword. New respect for the men who used these weapons formed beneath the layer of growing panic that drove her to try yet another implement.

A wicked spiked iron ball on a chain draped from a hook attached to the rack, and she grasped the handle firmly in one hand. The weight of it dragged her arm downward, and the spiked ball made a loud cracking sound as it hit the floor. She left the mace there, and reached for a short sword that was half hidden behind another.

Hefting it, she found it more easily managed; the double-sided blade ended in a sharp point, and the hilt fit her hand well enough.

With the sword in her right hand and the torch in her left, she made her way back up to the hall.

As she emerged from the narrow passage, she heard the crashing of wood and shouts of men. In all her years, she'd never seen a battle, though there had been times when it had raged close. She thought of the wine below, wished she had a cup of it, and braced herself as the door to the hall burst open with a thunderous clap of wood against stone.

The rasp of steel against steel was loud and terrifying as men ranged into the hall. She recognized Archie MacCallum just inside the doors, bellowing fury and swinging a sword as if it weighed no more than a broom-straw. Blood spurted, and a man went down before the force of Archie's blow.

Wounds aplenty she had seen in her days, but never the giving of them, and she looked away, near desperate with fear and uncertainty. Where did she go? What could she do?

A sudden movement to her left drew her eyes, and she saw a huge, bearded man bearing down on her, a grin slashing his dark beard. Though he carried a sword, he held it up and out as he charged, and without thinking, Judith brought up her left arm and the sputtering torch. She thrust it into his face before he reached her and heard his howl of pain and rage. He backed away, shaking his head, his free hand hastily slapping out smoldering fires on his jaw.

His eyes narrowed, and he snarled at her in Gaelic that she had earned herself a rough night now. This time he held his sword as she had seen Rob do, an easy twist of his wrist and flex of arm that looked suddenly expert and deadly. She hesitated but kept the torch held in front of her. Heat beat at her, sparks shedding onto stones and her wrist, but she dared not put it away. It was a far more effective weapon than the sword would be in her unskilled hands.

In earnest now, his grin replaced by lips curled back from bared teeth, he advanced. Judith waited, and when he was close enough, she jabbed the torch at him again, lower this time, aiming for his waist and below.

His sword flashed, neatly cleaving the torch in two. The flaming rushes bounced onto the floor, and she was left holding a shortened stick. It all happened so fast; he was still advancing, triumph flaring in his scorched face as he reached for her, and she brought up the short sword without thinking about it, lifting it from the tangle of her tunic.

There was a jarring bump against her, and she staggered, dropped the torch shaft to grasp the sword hilt with both hands and hold it steady, and then realized that the man had impaled himself upon it. Surprise lit his eyes briefly, his mouth sagged open, and he released his sword to grab at the blade she held, but it was halfway into his belly, his wool tunic scrunched around it.

The light in his eyes extinguished like a candle dipped in water, suddenly and completely, and he folded over the sword and collapsed atop her, taking her down with him to the floor.

Shuddering, she shoved at him, his body limp and heavy and pressing her into stone. Vaguely, she was aware of the noise in the hall, the metallic beats and shouts of men. The turmoil raged. Yet the world had narrowed to just this, the desperate struggle to free herself.

Her skirts tangled around her legs, and even though she knew he was dead, she beat a hand against his shoulder, palm thrusting against him to dislodge him. His beard brushed over her cheek, and something warm and wet smeared on her face, and her throat clenched.

And then, at last, the weight was lifted free, and she rolled quickly away before he could flop onto her again, scrambling to her feet, hands searching the rushes for his discarded weapon. Her fingers found the hilt just as a hand grasped her shoulder and she struggled to lift it, panic surging through her. The sword dragged, and as she felt the grip on her tighten, she abandoned the weapon and snatched her eating knife from the sheath on her belt.

Twisting away from the hand, she whirled, slashing with the sharp dirk, and heard a loud yelp of pain. She jabbed it again, the man a threatening blur, and he stepped swiftly to one side, letting her momentum carry her past him. She stumbled, and he grabbed the neck of her tunic and hauled her back, his free hand flashing out to snap against her wrist and send the dagger spinning out of her hand.

"Christ above, Judith!" came the protest when she turned with clawing hands, "I fought for two months without getting a scratch, and must come to my own keep to be sore wounded!"

A sob strangled in her throat, and through the haze of fear and relief, she was able to whisper, "At last," before she collapsed at his feet.

Chapter 21

✝

"A MOST NOVEL welcome, my lady," Rob said with wry amusement and saw her flush. "I see you have kept busy in my absence."

Judith maintained a dignified silence. She dipped the cloth into the herb-scented water again, wrung it out, and dabbed at the vicious gash in his arm. It stung, and he focused on her to keep his mind from it. Her plaide was gone, but she still wore the torn and dirty tunic, blood smears on it from the man she'd killed. Wisps of rushes from the floor clung to her hair, and her plait had come undone. Her lashes made long shadows on her soot-streaked cheeks.

He glanced across the hall. Fire had blackened stones and walls in places, ignited by the severed torch, the new wood charred. Simon lay on a cot, wounded but not mortally, moaning about the costs of the damage to hall and fields.

Rob thought of the woman in Weardale, pleading for

her beasts, her house in ruins behind her, and understood. It had surprised him then that she did not rage for the loss of her house but wanted only the promise of tomorrow. That was what those beasts had meant to her: food for herself and her children. He was glad he'd given her the purse of silver, though Douglas had called him daft for it.

He looked back at Judith. Her hands moved over his hurt in gentle efficiency. A fierce lady, and he thought again of the sudden panic that had clutched him when he'd seen her across the hall, thrusting a torch at her attacker. Fear for her, and anger that she'd left the safety of their chamber, had lent savagery to his blows, and he'd quickly dispatched the man who barred his path. But still, it had seemed as if he trod through chest-high water that dragged at his stride as he fought his way to her, aware all the time of her danger. He'd not seen her killing blow, for the men who checked his progress, but had seen the result of it when finally he had reached her.

"How came you to be hard on the heels of the invaders?" she asked quietly, and he leaned back against the pile of plaides she had put behind him.

"We were not chasing them. Until I saw the fires set upon the crofters' huts, I did not know the keep was under attack." He reached out, touched her lightly on the cheek, and she looked up then, green eyes shadowed with an emotion he could not identify. "Sweetling, what is it?"

She tied the strip of linen around his arm, then her hands grew still, lashes lowered as she looked away from him. Her husky voice was strained, muffled.

"I have never killed a man before today."

Of course she had not. Unthinkable, that she would need to fight for her life, yet he had left her vulnerable to it. A bitter heat flared in his throat, and he swallowed it.

"He would have hurt you, Judith. These men came to take what pleased them, chattel or silver, it did not matter.

If you had not killed him, he would surely have killed
you."

"Yes. I know that. I am not sorry that I did what must
be done. . . . I just regret the reason for it." When she
looked up again, some of the shadows had faded from her
eyes. "Your arrival was most timely."

"If I had not been delayed, I would have been here two
days ago." He paused, put his hand beneath her chin,
scraped his thumb over the velvety softness of her skin,
thought again of the impatience in him at being so delayed
by the division of the English spoils. Some for the crown,
some for the men, few quarrels during the just division,
as Douglas countenanced no strife. "I have a full purse to
add to the coffers, though now much of it will go to re-
pairs of what was already done."

She looked around, shuddered delicately, and nodded.
"Simon will be most glad of it. He has complained heart-
ily and constantly about the cost of everything from candles to nails."

"Simon should be the king's Exchequer. All of Scotland would then be pinchpenny."

A smile bloomed, and the simple sight of it struck him
hard, left him fumbling for thoughts of anything but this
lady who ever surprised, ever humbled him. His hand left
her face, curled into a loose fist in his lap.

"I chanced upon your brother in Weardale."

Her smile faded, and he had a moment of regret for its
loss before she asked, "Which brother?"

"Sir Payton."

"Ah." Silence fell between them, while across the hall
the hum of activity continued. "Was he well?" she asked
at last, and he nodded.

"Well enough for a man without boots or horse." Her
glance was startled. "He was taken in a skirmish and left
tokens of his regard in form of gear and mount."

A smile quivered on her lips, and there was laughter in her voice when she said, "I imagine he was not happy."

"That is the sense I got from him." He paused, took her hand in his, and scrubbed his thumb over her knuckles. They bore marks of her struggle in the form of cuts and scrapes. "He asked about your health."

"And you told him I am well."

"Yea." He paused, wondered if he should tell all that had passed between him and Sir Payton and then said, "It was the English king who was loathe to exchange Scottish lands for you, not the earl, if your brother is to be believed."

Her brow sketched an arch of surprise. "Is it so?"

"That is what he said, lady fair."

She was silent for a moment. Firelight glided over her face, made shadows of her lashes. Then she smiled.

"I am glad to hear it. He should have told me."

"Would it have mattered overmuch, the reason for it?"

"Yea, for if I had known my own kin valued me enough to barter with a king, I would not have felt so worthless and unwanted."

"Unwanted . . . ah, lady, lady, I cannot think you have ever been unwanted." He reached up, tunneled his hand into the unbound mass of her hair, cupped his fingers around her neck, and drew her closer to him, so that he felt the warmth of her breath across his cheek. "You are wanted here."

She put a hand against his jaw, fingers rasping over the beard stubble in a light caress. "I was not always wanted here."

"A lifetime ago. Another land, another time, another man. I want you. I want you now, I wanted you then, though I did not know how or why."

"And now you do?"

"Oh aye, lady mine, now I do."

The loose fall of her hair was a pale curtain that veiled the kiss he pressed upon her mouth, his lips moving over hers with unfamiliar, unexpected tenderness. She tasted of spiced wine, as he must, heady and potent.

A loud *"Harrumph!"* summoned him from the bower of wine and soft emotion, and Judith dropped her hand and sat back. Rob tilted his head toward this unwelcome intrusion and saw Archie MacCallum grinning like a mummer's fool at him.

"Grant pardon for the interruption, but I was sent to tell ye that one of the prisoners has information ye might want to hear. Should it wait?"

"No." Rob sat up, reached for the plaide he'd discarded when Judith tended his wound, and stood, wrapping it around his shoulder and waist with practiced ease. He flexed his arm and grinned, satisfied that it would not hinder him.

"Take me to him."

Black Douglas leaned against a wooden post, arms over his chest, a faint wild gleam in his eyes.

"This man's claim may be of interest to you, Glenlyon, for he has news of a mutual acquaintance."

One of the raiders knelt in the straw-littered dirt; he looked up. His face was battered, bloodied, bruises swelling one eye and darkening his cheek. He touched his tongue to the corner of his mouth.

"Water . . ."

"When you have given the laird your news." Douglas prodded the prisoner with a booted foot. "I may be patient, but the Red Devil's Cub is not."

A shudder ran through him, and the man jerked his head. "Aye . . .'twas Argyll. He sent us, twice now, but we were too few the last time. . . ."

"Sent you here? To plunder?" Rob stepped forward

when the man hesitated with a sideways glance, his voice low and fierce as he said, "Or to take the lady. . . ."

"Mercy, crave mercy . . . we were not to hurt her, but to take her to him along wi' the paper."

"Paper?" Ah, Argyll had not found it then. A taut smile bent his mouth. He dropped to one knee beside the prisoner, said so softly few could hear, "Tell me of this paper you were sent to find."

"I have not me letters. . . . It bears a seal, he said, the king's own."

"Yea, so it does, man, so it does."

Rising to his feet, he looked at Black Douglas, who had listened to all with unabashed interest. Dark eyes danced in the thin face, his grin wide and cocky as Douglas said, "I shall see that he gets water now."

Rob understood, and shook his head. "Do not foul my well, Douglas."

"Nay, I would not. We shall see how much he drinks from the loch." He turned, smiled down at the wide-eyed prisoner affably. "Do you swim, good fellow?"

†

ROB FOUND JUDITH still in the hall. Her steps flagged, her shoulders bent wearily as she moved among those wounded, tending with herbs and soothing words. He moved to her side. When she looked up, he put out a hand.

"You shall need tending next if you do not rest, lady. Come with me."

It was indicative of her exhaustion that she did not protest and went with him up the curve of steps to the second floor. There was no damage here, save for the taint of smoke, and he saw the chamber door ajar. She was pliant, quiet, and he led her to the wide bed against the far wall.

"Sit here, while I fetch Morag and hot water."

"Nay," she said faintly, a hand brushing back loose hair from her eyes, "Morag is also weary—"

"Not too weary to heat water. Stay, I tell you, or I'll bind you to the bed with ropes."

She looked startled but gave him no more argument, and when he returned with hot water and a huge wooden tub slung between two stout men, there was a fleeting glance of gratitude from her.

He waited until the men had left, then shut the door behind them and let down the bar. Light flowed in through the window, distorted by the glass into hazy prisms that crept across the floor with the rising of the sun. He went to the bed and lifted her gently to her feet. She stood as docile as a newborn lamb while he untied the laces of her léine and unbuckled her belt. Then he put his hands in the neck of her linen tunic and rent it in two.

Startled, she looked up at him, protests on her lips. "It cannot be mended! I have but two—"

He put his finger over mouth. "Peace, lady. There is time enough later to fret over linen."

The léine pooled on the floor at her feet. Light was her only garment now, soft and velvety on the high, firm contours of her breasts, the curve of hip and thigh, the pale shadow below her belly. A knot settled in his throat; heat rushed to his groin. He marshaled his resistance and concentrated instead upon guiding her to the wooden tub.

Steam wafted upward, gauzy drifts of scented cloud, and she lifted a brow. "Heather."

"Yea, lady mine. 'Tis my favorite fragrance these some months past."

He'd bought it for her, purchased it with good coin in a Glasgow shop, awkward with the selection. Never had he purchased gifts for a woman, save for his mother when he was but a greenling. Buying items he thought would be dear to a female heart had taken more time than he'd considered, until James Douglas had come looking for him. Among the more bawdy suggestions he'd had for gifts had been a very practical recommendation that he purchase scented soaps.

"It has been my experience that women find them most pleasant, and my delight in discovering that their use is even more so," Douglas had drawled.

There had been no question of which fragrance to choose for Judith. He still carried the sprig of white heather in the pouch on his belt to remind him of her.

An unnecessary reminder, for she inhabited his dreams as well as his waking thoughts.

With a hand beneath her elbow, he helped her into the tub, watched the lines of strain ease in her face as she slipped into the heated water until it reached her breasts. He pulled a stool close to the tub, straddled it, and picked up a pot of soap.

"Ah no," he said when she reached for it, "lean back against the sides, and I will bathe you."

Her cheeks were pink, whether from the hot water or emotion, he wasn't certain, and she gave him an almost shy glance.

"That isn't necessary. You must be weary and need your own ease."

"Yea, but that will come later." He dipped his fingers into the pot, scooped out a generous portion of heather-scented soap, and rubbed it into foam. His hands were slick as he slid them over her arm first, starting at her hand and working soap over each finger in turn, then massaging her wrist, forearm, and elbow before he soaped her upper arm. She lay back against the tub's edge, eyes half closed now, her first tension easing under his hands.

He washed her arms, then reached beneath the water to lift her leg, ignoring her startled breath as he soaped her foot with strong, sure pressure that made her moan. Delicate bones, as fragile as a child's, yet there was a strength in her that could exceed the best of men. He'd seen it.

His hand slid along the slick curve of her calf to her knee, then upward along the cushion of her thigh and hip. As he skimmed his hand over her belly, she looked up at him through brown lashes, lips parted expectantly.

It took more constraint than he knew he had to ignore that veiled invitation, and he washed her other leg, ending this time with her foot, a steady massage of the pads of his thumbs on her instep earning her luxurious sigh. She slipped lower in the tub. Water lapped at her breasts, tiny drifts of soap froth teasing pink nipples like rosebuds.

Heat washed him, steamy and rife with promise, but he kept to his intent and did not yield to the aching need that grew with each stroke of his hand over the soft cushion of her body. Yet he could not help his own reaction as his hand moved to ply soap along the curve of her collarbone, then lower. Torment, to touch her there and not follow his urges.

He straightened, took up another pot that sat on the floor by the tub, and uncorked it. She watched him with eyes half shut, her hair floating on the surface of the water in dark, wet ringlets.

Lifting a strand of her hair, he reached behind her to scoop it from the water and rubbed in more soap. He worked in soap until he had a fine lather, then dragged his hand through her hair, admiring the sleek beauty of it, even wet. Her eyes were closed again. His hands moved to the crown of her head, flexing against her scalp, removing all traces of grass and dirt and blood. When the soap was rinsed from her hair, he lifted a soft towel from the floor.

She lay still, her arms draped along the edges of the

tub, her knees bent and feet braced against the side, water slowly cooling.

Gently, aware that she was near asleep from his efforts, he lifted her from the tub and wrapped her in the linen towel, then sat her on a stool before the low fire. She leaned back against him, her damp hair wetting the front of his tunic. He wound the towel around her head and rubbed her hair until it stopped dripping, then took a hairbrush from the chest and dragged through the length until it began to dry in lazy waves down her back.

The silence in the chamber was soft and soothing, lending a sense of peace that he hadn't felt in longer than he could recall. Never had he brushed a woman's hair, and the unusual act lent its own sense of peace as well. Before, he had always watched, perhaps admiring the grace of motion as the hairbrush slid through glossy locks, but it had never occurred to him that it would be so soothing to slide brush and hands through damp, drying hair that felt like threads of silk in his palm.

Outside, he heard the distant barking of a hound, the clap and rattle of men and carts, the familiar workings of a keep. Inside, he heard only the steady thud of his heart.

His hands stilled in her hair. Standing behind her, he saw that the towel wrapped around her had slipped open. Her hands were curled into loose fists in her lap, and her breasts rose and fell in a steady rhythm. She slept. He stood for several long moments, relishing the simple trust that allowed her to relax so completely in his care.

Her eyelids fluttered but did not open when he carried her to the bed and lay her gently upon the coverlet. The fragrance of heather surrounded him, from the mattress to the scent of her body, welcome and arousing.

He lay beside her, drinking it all in, the sight and feel and smell of her, real at last after the months of having only dreams in his comfortless bed.

A wry smile curved his mouth. This was not the welcome home he had imagined on the ride north, his impatience to reach Glenlyon and his lady pressing him on until even James Douglas voiced protest at the pace.

But, perhaps, he reflected, it was the welcome home he needed. There was something so gratifying about just holding her without expectations of anything other than the moment.

Chapter 22

THIN BLUE LIGHT sifted through the glazing. Judith felt it first, then opened her eyes to the deep shadows that lay in the corners. The wooden tub still sat on the stones before the hearth, and by it, the three-legged stool and open pots of soap. She was alone. The depression beside her on the mattress was still warm, her hand testing it, then lingering as if she could feel him beneath her palm.

It was late in the day by the reckoning of the light, and she had slept through. He must have lain with her for hours, holding her, and she recalled the uncomplicated sense of sanctuary that had eased her into sleep.

How rich and rare it was, a tenuous thing, to feel so safe when the world was so dangerous.

Loath to rise, she knew she must. There were those who needed her care, men who had been wounded in the fray with the raiders. She still wondered who they were and why they had come now. It would have made more sense to wait until all the rents were in, when the stores were filled to the roof with goods for the long winter.

Simon MacCallum would be grateful they had not.

Simon . . . his wound was deep but not fatal; his expertise lay in wielding a quill and not a sword. He was proficient enough, she knew, for she had seen him with the others in the bailey, his brothers and cousins who had come one by one and two by two to enjoy Glenlyon hospitality. A plan, she thought, to fortify the keep without being obvious. It must have worked well, for the invaders had been repelled not once but twice.

This last, the damage was immense. Crofts beyond the walls were burned and fields laid to waste, smoke still thick in the morning light, but no one had been killed. Inside the walls, where there had been resistance, the casualties were on the raiders and not the inhabitants, save for wounds. Damage to the keep could be repaired.

Rising, she hugged the linen towel around her and slid from the bed. She hurried across the floor to the chest, her bare toes curling up at the chill of stone beneath her feet. Her tunic lay in tatters, leaving her only the one she had been given in Glen Dochart. If she had a loom, she could weave more cloth, and during the winter months there would be plenty of time to sew new garments.

She knelt, unfastened the clasp on the chest, and lifted the heavy lid. Still holding it with one hand, she saw an unfamiliar bundle atop the few personal items she possessed. It was a length of green velvet, and she drew it out.

It was bulky and thick. She lowered the lid and set the bundle atop, then unfolded the edges, her hands trembling as she saw a shimmering patterned silk. It seemed to slither free of the bundle, a glorious emerald shade, rich and sumptuous.

"Sweet Mary," she murmured, her hands sliding over the elegant stuff, and she lifted it to see that it was a gown sewn in the English fashion. It was simple in style, with a narrow waist and full skirt, the sleeves long and tight, and the oval neckline decorated with glittering gold embroidery. The bundle yielded a pair of soft slippers and small boots, as well as two pair of fine-knit stockings. A soft linen undershift and kirtle were folded beneath the stockings.

Where had he gotten them?

Overwhelmed, she knelt there on the stones so long that her knees began to ache, and she was shivering with chill. It was unexpected, startling, another facet of this man she still knew so little.

"I thought 'twould be more fitting than a pretty bauble or two," a voice said from the doorway, and she turned.

"Yea, so they are," she said softly.

Rob remained in the open door, obviously uncomfortable, and she rose, still clutching the green gown. He looked away from her, then back.

"Douglas departs in the morning. He goes to meet the king, who has newly returned from Ireland."

She tensed, and her eyes must have betrayed her, for he added with a faint smile, "I declined to join them but have sent my regards."

Relief eased through her, and she nodded, the linen about her shoulders sliding a bit. "When I'm properly garbed, I will come down to share the evening meal."

She sounded so stilted, so detached, when she wanted to say what was in her heart, the words sometimes springing to her lips and almost out before she caught them back. But it was not the time, not yet.

It was easier, so much easier, not to risk the anguish of loss, but the absence of sweet tenderness would be worse. How did she tell him? How did she say the words that she'd never said to any man, when she wasn't certain how he felt?

Plain enough that he wanted her in his bed, but there were many men who plied heated caresses without thought for anything but their own pleasure. And yet . . . remarkable that he had cared for her so tenderly, his hands gentle but not intrusive on her when he bathed her as any servant might do. She should ask for the words—

"I'll await you in the hall, lady," he said, and backed out the door in a single step, closing oak behind him.

Uncertainty changed to anger when he left, at herself that she was so cowardly. At the moment, she would rather face another raider than ask Glenlyon if he loved her. Daft reluctance . . . but perhaps there was another way to ask.

She wore the emerald patterned silk when she joined them in the hall, the kirtle laced over fine linen, and the dainty slippers on her feet. Beneath the garments, she'd found lengths of ribbon and wound two through the weave of her braid, letting the ends trail free and the rope of hair dangle over her shoulder. There was no need for jewelry, for heavy necklaces or flashing earrings; the gilt thread at neck and sleeves gave off sparkles of light enough.

James Douglas saw her first, and he rose to his feet in a gallant greeting that drew Rob's attention from the large, beefy man at his side.

"Good even to you, my lady."

"And to you, Sir James."

She felt Rob's eyes on her, saw from the corner of her eye that he had abandoned his companion and had come toward her at once. His hand was warm, swallowing hers.

"You are rested now, my lady."

His tone was low, intimate, and she felt a flush rise to her cheeks though there was nothing said to warrant it.

"Yea, well rested."

"There is a place at table beside Simon. He frets that you are unwell."

She smiled. "When he sees that you have spent good coin on frivolous silk and ribbons, *he* will be unwell."

"Yea, it may well see him stretched his length upon the hall floor," Rob said with a laugh.

"Shall I tell him Sir James bought them?"

He put his hand over the fingers she'd laid on his arm and squeezed. "Not if you like Sir James at all."

It was a pleasant evening, despite the ruin evident in the hall, with wine and the retelling of the exploits in England. She felt Rob's glance a time or two when one of the men were less than charitable about their English foes, but nothing could disturb her this evening.

Nor did the evening end when all sought pallets in hall and corners, men bundled in their plaides for sleep. She stepped around slumbering forms, some drunk on wine and snoring openmouthed and oblivious, Rob at her side as they made their way up the stairs to the second floor.

Privacy was such a rare thing, treasured all the more when it was found, and the gloom and silence in their vacant chamber was welcome indeed.

"Solitude," he said, closing and barring the door, his remark an echo of her thoughts, "is fleeting."

"Yea," she agreed, and moved to tidy up discarded cloths still left upon the floor. The tub was gone, taken to be used elsewhere, no doubt, but no one had come to tidy the chamber. Understandable, in light of the chaos.

"Leave that," Rob said, coming to her side, "for the morrow."

She turned into him, the damp cloths forgotten. He smelled faintly of soap, and her head tilted back to look up at his face, so dear above her, shadowed on one side, lit by the fire glowing in the hearth on the other.

"You smell of soap," she said, and he laughed.

"Not heather, I trust. There would be those who think it strange for a sworn knight to reek of flowers."

She pressed her face against the front of his tunic. "I have known many men to wear scent."

"Aye, but I am not among them." His hand moved to cup the back of her head, gentle and firm. " 'Twould be said the Red Devil's Cub seeks to mask the taint of brimstone."

She closed her eyes and breathed in deeply. "Heather or brimstone, you smell like heaven to me."

His laughter stirred her hair, warm and reassuring. "Ah lady mine, you ever flatter me."

"Nay." Her head tilted back to gaze up at him, at the shadowed angle of his jaw, the tiny white scar etched into his skin, and the smoky eyes that regarded her through the brush of his lashes. Her heart clenched with the sweetness of her love for him, and she whispered, "It is the truth."

His smile faded slightly, and a gleam she knew well lit his eyes. "Sweet lady, you undo me."

"As you do me, Robert Campbell of Glenlyon, as you do me."

Her breath came a little raggedly now as his hand drifted downward from her hair, pressing lightly into the small of her back.

"Loose your hair," he murmured, tugging at a ribbon, "I would see it free around your face."

Reaching up, her fingers sought and found the trailing end of ribbon, pulled it free to release the bound plaits in her hair, then combed her fingers through the length until it lay upon her shoulders. He watched her, eyes reflecting silver light.

"You seem as an angel, lovely and unsullied by trials or strife."

"I am," she said, "no angel but a woman. A woman who longs for your touch, for your love."

Her heart beat a rapid thunder in her ears. She yearned for words that would vow his love, for the assurance that he had yet to give voice.

"Lady mine," he said softly, and reached out to draw her close, "I could give you nothing less."

His head bent, and he kissed her, not with tenderness as she expected, but with a hot, wild urgency that surprised her in its intensity. His fingers curled in her hair as his mouth devoured hers, a plundering kiss that swept away the words still trembling on her lips.

Lightning flashed, seared a path through her body as he drew her hard against him. Moaning against his mouth, her hands splayed on his chest, soft wool and linen beneath her curling fingers when she gripped tightly. His heart beat a heavy rhythm beneath her palm. Hotter and higher, his kiss burned away everything but the need to be with him, to lie beside him in the bed and shut out the world.

Heat shimmered as they found the bed, blindly locked in shared desire, hands swift and certain on laces and linen. His touch on her summoned shivers and fire, and she sighed as his hands slid over the curve of her ribs and down, skimming bare flesh, spreading on her back. They sank into the soft, scented mattress, surrounded by heather and shadow, as if they lay in a field beneath the Scottish sky.

Fitting his body to hers, she felt the length and need in him, the arrant sensuality of his bold intent pressing into the cleft between her thighs. Heat spiraled through her, sharp and insistent, and she slid her hands up to curve behind his neck.

"Rob . . ." His name was a soft sigh on her lips, a wish and a prayer combined. He answered her with a slow, luxurious push that gained him entry, and she gasped at the sweetness of it, the wild, hot need that ignited with each thrust and drag of him inside her.

"Rob . . . please . . ."

Perhaps he answered her; she wasn't certain, the sound was lost in the haze that enveloped her as his mouth traced a flaming trail from her ear to her cheek, then her lips. He lingered there, tongue teasing them apart to explore in light thrusts that mimicked the movements of his body. Then he was moving lower, his mouth finding and surrounding the tight, aching peak of her breast as she cried out softly and arched into him. Sweet ecstasy, a fusion of fire and need as he drew her into his mouth, his teeth a gentle nip that sent shudders spiraling into her belly.

She wrapped her arms around him, fingers sliding over the slick muscles of his arms, up and down, a fretful caress that signaled her release. It hovered, waiting, while he stroked inside her, inhaled the bud of her breast and teased her other nipple with clever fingers, until finally it exploded like wildfires in the night, all-encompassing and endless, wave after wave a shuddering bliss that took her beyond even her most precious dreams.

Drowning with it, sinking into the heated sea of joy and release, she knew that if all the rest of her nights were as wonderful, she would be content whether or not she ever heard the words he had yet to say.

It was, she thought, enough that he gave proof of how he felt, even without the words.

✝

SUMMER DAYS HAD dwindled into cooler nights with the promise of winter on the wind's breath. Days were filled with preparations, with the rebuilding of the square keep and the crofter's huts that had been destroyed. A surge of urgency filled him, and Rob relentlessly goaded workers into a faster pace. Argyll would send more men. He had not gained what he sought and would not relent until it was in hand.

There was a sense of purpose at hand now, and the king had marshaled fresh troops and marched into Northumberland at their head. Victory hovered, a threat to men like Argyll, who waited to sway loyalty to the winning side. To choose in error would be fatal, to delay too long just as deadly. King Robert Bruce dealt harshly with traitors.

It was nearly time.

Not again would he leave Judith unprotected, for when he left Glenlyon to execute Argyll's destruction, he could not be distracted by worries for her safety. He hadn't told her yet of his plans, and when he did, he would not tell her all. It would only generate fresh fears that he could not ease.

Christ, but there were no words to tell her how he felt, and it would be unkind to make promises he may not be able to keep. If Argyll succeeded in his goal, she would be in danger unless he made provisions. A betrayal in its way that she may not understand. How did he tell her? How did he warn her that his life would be forfeit if he failed, but to take no action would be certain death? Argyll would not halt until he was dead or triumphant.

And now he had only to wait for the right moment, and it was soon at hand. Bruce had divided his forces, with one surrounding Norham Castle and the other installed at Alnwick, passing the time until it could be starved into submission by conducting formal tournaments outside its walls—a clear indication of confidence in success.

Word traveled like wildfire through the shires and over lochs and burns that the triumph of the Scots was nearly complete. Robert Bruce left his troops to make a leisurely progress through the countryside, hawking and hunting as he went. The wily king let it be known that he intended to parcel out the northern counties of England to his loyal followers upon their fall into his hands.

It sent a shock wave of terror and anger through the English and wild elation through Scots hearts.

Yea, the time was almost upon him for retribution, and Rob readied his tower keep to withstand his absence. He spoke to Simon of his intentions.

Silence followed, then Simon asked, "And of the lady? If you do not return—" He halted, unwilling to finish the sentence, but Rob completed it for him.

"Should I not return, we are handfasted, a legality that should see her protected from law but not Argyll. You are charged with her return to Wakefield. Send word to Sir Payton of Langdon below the River Wear. He can meet you at the border and take her into his custody."

"The lady is strong-willed. She may not go."

It was said with a sighing conviction, and Rob grinned. "Aye, she is that, but I have faith in your ability to endure much abuse."

"Aye, I have endured yours for many a year."

"So you have, faithful comrade, so you have." He put a hand on the broad shoulder. "Call to arms all of your kin who will answer, and know that Dugald MacNeish is sworn to my standard should he be needed."

Simon's snort signaled his low opinion of the De'ils Dugald MacNeish. "There would be so much fighting between the MacNeishes and MacGregors that any raiders would be lost in the fray."

"Probably," Rob agreed, "but the lady would be safe."

"When do you leave?"

"A sennight, no more."

Seven days or less to be with Judith, to absorb all of

her he could before he left to an uncertain fate. He intended to fill them with as much of her as he could.

He found her in the kitchens, wearing the saffron léine that had been a gift from the MacNeish, the hem tucked into her belt to lend freedom for her tasks. A silver ring of keys dangled from the same belt, a mark of her authority and stewardship of household duties. Despite the depredations of the raiders, the larders bore evidence of her husbandry, and the Martinmas rents were not yet due. With Simon and Judith as such able stewards, he would never need for food or coin, save complete disaster.

A savory dish simmered in a huge cauldron slung over the fire, and he caught the pleasant scent of bread baking in the ovens.

"Bannocks," she said when he asked, and turned to him with a scolding smile. "And the stew you're tasting. Put down the ladle, or you'll not get your share later."

He grinned, the taste of simmering stew hot and tasty on his mouth. "Come, my goodwife, and while away a few hours with me."

"Idle hands, good sir?" Her brow rose. "There is much yet to do, I fear. Butter and cheeses to be stored, and pots of honey to be properly laid by—"

"They will wait." He took her hand, ignored her protest that she could not leave Morag all alone to instruct the village lasses in selection of spices, and pulled her with him to the stables.

Her reservations faded away when they rode out of the gates at last, and she'd pulled up the hood of her léine to cover her hair against the brisk wind. The autumn season lay just ahead, evidenced in the cooler days and chill nights. Soon would be the harvest of the fields, time for farmers to lay their bonnets on the ground and the reapers to toast the hairst. If possible, he would be back for the

kirn. It would be a most welcome feast this year, in light
of all that had been lost to the raiders.

It was a fine day, the sky a bright blue bowl overhead
and the sun warm upon their backs. Here and there, scorch
marks lent evidence of the raiders, but new turf walls and
cottages replaced the burned ruins. A flat plain stretched
eastward, marked with huge standing stones.

" 'Tis said the ancients put them there," he told her
when they paused in the shadows of towering boulders
like granite trees, "but it's not known for what purpose.
There are hollows carved in some."

Dismounting, Judith let her horse graze on high grass
and moved to drag her fingers over the ancient stones.
"Old tales say the stones can speak," she murmured.
"What do you think they would say to us?"

He smiled at her whimsy. His horse shifted beneath
him, tossed a restive head, and he loosened his grip on
the reins to allow the beast to graze.

"What do you think they would say?" he replied when
it seemed she expected an answer, and she looked up at
him, a hand curved over her eyes to shade them from the
sun.

"Perhaps they would warn us that life can change too
quickly, and we should cherish each hour we have."

His smile faded. The wind blew tall grass in a rustling
dance around them, as if fairies whispered between the
stalks. Beyond the tree-choked humps of hill and crag lay
the glittering waters of Loch Tay. She knew. Perhaps she
did not know when or why, but she knew he was leaving
soon.

He drew in a deep breath as he searched for a reply,
but she said before he could, "I want to go with you."

"No." He didn't ask how she knew. It didn't matter. "It
is not safe for you, Judith."

"Do you think that matters to me? It was not safe for

me to stay behind the last time you left me here. If you do not return, there will be no safety for me anywhere in Scotland."

"If I do not return," he said flatly, "you will be taken to your family in England."

Sunlight picked out the flare of shock in her eyes. "You have already made your plans."

"Judith—"

"When was I to know? When I awoke and found you gone, perhaps?" She moved from beside the stone to put a hand on his leg. Her touch was warm, pleading. "Take me with you, Robert Campbell of Glenlyon. Do not leave me to the anguish of uncertainty."

"Lady . . ." A helpless sigh escaped him and he bent to cup her chin in his palm. "I cannot. To have you near would be a fatal distraction."

Her eyes closed, dark brown lashes shadowed her cheeks, and her mouth quivered slightly with emotion. After a moment, she opened her eyes and said simply, "Then give me one more memory for my dreams."

They made love in a bower of woodbine and feathery ferns, long hours that whiled away the rest of the day, so that dusk shadowed the road when they returned at last to the keep. She rode his mount with him, held in his arms and his plaide wound about them both, her horse trotting behind.

As the keep came into sight, so did armed troops that waited without the walls. Reining his beast in a half circle as he surveyed them, Rob recognized the standard. It snapped cleanly on a lance, white and red and familiar.

Judith's hand curled into his arm, her voice fearful. "Who is it?"

"Lochawe."

Chapter 23

"I WAS SENT to fetch back the woman," Angus Campbell said curtly, eyeing his son over the rim of a cup. "She has been ransomed."

"That no longer holds. We are handfasted."

Silence greeted Glenlyon's cool reply, and Judith held her breath. She perched on the edge of a bench in the hall, while her future lay in the hands of the two men before her, father and son, sworn enemies now, with divided loyalties.

Lochawe finally lifted his shoulders in a dismissing shrug. "Och, well, that doesna matter. I have a king's writ. Ignore it, and ye'll have a royal army at yer gates."

"Scots or English?"

Lochawe swore foully at that and took a step closer to his son. " 'Tis not I who am named traitor! Look to yer own deeds as proof of treachery. We swore to Argyll, and ye have betrayed that oath and dishonored the Campbell name."

"My allegiance to Argyll was disavowed, but even were it not, I would not allow her to go with you. Her safety as a hostage was compromised."

A sneer curled his mouth as Lochawe shook his head. "She has bewitched ye true, but 'tis not for me to deal with that. I am to take her to Argyll at Innischonnel."

Cold dread formed a tight knot in the pit of her belly as Judith recognized the implications.

"Refuse me," Lochawe continued, "and ye have refused the king's official writ. An army will be at yer gate, and every stone of yer keep will be pulled down before it ends."

Disaster loomed before her. She sat with the dawning realization that Rob would defend her to his own death, and she could not allow that.

"I will go," she said into the gathering silence that was fraught with tension, "and Argyll may have his ransom." She turned to Rob, who glared at her with a thunderous scowl on his face, and said softly, "It is the only way. I cannot risk your destruction."

"You have no say in the matter." His cool reply was as sharp as a slap, and she recoiled slightly. " 'Tis my keep, my life, and you are handfasted to me. By your own vow, you are mine, and I will not allow you to go."

Rising to her feet, she stared at him. If he had given words of love, or even loyalty, she would understand. But not this cold reminder of her subjugation.

"Handfasting is not binding," she said miserably.

"A year and a day, lady mine, and that has not passed."

"Much good it will do if you are dead!"

Aware of Lochawe's narrowed regard and Rob's intense gaze, she tried to sort through the tangle of emotion and cloudy reason that muddled her mind. If she stayed— and oh Mary and all the saints, she wanted to!—he would earn harsh reprisal. But if she allowed herself to be ransomed, then he would be left free and she could return at the very first opportunity. If only she could have a moment alone with him, she could tell him. . . .

"The woman has more sense than ye, it seems," Lochawe said dryly, and Rob turned back to him.

"I will give you my decision in the morning." When his father's brow rose, he added, "You will find the fields outside my gates most comfortable for your night's rest."

Summarily dismissed, Angus Campbell hesitated only for a moment, then accepted it, as he had little choice. Come the dawn, he would have his answer, like it or no.

Left alone with her glowering laird, Judith resorted to silence until he could speak to her calmly. Fury was obvious in the narrowed glance he gave her, in the set of his jaw and the muscle in his cheek that ticked a warning.

Simon MacCallum retreated to the far side of the hall, whether to give them privacy or for his own safety she wasn't certain. With hands folded in front of her, she stood and waited for Rob's anger to subside.

"You spoke foolishly," he said at last, and there was an edge to his voice she couldn't identify.

"Not so foolish, if you consider the alternative. Do you think I want to go?"

He flicked a smoky glance toward her, shook his head. "No, I do not think that. I think you act out of misguided loyalty."

"Misguided? Are you not worth my loyalty?"

" 'Tis not what I mean, for the love of all that's holy, but you don't know how treacherous Argyll can be."

"If the king—"

"Christ, the king will not be there, Judith. Argyll is not to be trusted. I know." His laugh was unpleasant. "I know full well how far he can be trusted."

He raked a hand through his hair, the gleaming black strands catching light from the fire. Pacing back and forth in front of the hearth, he finally halted, shot her a dark glance, and said, "I spent three years in an English prison for trusting unwisely. I will not do it again."

"Argyll is Scottish—"

He laughed harshly. "Argyll is not one or the other, to my way of thinking."

Sudden clarity illuminated his reasons for mistrusting Argyll, and she began to understand.

"He betrayed you."

"Aye, he betrayed me. And worse." When she would have asked how it could be worse, he stepped close to her, so that his face was only a handbreadth away. "If you have some foolish notion of throwing yourself on his mercy, take heed; it could be the death of you."

"That is unlikely." She met his angry gaze steadily. "My father is an English earl, powerful and worth much as an ally. As an enemy, he can be formidable. No doubt, Argyll has cultivated his favor with the promise of my return for coin instead of land, a more acceptable exchange to my father, and to King Edward and his needy coffers."

"More acceptable to Argyll, whether or not the king is likely to profit." He frowned down at her. "I will not risk you."

"If you do not, it's quite possible that there will be the king's troops at the gates. They'll raze the keep, kill beasts and people much more efficiently than raiders."

"I can protect my own."

"Can you? With the men you have here?" She swept out a hand to indicate the hall, and knew she'd made a telling point. "What if they come when the MacCallums are gone? It is not beyond ken. Many a keep has fallen to Edward, and if he has Argyll's help. . . ."

"No," he said finally, and there was grim determination in the steely eyes, "I cannot risk you."

"Not even for the lives of those here?"

"Not even for my own life."

She inhaled sharply. God . . . he would die for her before he would yield. But could she allow that?

It would be a simple enough thing to allow the ransom, then return to Scotland. There were no marriage lines to honor now, no disputed lands, no war to keep her bound. She would be free, and Rob would be alive.

She looked around the hall. Simon bent over a table on the far side, perusing his eternal ledgers. Morag was in the kitchens, no doubt, contentedly cleaning and cooking, with the young village lasses at her heels. Beyond the square keep lay the crofters' huts that looked to Glenlyon for protection, and near the field with the standing stones, new shops had been built on the narrow street by the ancient yew, thriving with the workmen who had come to labor and remained in the area. It prospered here. Vengeance from Argyll or royal troops would hurt so many.

And she knew what she must do.

†

LOCHAWE DIDN'T SEEM surprised to see her. She stood shivering in the bleak light of a new moon, wrapped in hood and plaide. The wind whipped her plaide into a dark billow around her.

"He doesn't know ye are here, I wager," he said and laughed softly.

"No." She stared at him, trying to see some of his son in this man, but failed. "He sleeps still."

"Aye?" Angus lifted a disbelieving brow, but she had no intention of confessing that she had drugged Rob's wine. It would likely earn her another accusation of witchcraft.

"As I could not bring a horse with me, I suggest you find me a mount and hasten from this glen. Unless you wish to meet Glenlyon in battle."

"He'll not thank ye for it," Lochawe said, "but ye have done him a favor by leaving him."

"Understand me," she said coldly, "I do not leave him for hate but for love. There has been enough bloodshed, and I will not see father set against son."

"Ye had nothing to do with that, woman. It was set long before ye bewitched him."

There was nothing to say to that, and when she was mounted, Judith cast a last look back. Outlined against a night sky, the square keep rose strong and proud, a symbol of such brief contentment, such brief happiness. Pray God, she would see it again.

And pray, too, she thought miserably, that Robert Campbell would forgive her.

‡

ANGUS CAMPBELL WAS no fool, and it was obvious he had no desire to cross swords with his son. He set a hard pace, and she was reminded of the arduous ride from Caddel Castle to Lochawe. Terror had been her companion then, and sweet Mairi. If she had known what she would discover at the journey's end, perhaps she would not have been so frightened of it.

Shielings dotted the slopes of Ben Lawers, empty now, with sheep and the shaggy Highland cattle gone from summer pastures. Soaring high above Loch Tay, with serrated ridges and jagged rocks, the slopes disappeared in green folds beneath billowing clouds. Rain threatened in a low rumble of thunder.

She thought of the last time she had ridden this path,

fleeing from the very man she had chosen to ride with now. It was a circle, and she had come full round it. Misery rode every step with her, dulled her senses so that she could hardly think for it. Her head pounded, grief an ache that settled in her chest. So many losses through the years . . . she had thought leaving Mairi behind was the worst . . . until now.

The press of hot tears stung her eyes, and she blinked them away angrily, not wanting to give in to the weakness. It was not—could not be—forever. How could she bear it if it was? No, it was only for a short time, and she would be with him again. He would understand then why she had gone.

Engulfed in her misery, she did not at first comprehend the ripple of excitement in the men around her, not until she heard one mutter, "The Devil's Cub," and her head whipped around to see the cause. Her heart leaped.

Glenlyon. With him were MacCallums and Mac-Gregors, and she recognized Archie MacCallum riding at Rob's side. They came fast, horses quickly closing the distance between them, and she heard Angus curse. A faint smile curved her mouth. All for naught—her sacrifice and risk had gained nothing, yet she couldn't help a sweeping surge of relief that he had come, and then stark fear that he would be harmed.

She glanced at Lochawe. Fury glittered in his pale eyes and marked his face. Before she could spur her mount away, he reached for her, his arm snaking out to grab her by the back of her tunic and yank her from her horse.

Dangling at the side of his horse, she felt him shift to put an arm around her waist. She grabbed at him with both her hands and tried to pry free. He held her fast, cutting into her with fierce pressure every time she moved.

"Aye, I've not forgotten the last time I had ye like this," he muttered, "for I still have the marks of yer teeth in my arm. Be still before ye wear the marks of my fist on yer cheek."

She had no doubt he'd do it.

Helplessly, she watched as Rob and his men rode within twenty feet of them, then came to a sudden halt.

"Release her," came the growling demand, and she wanted to weep at the anger in his voice.

"Nay," said Angus, an expected reply, and through the tangled veil of her loosened hair, she saw Rob's mount dance in a half circle. "If ye want her, come for her, lad."

Judith gasped as he moved abruptly, and then she felt the cold edge of a dirk pressed against her bared throat. When Rob swore at him, Lochawe laughed harshly.

"She'll not be much good to ye with her throat cut, but that will be yer choice."

"She'll not be much good to Argyll with her throat cut, I warrant," Rob snarled.

"Argyll is not so particular. Wakefield might be, but he was promised only that his daughter would be returned. Nothing was said about the state of her health."

A dark wind sprang up, snapped the edges of her plaide as Judith hung from Angus Campbell's arm, the world narrowed to the cold steel and her trembling fear.

"Christ above," she heard Rob say, "you have become as treacherous as Argyll."

"Fine words from a man who forswore his oath!"

"And have you ever asked the reason for it?" Rob rode nearer; she saw his black horse prance over stone and turf. A rumble of thunder growled, closer now, and loud. The wind caught his hair, blew it back from his face. His drawn sword glinted dully. "Christ, did you never wonder why?"

The arm Lochawe had around her tightened slightly. "If there had been good reason, ye would have told me."

"There was good reason. I spent three years in an English prison for his betrayal."

"Aye, so he told me. But ye know he had little choice in the matter; the English were on him so fast and hard he had to retreat."

"Is that what he told you?" Rob's laugh sent a chill down Judith's spine. "Aye, he would concoct a facile lie."

"Do ye deny it?"

"Yea, I do." He leveled his sword and pointed it at Judith. "But this is not the time. Release her."

She felt a hesitation in Lochawe, in the faint loosening of his taut muscle, but then he tightened his grip again. "I will not."

A rumble of thunder rolled down the rocky slope of Ben Lawers, so loud the ground shook beneath the horses' hooves. A thread of lightning spiked across the sky, and a hot smell filled the wind. Nervous beasts pawed the ground, snorted, and Lochawe tried to hold her and control his horse.

Turbulence coiled around them like a demon's breath as a sudden blast of wind and rain tore from the sky. Slashing down, it pounded against rocks and men in stinging pellets. Chaos erupted, in shouting men and frightened horses, and she heard over the tumult the first clash of swords.

Clinging desperately to Lochawe's arm, Judith was only vaguely aware of the clumsy retreat, his swearing commands to those with him, and the sharp-shod hooves of his horse flashing just past her dragging feet. She half hung from his arm now, with his fist tangled in her tunic and towing her along like a sack of grain. There was nothing to hold onto save his arm, and she feared that at any moment she would be trampled beneath the horses.

And then she was suddenly thrown free, tumbling through the air to come up sharp and short against the white face of a stone thrust up from the ground. Stunned, she lay there in the pounding rain, gasping for air, but sucking in wet hair and icy rain.

The world tilted awry, spinning away from her as she tried to hold to the ground and her senses. Everything was a blur of rain and motion, a flash of steel and streak of plaides, men shouting. A hand clamped around her arm, and she began to struggle until she heard Rob's voice against her ear:

"Be still, Judith—"

And above that, another voice, harsh and triumphant, "I have ye both now, by hell!"

Chapter 24

†

DEGRADING DEFEAT. THE return to Loch Awe was not as he had planned but atop his horse with his feet tied beneath its belly. Angus Campbell had taken no chances that his traitor son might escape.

Rob leaned his head back against the clammy stone of his cell. Innischonnel. A sturdy keep built upon an island in Loch Awe. There was little hope of escape from here.

Perhaps this had been inevitable. He had only delayed it. How else to explain the convoluted path that had brought him to this end? And Judith . . . God. She had become entangled in the mire along with him, given over to Argyll by now, or even to her father. It didn't bear thinking to consider what else her fate might be.

He thought of her as he'd seen her last, sitting stiff and erect atop a shaggy Highland pony, green eyes awash with tears as he was led away. It was the first time he'd seen her weep or even glimpsed tears in her eyes, save for that stormy day in the solar.

A shaft of light pierced the barred wicket of the door, a faint flicker lighting the gloom, though he would almost have preferred no light at all. It was easier to contemplate the darkness of the grave when he did not have to endure the light.

He tried to remember how many weeks he'd been here, but they had blended one into the other without much to separate them. Two? Three? He counted time by the changing of the guards. Argyll's prison was larger than he'd thought, and he was not alone in this bleak and hopeless hole. There were others. He heard them, the sounds of despair in wavering cries that rent the night.

The muted sounds of clanging iron and men's voices drifted down the narrow corridor to his cell. The guards exchanged places again. Another day gone. His belly growled. Food—or what passed for it—would arrive soon. Just enough to keep him alive.

Scraping a hand over his jaw, he felt the rough bristle of his half-grown beard. He'd had time to think more clearly while here and had planned a defense when brought before a council to answer for any charges Argyll had produced. That there would be charges, he had no doubt. Even Argyll would have to have good reason to hang a man the king had knighted on the heights of Sutton Bank.

Ah, the king. Not for a moment had he believed that the Bruce had signed a writ against him, but it had been obvious that his father did. He would add forgery to the growing list of crimes to lay at Argyll's feet—though treason alone was enough to see him executed.

And it had been treason. Argyll had sworn to one king, then to another, but had betrayed them both for his own ends. Rob smiled grimly. He had the document to prove it. Still had it, though Argyll had sent men to find it. For a time, it had been all that stood between him and an assassin in the night. Now its use as a barrier had come to an end.

It was all that would save him now, and he had no way to get it unless he was free. Or dead—a searing irony.

Bending his legs, he crossed his arms over his knees and laid his head on his folded hands. He wore no chains. It wasn't necessary, for escape was impossible. Even if he did manage to escape his cell, he had to get past guards, and once outside the prison, he would have to swim the loch to reach the mainland.

Another rattle clanked in the corridor outside his cell, and Rob looked up, expecting to see the guard with his daily meal. A key fit into the lock, turned with a squeal of iron, and the door swung slowly open.

Torchlight was briefly blocked, then danced inside the cell again.

"Well, well, it has been a while since last we met," came a smooth, unctuous voice he'd never forgotten, and Rob rose slowly to his feet.

"Have you come to take my place, Argyll?"

Soft laughter drifted from behind a scented square of cloth he pressed to his face. "Ah no, I must dash your hope for that, it seems."

"A pity." Rob's hands curled into fists at his sides, but he did not move toward Argyll. If only he had his dirk . . .

"Yea, a pity that you were not more clever. For a while I despaired of success. You eluded my most determined effort to snare you." The cloth square fluttered with his words, wafting scent across the cell. "Your father has proven an invaluable ally."

"My father is loyal, a virtue that has been misplaced in you."

"Ah, loyalty. It has its place and uses." Pale hair gleamed in the torchlight, and the eyes that looked at him over the edge of the cloth were opaque. "I am not a callous man, Glenlyon. Tell me where you hid it, and I'll set you free."

"I was fool enough to trust you once but learned my lesson well. I had three years to reflect upon my folly."

"Yet you are alive today." A shrug lifted his narrow shoulders. "You were not executed. War is a capricious master. Men often are forced to acts they would not commit otherwise."

"That is not the case where you're concerned. As you know well."

"You force me to harsh retaliation," he said sharply. "I will have the document in my possession, or you will die."

"All men must die."

"And all women. Ah. I see you do not like that." He paused, then said softly, "For the moment she is comfortable enough, but that can change."

"Wakefield—"

Argyll gave a dismissing flick of his fingers that cut him off, saying, "Is used to disappointment. Lady Lindsay—or is it Glenlyon now?—has been accused of witchcraft. You are aware of the fate of witches, I presume. However, should I be satisfied with your cooperation, she can be ransomed by her father and no one need ever know of the accusations against her."

Disaster loomed before him. Argyll must have sensed his resignation, for he laughed softly. "I have often said that women are usually the death of a man."

"If I relinquish the document to you, you must first set her free."

"Ah, but much like you, I find it difficult to trust. I will set her free once I have the document."

Impasse. His mind raced from one possibility to another until finally he said, "A document for a document. Draw up a pledge that you will ransom the lady to her father—

alive—and I will tell Lochawe where I have hidden the document. He will make the exchange."

"You trust the man who brought you to me?" Surprise was evident in Argyll's voice, and Rob smiled grimly.

"Aye, for he acted out of loyalty and not treachery. We may disagree, but he is not a dishonorable man."

Argyll was quiet for a moment; then he said, "The idea has merit. I will consider it."

"Before I tell anyone where I've hidden the document, I want proof the lady is well. I want to see her."

"She may not want to see you once your stench reaches her, but I see no harm in it. For a brief time, of course. Farewells can be so difficult."

When the cell door closed behind Argyll, Rob leaned back against the wall and slid down it slowly, weariness and finality seeping into his bones. It was nearly over.

†

SHE HAD MOVED through the days as if in a dream, light and shadow ebbing and flowing around her, voices filtering through the fog that seemed to never fade. Then came the promise of seeing him and the world righted itself, was once again unclouded. There was so much to tell him. . . .

Impatience pricked her sharply, and she asked so many times when the hour would be at hand that her guard gave in and escorted her from the chamber earlier than he should. It was a bright day, sunlight glittering on the loch that surrounded the keep. She paced the small courtyard, waiting, filled with excitement and dread both at the same time.

Finally, she heard the clomp of booted feet on stones and the faint rattle of pikes, and she turned toward the sound. She clasped and unclasped her hands, nervous at what he may say to her. Would he be angry? Would he even listen to her reasons for what she'd done? Oh, if only she'd been able to talk to him on the journey to Loch Awe, she would know how he felt. But he'd been kept distant from her, surrounded by his father's guard, so that she scarcely caught a glimpse of him.

And then that horrible day when they had come here, and he was put aboard a small boat and taken across the water, and she could only weep with regret and despair.

Fret filled her, and uncertainty for the future. Surely Lochawe would not let his only surviving son be imprisoned. If she was ransomed, then that should be an end to it. They would release Rob, and he could return to Glenlyon.

Her heart leaped as the guard came into view, and she caught a glimpse of Rob, sunlight shining on his black hair. He was flanked by two men, with four more ranging behind him with naked pikes, as if he was a vicious murderer bent on mayhem.

Unable to wait for him to reach her at the far end of the walled courtyard, she moved forward but halted sharply as he drew near. Her throat clenched, and she put a hand up to her mouth, fingers trembling. This was not her bonny laird but a changeling. His hair was matted, his tunic torn and filthy, and cuts and bruises marred his handsome face.

The wind behind her tugged at her skirts, gave her the push she needed to move again, and she forced her feet into motion. He stopped in the middle of the courtyard, waiting.

Even bruised and bloodied, he radiated a fierce sense of strength and pride, and she fought the urge to weep.

"My lady," he said softly, and his voice had lost none

of its power to ease into her very soul. "You smell of
heather."

"Yes. I . . ." She stopped, swallowed hard, then continued calmly, "I have been allowed a few conveniences."

He smiled, a crooked tilt of his mouth. The urge to
weep grew stronger, and she held it at bay.

"What of Archie MacCallum?" he asked, and aware of
his guards, she chose her words carefully.

"Safe, as are the rest." It was true as far as she knew,
for she had seen them flee once Rob was captured.

"Ah, that is good to know."

He searched her face, stared at her as if he had never
seen her before—or would never see her again. A cold
chill chased away the warmth of the sunlight.

"I am to be ransomed," she said, the words swift and
reassuring, "but once my father has paid, I will choose
my own fate." When he nodded, she felt the same nagging
sense of doom clutch at her, and she tried to drown it with
assurances of the future. "I have some lands of my own.
They belonged to my mother. I can sell them—"

"Keep them, sweetling." It was said kindly, and there
was a quick, bright light in his eyes. "You may need
them."

"Why? Will I not . . . We are handfasted." A trembling
began inside her, spread to her hands and mouth. "We can
be wed on All Hallow's Day. You haven't forgotten?"

"Ah no, not for an instant. I remember it all. My hours
are spent in memories, and all are of you." He paused,
his eyes shifting to gaze out over the loch. "I can still see
you that first day, sitting atop the pony and holding onto
Mairi with your hair tumbled loose around your face and
only one shoe. You were so brave. I think I fell in love
with you then."

She caught her breath. He had said the words she

longed to hear at last, but why did they sound like a farewell?

A slow, steady pounding tolled a warning that penetrated at last, and she looked from one guard to the other, the enormity sinking in.

"Tell me," she whispered through lips that felt like ice, "what is to come."

His gaze shifted back to her, lingered, then he lifted his hands, and she noticed now his wrists were bound with stout rope. Dragging his finger over her cheek in a light caress, he said, "You will go home, sweetling. It is what you have wanted for far too long."

"No . . ." Wildly, grief rising up in a choking wave, "no, that is not what I want—not England. I want to go home with you, to Glenlyon. To *our* home! Oh God, Rob, what have I done to us? To you?"

"You did nothing to me. It was done long before we met. This has nothing to do with you, Judith. I swear it." He paused, and there was a harsher edge to his words when he said, "This has to do with an earl's treachery, nothing else."

There was so much more she wanted to say, to ask, but the guards were too close—and then they were saying it was time, that the visit was over.

"Wait!" She threw out a hand imploringly, and lifted to her toes to take Rob's face between her palms. Pressing her mouth to his, she whispered, "You cannot give up now, Robert Campbell, for the sake of our love and our child."

A hot, fierce light flared in his eyes. Then they were taking him away, and she was left standing alone in the empty courtyard, feeling her world crashing in on her like falling stars from the sky.

Chapter 25

✝

"WELL?" ARGYLL DRUMMED his fingers impatiently against the table. "Is it to your satisfaction, Glenlyon?"

Rob read the pledge again, looking for ways it could be circumvented. The Latin words were familiar enough, and the gist of the document would give Judith safely into the care of her family, "in good physical and mental health, as she was found, and with all due haste and respect for her person and possessions."

He looked up at Argyll. "Your grasp of Latin is tenuous at best, but it seems in good order. As your scribe has made two copies of it, sign them both, one for your use, and one to be sent with the lady."

A faint sneer curled Argyll's mouth, but he nodded. "It will be done." He glanced at Lochawe, who stood across the hall, and beckoned him forward.

Rob felt his father halt beside him but did not turn. Too much depended upon Angus Campbell's innate sense of honor. He would live or die by it, so he must choose his words carefully.

"Lochawe," Argyll said, leaning back from the table to gaze at his liegeman with heavy-lidded eyes, "you are to be entrusted with a solemn task. Your loyalty to me has been unquestioned, proven without doubt by delivering up the lady and your own son."

"Aye," Angus said, a clipped note that betrayed his disquiet. "Never have ye given me cause to be disloyal."

"That is true. You were well rewarded for bringing the little heiress to Loch Awe, and for that I am also grateful. Your service to me has been invaluable, and I require your discretion once again." He paused, his gaze shifting to Rob and then back to Lochawe. The velvet tunic he wore was a bright blue that made his skin look sallow. His agitation was palpable, his smile too quick.

"I am at yer service," Angus replied as expected, and Argyll leaned forward.

"Glenlyon has possession of a certain document. 'Tis a forgery, but a clever one that could cause me much grief. I desire it to be brought to me."

Rob's brow rose. Ingenious earl, to allay suspicion with a claim of forgery. Would Lochawe see through the ruse? There was so much to lose; his life would be forfeit if his father held to blind loyalty.

There was a moment of thoughtful silence before Lochawe said, "If that is what ye require, I will do it."

"Excellent." A flick of his eyes hid the sudden flare of exultation, and Argyll said smoothly, "Tell him where it is hidden, Glenlyon."

"Sign the documents first, as we agreed." Rob felt his father's tension, his quick jerk of surprise when he added, "My father can sign as witness."

Displeasure showed briefly on Argyll's face, but he nodded as affably as if all was in perfect order. A quill was sharpened, ink unstopped, and a shaker of sand put to use, and the documents that would see Judith safely to her father were signed and witnessed. That much, at least, he had done for her. Argyll could never say now that he had been coerced or that he had not signed them.

"I have fulfilled my end," Argyll said sharply, "keep your word to me."

A faint smile slanted Rob's mouth as Lochawe turned to look up at him, and he recognized the troubled glint in his eyes. "The document Argyll is so anxious to have lies at my mother's feet," he said, and he saw his father's brow lower.

Angrily, Argyll said, "Curse you, Glenlyon, do not dally with nonsense!"

"I do not." He didn't look away from Lochawe's face. "My mother's loyalty lasted until death." Loyalty—a trait represented by the little carved lapdog at his mother's feet in the family crypt. There was a small chamber beneath the stone dog, and the document lay hidden inside. Would his father think about what the dog represented? Or that seven of his sons also lay in that crypt? Would he weigh loyalty to Argyll against his own blood? Rob waited uncertainly.

After a long moment, Angus turned to Argyll. "I will fetch the paper and see it delivered."

When Lochawe had gone, Argyll laughed softly. "You have lost all, Glenlyon."

"Aye, so it seems."

⸸

SHIVERING, JUDITH PEERED through the shadows, her hands wrapped in the thick plaide around her shoulders. Lights bobbed from the galley mast, reflected on the waters of Loch Fyne. It seemed that they would never arrive at the voyage's end. She wanted to rage, to scream defiance and refusal, but it would only be futile. She had already made protests, useless and time-consuming, before she had relented.

So now she stood on deck a galley that bore her along the west coasts of Scotland toward Dumbarton, where she was to be ransomed. Hateful fate, that saw Argyll as her escort, his heavy-lidded eyes an unnerving regard.

"Your silence is an accusation, Lady Lindsay," he said, and she turned to stare at him.

"I have said nothing."

"Yea, that is my complaint. Do you think I have killed him?"

His blunt question took her back. "Have you?"

"No." He laughed softly. "The temptation is great, 'tis true, for Glenlyon was a thorn in my side even before he won spurs and a king's favor."

"Hardly a good reason to imprison and kill him, my lord."

"Ah, well. I have my own reasons. He was my sworn knight once. Did you know that?"

She hesitated, unwilling to betray too much. Finally, she said, "Yea, I had heard that to be true."

"He disavowed me. You heard that as well, I'm certain, or you would not gaze so prettily out to sea instead of look at me. Ah, never fear, I am not angry about it. His father is my loyal vassal, as Campbells of Lochawe have been."

"Why tell me all this, my lord? We have an agreement, you and I, and it changes nothing."

"Ah yes, our agreement. You are wise as well as lovely, and I envy Glenlyon your loyalty."

Bitterly, she said, "You gave me little choice. If I had refused, would you still release him?"

"No." He reached out, touched her lightly on the cheek, and she recoiled with a shudder. His hands were cold, like the claws of a hawk. His hand fell away, and his tone was suddenly mocking. "Just think how glad your brother will be to see you. Does he know that you are Glenlyon's leman?"

"We are handfasted," she said stiffly, but heat seared her cheeks at the contempt in his voice.

Argyll flicked his fingers in a gesture of dismissal. "It gives you rights for a year and a day, 'tis all. Hardly as binding as a priest. But I'm certain Glenlyon didn't tell you that."

"I am aware of it."

"And still you rise to his defense. How virtuous. I suppose you think yourself in love."

When she didn't answer, he laughed again, a nasty sound that made her heart sink. Her fingers curled into fists, nails digging into her palms to keep from saying or doing anything that would cause Argyll to go back on his word. He had sworn to release Rob if she would sign the letter to her father, and she had done so at once. She would have done almost anything to ease the last memory she had of him, of the finality in his eyes and voice.

If only she could have seen him again before leaving.

It was nearly dark when the galley finally entered the mouth of the River Clyde and slipped under the towering basalt rock of Dumbarton. Atop the clefted crevice where Scottish thistles grew rampantly, the castle sprawled, in Scottish hands once more after years of being English held.

She was weary; it had been a long journey, and the incessant motion of the galley had made her nauseous. She wanted to lie down in a shadowed room, not fence with the earl as they had done the entire time. He taxed her, and she had still her father or her brothers—or all—to deal with very soon.

What would they say when she told them she intended to stay in Scotland?

She didn't know whether to be relieved or disappointed when she discovered that only her brother had come for her. He waited in one of the anterooms, and when she entered, he came toward her easily.

"Payton . . ."

"Sweet sister." He grasped her outstretched hands and held them a moment, smiling.

Oh, he was so much older; seven years had passed since last she'd seen him, of course, and he had been but a youth then. Now he was a man. Tall, broad-shouldered, with fair hair like her own, though his was streaked with brown. He wore a beard and mustache, close-trimmed and darker than the hair on his head, but flecked with touches of gold.

"You . . . you've grown!" she said, and they both laughed.

"Yea, so I have. And you have grown more lovely than I remembered you."

"We have our mother's eyes."

He nodded. "Our father says we favor her greatly."

"And is he well?"

"Well, but worried. We all are. Matthew and I have wanted to bring you back to England for some time, but it was not possible until now." He pressed her hands again lightly, then released them. "Argyll has been cooperative, much more so than those at Caddel Castle."

"Yes, so he has told me." She paused, realized she must tread delicately where Argyll was concerned. Nothing could go awry until Glenlyon was safe!

As if conjured by the mention of his name, the earl and the Dumbarton castellan joined them. Vexed, Judith saw that Payton would have preferred privacy for their discussion as well.

Argyll gestured to a table and some benches as if he was castellan. "Sir Walter has sent for wine and cakes. We have much to discuss."

Payton frowned. "The terms are fairly straightforward, my lord. You have two thousand pounds, and my sister is free to go home to England."

Judith smothered a small gasp. Two thousand pounds? It was exorbitant! She thought of Simon and what he could do with that much coin. It was a princely sum, indeed.

A smile spread over Argyll's face. He flicked a glance toward Judith and shrugged his narrow shoulders. "It would seem fairly simple, yes. I am afraid it is more complicated, however."

"Is it." Payton sounded unconvinced and impatient. "If you will forgive me, Lord Argyll, I traveled here at great speed. My men are weary, as am I, and certainly the lady must be so after her long journey. There is time tomorrow for a discussion."

"Surely you do not begrudge me? Alas, I must leave early in the morn, as I have pressing business awaiting my attention." There was no mistaking the swift, malicious glance he sent her, and Judith shuddered. "I merely wish to assure you of my distress in not being able to save the lady from the depredations of my vassal."

"It was my understanding that you sent men to abduct the Caddel heiress," Payton said with a lift of his brow, and Argyll's mouth tightened.

"Yea, that is true, but my orders were not to abuse the hostages in any way."

Judith, who had taken a seat when Sir Walter very courteously pulled out the bench for her, surged to her feet. "It is apparent what the earl intends, so I shall save him the embarrassment of saying it. While I wasn't abused, it is my full intention to remain in Scotland. Forgive me, Payton, but I know of no other way to say it."

He stared at her, green eyes turning to ice, and she wondered if hers did the same when she was angry.

"That is impossible. The ransom is paid, and you will return to England with me on the morrow."

"I have acted in good faith," Argyll said, "and abided by the terms of our agreement. The money should not be forfeit."

"The money will not be forfeit," Payton said tightly, "because the lady will be leaving in my custody. Our father is expecting her home, and that is where she will be."

"I will not." She did not raise her voice, but her determination was clear. "I am remaining at Glenlyon."

Soft laughter slipped from the earl. "She is a defiant lady, it seems."

"The lady," said Payton, "will be under guard until we are once more in England."

There was a finality to his words that she recognized. He would do it. If only they were alone, she could appeal to him, tell him of Argyll's treachery as well as Glenlyon's plight . . . impossible, and made so much worse by Argyll. What could she do to convince him?

✝

WAITING WAS INTOLERABLE. Rob had never been a patient man with such things, and now it seemed a cruel torment. Not as cruel as the torments Argyll would prefer, but vicious in his current state of mind.

New hope shattered the dull sense of acceptance that had clouded his mind, but it made the waiting worse. Resignation to his fate had been kinder, if fatal.

He paced the small cell, six steps one way, four the other, kicked at clumps of fetid straw, peered out the bars of the wicket time after time. Monotony stretched tautly, and he thought again, as he had a thousand times a day, of Judith standing in the wind-whipped brightness of the courtyard with her heart in her eyes and salvation on her lips.

A miracle . . . the lady true through all, faithful in love and deed. She'd saved him. And he meant to live long enough to wed her, long enough to see his bairn.

Six days passed, marked by the changing of the guard, his mood fretful and angry by turns. Would Lochawe hand over the incriminating paper to Argyll? Christ, he'd time enough to walk to the crypt, then back to Innischonnel on the east side of Loch Awe. More than time enough to ride.

It was early on the morn of the seventh day when the summons finally came, a guard escorting him once again to the hall where Argyll waited. Every fiber of his body was taut and strained, tension riding him hard.

Lochawe waited with the earl, his familiar red-and-gray-streaked head turned away from the door as Rob was brought in. Alarm thumped deep in his belly. Argyll beckoned for him impatiently.

"Come ahead, man, come ahead. I would have this matter over and done with no more delays." His opaque eyes shifted to Lochawe. "He is here as you requested. Now I will have the paper."

Rob watched with black dread coiling inside him as his father took out a leather pouch. He recognized it as his own. He had lost, then. He had gambled on Lochawe's honor to see him saved from Argyll, and he had lost. Tradition won, the long-held tradition of a Campbell's fierce loyalty to an overlord, no matter how treacherous. Bitterness settled in the depths of him, sinking into the black void where hope had so briefly gleamed.

Lochawe tossed the leather pouch onto the table between them and Argyll, his voice heavy. "A forgery, ye said."

"Aye. Cleverly done. The seal very like my own." His hands closed on the pouch, dragged it to him, satisfaction a smug smile on his face.

"Ye sent me for the proof of my son's dishonor, yet I found a lie," Lochawe said, and this time there was an odd tremble in his words.

"Aye, as you were told." Argyll was impatient now, one hand tugging at the cords that closed the pouch. " 'Tis all a lie—it's not here." His head jerked up, eyes narrowed. "The pouch is empty."

"Aye, so it is."

"Where is it, you old fool? I would have that paper now, or your son's head will be on a pike before the hour is out!"

"A lie," Angus repeated, shaking his head. "Yer whole life has been a lie. I've looked the other way time and again. Campbells of Lochawe have always been loyal. I gave seven sons for yer cause, and not once have ye acknowledged the heavy price."

"Christ above, man, I gave you a hefty purse! You were paid well for your sacrifice—"

"Seven sons!" Lochawe bellowed, slamming his hands down on the table between them, leaning forward to fix Argyll with a fierce gaze. "And ye not worth so much as a hair on any of their heads. Nay, nor worth the steel it would take to sever yer head should Robert Bruce read what I found hidden."

Argyll paled. His hands shook. "I played you fair—"

"Ye have played me false, by hell, from the first."

Sucking in a deep breath, Lochawe took a step back from the table. He raked a hand through his hair so that it stood up in a wild fringe atop his head, giving the appearance of spiky flames.

"Glenlyon was right," he said softly then, "and I did not listen. Nay, do not protest to me, George Campbell of Argyll, for I know now who ye really are. Ye're not worthy of the Campbell name, not fit to lick the boots of yer own father, God rest his soul." He held up a hand in warning when Argyll surged to his feet. "It would behoove ye to lend an ear to what I say next, for it could well mean yer life."

It was no idle threat. Robert Bruce had little mercy for traitors. Rob stood silent, fierce hope a blaze now in his chest.

Impotent rage flared in Argyll's pale eyes, but he held his tongue, though his hands were clenched into fists around the empty pouch. Lochawe nodded.

"The letter ye wrote, signed, and sealed is where I put it, where it will be delivered to Robert Bruce if I am dead by foul means, if me, my son, or any of my kin are harmed by yer hand or desire. Heed me well; I am not called the Red Devil for naught. That paper is all that stands between ye and death, and well ye know it. 'Tis yer safeguard and mine. Deal fairly, and the paper stays hidden. Deal treacherously, and ye will rue it."

Silence spun when Lochawe finished. It settled heavily over them, while Rob waited for Argyll's decision. He could well refuse, seize them both, and cast them into the cells below and never free them. It was a great risk.

Finally, Argyll snarled, "Glenlyon resisted the king's writ and must be tried by law."

"Another forgery. Robert Bruce is busy in England, too busy to meddle in the quarrel over a hostage." Angus leaned forward. "The English have sued for peace. Bruce will soon return to Scotland and will have time enough

then to deal with traitors on his own soil. What say ye,
Argyll? My son's freedom for yer own?"

"Done, by Christ, and be damned to you both!"

"I'll have a paper signed on that, a bill of innocence
from the charges against him."

"Will you!" Argyll looked a little wild, and Rob shifted
from one foot to the other.

"The lady," he said, the first words he'd spoken since
coming into the hall, "what of the lady?"

Argyll shot him a bitter glance. "Ransomed, as agreed."

"By hell! When?"

"Four days past. Nearly across the border into England
now, I warrant, well out of your reach." A nasty smile
bent his mouth. "Sir Payton seemed most eager to leave
Scotland."

Gone, and once in Wakefield's hands, he was unlikely
to get her back again. Disaster loomed, hope unraveled.
So close, and now he was undone.

⸸

LOCHAWE CAUGHT UP with him on the mainland and
curbed his restive mount with a firm hand. " 'Tis a long
walk to Lochawe from here."

"Long enough," Rob agreed, never breaking stride, his
legs covering distance over rutted track and grass.

His father matched his mount's pace to Rob's, silent
for several yards before he said, "Ye go after the witch."

Rob jerked to a halt, pivoted to face him, looking up.
"I go after my wife."

A muscle twitched in Lochawe's jaw, then he nodded.
"Aye, so ye do."

Wind blew off the loch, cold and damp, promising the
arrival of winter. It must be October now, so long had he

been held in the reeking hole below Innischonnel.

Turning, he walked on, and after a moment, he heard Angus nudge his horse to follow. The clop of hooves was soft.

"Ye could do with a good dunking in the loch, lad. The stink is strong, even from here."

"Then ride on."

After a moment, he heard his father blow out a heavy sigh. "I never thought Argyll would try to hang ye, lad. I thought at worst, it would mean some time in a cell."

"You were wrong."

"Aye. About more than that."

"Yea, about more than that," Rob agreed. The wind felt good against his skin and in his hair, clean and fresh coming across the loch. There was the smell of pine in the air, and he thought instead of heather. White heather, and the lady who had given him a sprig for luck.

Angus rode alongside him, half in front, turning his horse to bar his path so that he had to stop. He held out a hand, palm up, fingers loose and uncurled.

"Come up, ye great stubborn ass, and I'll get ye to Lochawe much faster."

Rob looked at his father's hand, then up at his face, unmoving. The months, years, of strife between them had left marks on both. Never had he thought Angus Campbell would extend the hand of peace to him, when he had been soul sick from the wanting of it, the lack of it.

And yet . . . and yet there was an honesty in his father that had not betrayed him, nor his own sense of honor. Angus Campbell had remained true. It was, Rob realized, tradition.

He moved at last, took his father's hand, and swung up behind him on the horse.

"Christ above," Angus said with a snort, "ye smell like a hog byre."

"Then ride fast so the stench will be behind us both."

Laughing softly, Angus did just that.

A league from Lochawe, a stream of riders poured down a grassy hill, and Rob recognized them. "Hold," he said, and Angus halted their burdened mount to wait.

As they drew abreast, the riders slowed, then came to a halt. Archie MacCallum glanced doubtfully from Rob to Angus, obviously waiting for a signal. Behind him ranged MacGregors and MacNeishes, united in purpose, their feuds momentarily—and no doubt warily—put aside.

"Are there any left to guard Glenlyon?" Rob asked, and Archie nodded.

"Aye, MacCallums all, sae ye ha' no worries."

One of the MacNeishes snorted disdain and was tactfully ignored.

Archie cleared his throat. "We came tae rescue ye from the clutches o' the hangman."

"As you see, I am rescued. But there is work afoot, if you are game, men."

A hearty "Yea!" went up, echoing across the loch.

"For Lochawe, then," Angus said, and spurred the mount forward.

Chapter 26

†

A WET WIND sent a spiral of fallen leaves curling across the road in front of her horse, with a keening sound like a kelpie's call. The steed danced sideways, snorting, and Judith calmed it with a pat on the neck, flicking her glance to the road ahead.

They would reach England soon, and she had not been left freedom enough to flee. Her brother must have guessed her intention, for he'd set a relentless guard to her that was impervious to pleading or even bribery.

But she was as determined as he, and she waited still and watched, certain the opportunity would come. If it took longer than she liked, it would still be welcome when the chance presented itself.

A cold rain fell. She huddled beneath the wool hood of the brèid she still wore, blinking rain from her lashes as she looked down a sloping hill and across a boggy moor that stretched beside the narrow track of road. A few miles ahead lay the twisting ribbon of ancient wall that marked the line between England and Scotland in places, but much more than stones separated the two countries.

She thought again of Rob, as she had every passing hour since leaving Innischonnel. And she thought of Argyll, his arrogant certainty that he would succeed in ridding himself of Glenlyon. Worry was a constant thrumming ache. A sense of urgency filled her, and her thread of patience wore taut and thin.

A horse came alongside her, and she knew it was not her guards. They'd tasted her temper and found it best to trail behind by half a length.

"Still grieving for your Highlander?" Payton asked. Rain dripped from his metal helmet in thin rivulets.

"His name is Robert Campbell of Glenlyon." She slid her gaze to the road ahead, unwilling to even look at him.

Fairness bade her admit that it wasn't all his fault they had quarreled. He'd not expected her to refuse to go with him, and it had given Argyll great amusement for them to argue over her intention to remain in Scotland.

"Aye," Payton muttered now, wiping rain from his eyes with a bare hand, "I know his name quite well."

She slid another quick glance toward him, recognized the sullen set of his jaw. "So I understand," she said.

"He told you."

"Of your barefoot stroll? Yea, so he did."

When he muttered an obscenity under his breath, Judith said, "He could have held you for ransom, as I have been."

"Unlikely, under the circumstances." Another blast of wind and rain pelted them, and for several moments, any conversation was impossible. When the rain lessened, he rode his mount close to hers again. "He said you were well."

"And so I was. Did you doubt? Have we not discussed this in greater length while still at Dumbarton? We gave great entertainment to Argyll and the king's castellan."

"Christ, what did you expect? I risked my life and liberty to come into the enemy's lair to bring you home at last, and you tell me you'd rather stay with a Scot!"

"Did you ask my wishes?" Anger warmed her beneath the chill mantle of rain that wet her face. "No one ever asked my wishes, save Robert Campbell. All the long years I was left to languish in a foreign land, alone without even a husband to see to my rights and needs, and you think to berate me for saying at last what *I* want instead of yielding like a timid mouse to what *you* want!"

He recoiled slightly, eyes narrowed beneath the helm, familiar and yet strange to her, this brother she didn't really know. And that was the most illuminating thing, that she had longed for a home that was no longer hers, yearned for love and had not recognized it until almost too late. If she had not fled Lochawe, perhaps she would never have known it. Would never have known the sweetness of loving Rob. . . .

"You don't know what is best," Payton said harshly, "for if you did, you would not shame your family and your name. Best to go to a nunnery than live loosely—"

"Handfasting is the same as marriage, but without the priest."

"As I said—loose. And if you have a child? Saints help you, then, for it's sure you'll need it."

Her lips thinned into a stubborn line of silence. She had no intention of telling him that Glenlyon's babe already grew inside her.

"Judith," Payton said when they had ridden a while in cold, wet silence, "you have your lands near York. They're good lands, fertile, with ample rents. If the terms set out by the Bruce are signed by Edward, no Scot can own land in England, nor Englishman own land in Scotland. All contracts are null. You can wed again; there have been negotiations for you."

Surprise trembled through her, and she turned to look at him through the mist. "When?"

"Recently—"

"Then that is why you ransomed me? Not because you want me home but because there is an advantage for you?"

A dull color rose up his throat, and he looked away, his jaw clenching. "Christ, I told him . . ." His head snapped back, and he stared at her. "Marriage aside, you'll be safe in England."

"I don't want safety, I want love."

"Love is not necessary to survival."

She stared at him a moment, thought of another man and the same words, spoken about a child, then, but just as mistaken.

"Perhaps it is not necessary to you," she said, "but it is vital to me. I wed once for duty. When I wed again, it will be for love."

"It seems," Payton said softly, "that we are at an impasse."

"Yea, brother, so we are."

"You have learned how to be willful in Scotland."

"Nay, I have learned how to be loved."

✝

THE RAIN HAD stopped. A mist of gray light draped like a curtain over rocks and slopes. Judith's heart clutched, and unexpected tears stung her eyes. The mist reminded her of Rob, of the unique color of his eyes. Why did she weep so often now? It seemed as if she could not go an hour without the sting of tears behind her lids, she, who had rarely wept in her life, a veritable waterfall these days.

A wall snaked across the land, dipping into valleys and rising with the hills, built of Roman stones that had long been the dividing line between England and Scotland. It had been debated whether the wall had been built to keep the Scots out of England or keep the English out of Scotland, but the wall was there just the same, with the boundaries occasionally contested.

Just ahead lay the border, with the city of Carlisle not far beyond promising respite from cold and rain. Riding faster now within reach of a fire and ale, Payton's guard jostled around her, laughing and sharing tales of their plans for later. The road swooped in a steep glide down, then up again, rolling toward England.

Toward years without love . . . without Rob. . . .

Desperation seized her, a kind of madness borne of fear and even sorrow. She could not be led tamely back like a hound. Not without doing all she could to get away.

And then, the miracle. The chance she had been waiting for since leaving Dumbarton presented itself. Her guard relaxed vigilance, thought of their bellies and comfort rather than the woman they had been charged to escort. She seized the moment, slowed her mount, easing back a bit.

They rode ahead of her, riding down the brown ribbon of road into a gentle dale of green grass and grazing sheep, and she dropped back even more. At the head of the hundred-strong troop, her brother rode with his comrade in arms. No one seemed to notice that she flagged, and should they, she intended to pretend a necessary stop in the bushes. None would question that. She had made so many of those stops her brother had accused her of purposeful delay.

A damp wind curled the edges of her plaide around her, and her horse danced over muddy ruts, sliding a little.

She eased back onto the grassy verge near a copse of hazel.

No one noticed. They were some distance ahead now, dull light gleaming on the linked mail and domed helmets and weapons. Caked mud from hooves soared into the air, chunks flying behind like heavy rain, the slapping sound of hoofbeats fading.

One rider among so many, her absence not yet noticed.

Blood pounded in her ears, beat through her veins with a wild rush, and she turned her mount down the slope off the road and into the trees that edged a rocky stream. Faster now, urgency biting at her, she followed the winding brook that led away from the city until the ground became too marshy. She paused to get her bearings.

Stretching to one side lay the sloping hills they had just passed, and to the other lay the wall, moss-covered and draped in ivy, high as a man's head in places. She urged her horse through the high, thick grass, keeping to the wall's shelter for a ways, then cut across the undulating hills that led northward.

The horse stumbled slightly in ditches, clambering up and then down again, with mud flying up and grass whipping at belly and legs. Her hands were cold, her teeth began to chatter, and tension pulled tight inside her like a rope being stretched. She pushed onward until she reached a rocky ledge and brought her horse to a skidding halt. Snorting, he hung his head and shook it, blowing steam into the air.

Below, an angry torrent, swollen by the rains, surged over rocks, chewed at dirt banks, swallowed chunks of earth and grass in its hungry spate. It was too dangerous to attempt fording, with the dark water deep and treacherous. To cross, she would have to go around, using the bridge up on the road. A risk, but her only alternative.

As soon as she started around, she heard a shout on the

wind and looked back. Payton. And with him came the
hundred. They flowed across the fields toward her, a dark
wedge of determination. Panic swelled. No, not now, not
when she was so close. She urged her mount up and down
the banks of the raging stream, searching for a place to
ford it before they reached her. There must be a way
across.

And then she saw it, a crag that rose out and over the
water, grass-fringed, sticking out so far it almost reached
the opposite bank. Her horse was winded, flagging. Several feet of open air lay between one bank and the next.

Another shout, closer now, and she made up her mind.

"Shh, shh," she urged, circling the bay for a running
start. It snorted, danced, pawed restlessly at the ground,
and she dug her heels into its sides. Bounding forward in
a canter, she felt the smooth bunch of muscles beneath
her, the lengthy stride, and then the sudden lift into the
air.

For an instant, it was as if she had wings. *Dealan d'*—
Mairi's butterfly.

Then the bay landed on the opposite bank, a brief jolt,
and she was safe. She glanced behind her when she
reached the top of the next hill. Pallid light glinted on
pikes and helmets. They were already slowing, some separating to ride toward the road, but they would be too
late. She would be well into Scotland long before they
could catch up.

Exhilarated, she lifted her arm into the air, saw her
brother ride right to the edge of the flooded stream and
rein to a halt. He stared up at her with an expression of
baffled anger, and she felt almost sorry for him. Almost.

Wheeling her horse, she crested the hill—and saw
them, a band of near fifty men coming down the Carlisle
road.

Even from this distance, she recognized the rider in

front, the black hair swept back from his face, and the dark blue plaide that whipped behind him. Without a single glance or regret for what lay behind, she rode toward her future.

✝

HE'D SEEN HER streak across the fields, a solitary rider dark against the green, and recognized her at once. Even if not for the bright hair that spilled down her back, he would have known her. And if he had been close enough, he would have throttled her when she made that daft leap across the spate. Failure would have meant serious injury or even death.

Yet fierce joy surged through him when she turned her horse north. The wind snatched at her plaide and her hair, sent it streaming behind her like a banner.

"By hell," Lochawe said, "she rides like a Scot!"

Archie MacCallum and the MacGregors whooped with rising excitement, swords drawn and axes waving over their heads as they hurtled down the sticky mire of the road without regard for man nor beast. Like hounds on the scent of a fox, they spied their prey and gave voice.

Rob let them run a bit; perhaps it would give Langdon pause. Fifty Highlanders against a hundred seasoned English men-at-arms were fine odds. The Bruce himself had faced the same unequal odds and been victorious.

Not for him the fray, not when he had his lady so close now, near enough that he could see the wild light in her eyes and the gleam of her teeth as she came laughing toward him.

He waited, allowed her the moment, curbed his restive mount with an easy hand while she sidled alongside him. Rosy-cheeked from the wind and chill, she lifted a fine brow. Then the husky voice that had kept his dreams alive said, "You are late, Glenlyon."

"Yea, lady. But not too late."

"No," she agreed and leaned forward so that he caught the clean fresh scent of heather in her hair as she reached for him, "it is never too late to love."

Leaning toward her, he cupped her chin in his palm and brushed his mouth over her parted lips. "I shall," he said softly, "give you all the love you can bear."

Her hand came up to cradle his, fingers trembling slightly, the laughter in her eyes replaced by the burn of emotion. "It is liable to take you a lifetime."

"Then we had best begin now."

"Yea, or as soon as we convince my brother that I am not going on to England."

He followed the direction of her gaze and saw that his father and the MacGregors had incredibly come to a clash with Langdon's men. The chink of swords sounded muted by distance, but deadly nonetheless. Rob swore softly under his breath, and gave her a swift, hard kiss.

"Ride on, and I'll follow."

"No!" Instant alarm sprang into her eyes. "Payton would like nothing better than to see you slain—please, do not join the fray!"

"And what kind of man would I be to allow others to risk injury or death for my cause? Ride on, Judith, and let me meet with your brother or this will never end."

"If you think to persuade him to ride meekly away, you are a fool, for he would no more relinquish that which he considers his than you would."

Rob studied her for a moment, then nodded. "Aye, you are right. Stay here then, and whatever happens, you will be protected. Your brother would not harm you."

"If he slays you, he might as well."

Curbing his restless mount, he leaned forward again to

kiss her, then spurred away, riding to join his men.

Sir Payton saw him coming, and amidst the shouts and flashing swords, rode out to meet him. Heavy mist dripped from helmet and blades, dampened the air like rain as they rode within several feet of each other and paused. Horses danced, snorting, mud churning beneath lethal hooves.

"The lady goes with me," Glenlyon said before Langdon could speak, and watched anger crease his face.

"My sister goes home to England," was the snarling reply, and his sword gleamed dully when he lifted it. "We can settle this between us. I am no longer unhorsed or weaponless—do you dare?"

"I dare." Rob kneed his mount forward a step. "Do you have courage enough to keep this only between us? If I win, we leave unmolested. If you win, you take the lady and leave my men to return to Scotland."

"If I win," Langdon growled, "I will do what I wish in regard to your men."

"You were released unharmed, save for your donation of horse and arms," Rob said, lifting a brow. "Are you too craven to extend the same courtesy?"

Sir Payton considered a moment, then gave a jerk of his head. "Aye, then, the same courtesy. If I win, your men can walk back the way they came."

"Done."

Orders were given, and reluctantly, the MacGregors and MacNeishes quit the fight to group behind Rob, muttering in discontent, but compliant. Sir Payton had the same problem with his men, but they finally regrouped some distance away, watchful and waiting.

"I hope ye know what ye are about," Lochawe muttered, his expression registering doubt. "We could have won the day."

"And if I killed her brother? Would she love me for it, or would that always be between us?"

Angus Campbell looked startled. Mist dampened his face and clung in pale drops on his lashes. Finally he shook his head. "So that's what this is about, is it?"

"That's what it's been about for a while. What did you think?"

"I thought," Angus said after a moment, "that it was about her lands."

"It has never been about lands, but about her." Rob slid a glance toward Judith where she still sat her mount, fret in the agitation of her hands but a resolute expression on her face. He looked back at his father. "It has always been about her."

"God be with ye," Lochawe said after a moment. "Ye deserve the lady and her love."

Dismounting, Rob stood still and tense while Sir Payton dismounted and approached. It was quiet. The smell of rain and mud was thick. Rob wore only his tunic and plaide, but Sir Payton wore the red and yellow Wakefield tabard, with the leopard rampant upon his chest. Dull light glittered on the embroidered beast, and on the metal of his chainse.

A brisk wind caught the edge of Rob's plaide as he stood with legs braced, sword held at the ready, his stance alone a silent challenge. Sir Payton closed the muddy space between them in three long strides.

✝

JUDITH STIFLED A scream. Her worst nightmare had come true, the choice before her a grim one. How could she just sit and watch while the man she loved and her own brother hacked at one another with lethal swords? Somehow, her fist was in her mouth and she tasted blood, so hard did she press against her lips.

Payton wore protective armor, while Rob had only his tunic and plaide . . . the deafening clangs of sword against sword were so loud . . . so deadly. She tried not to look, but terror kept her eyes on them as they fought, slashing at one another, brittle light reflected from their blades, and both wore expressions of fierce concentration. She heard Archie MacCallum swear softly, knew that Lochawe scowled, yet it all seemed to be a terrible dream, with men moving as slowly as if the very mist that blurred them dragged them down.

Rob went down on one knee in the mud as Payton's blade forced him back, and Judith stifled a scream with both hands to keep from distracting them. Her heart pounded, and there was a loud roaring in her ears.

Oh Mary, Mother of God, let him live! she prayed as hot fear rose to choke her, and then, miraculously it seemed, he was on his feet again, swinging his heavy sword sideways to catch her brother by surprise. The blow knocked Payton back, his booted foot sliding in rutted mud, and he staggered but kept upright, barely able to turn away the vicious blow. It caught his sword beneath the hilt and sent it up into the air and spinning away to land heavily on the grassy verge.

Panting from his exertions, with sweat and mud coating his face, Payton grimly spread his arms out to the sides to indicate defeat. Judith wanted to weep. She was happy Rob had won, yet knew her brother would not accept his defeat graciously. He never had.

"Take her then," Payton snarled when Rob stepped back and away, "for no decent Englishman would have her after she's lain with the devil!"

Fine lines of fury marked the edges of Rob's mouth, his mud-smeared face just as angry as he replied, "I will take her, and be glad to set her free from men who care more about her lands than about her."

Payton shot a glance toward Judith. He looked angry and miserable. "It was never about the lands for me. She's my sister, my blood. I would never have turned my back on her as she's turned her back on me."

Judith nudged her mount forward several steps, until she was close enough to him to say softly, "Payton, you are my brother and I love you as a sister should, but my life would never be complete without Rob. I am sorry you don't understand. I have made my choice, and perhaps one day you will find it in your heart to forgive me, and understand why I have chosen love over all."

"I would never forsake family for a woman!"

She smiled sadly. "Then you have never been in love. I would forsake all I know for this one man."

"Aye, that's what you've done, it seems."

"Yea." She looked at Rob, who stood with his chest still heaving, and there was a faint smile on his mouth that confirmed her choice. "Yea, I have forsaken all for my laird, my love, and have no regrets."

Chapter 27

✝

BLUE HILLS BILLOWED and rolled like the sea beyond
Ben Lawers, cloaked in mist that diffused light and
shadow and lent an air of brooding majesty to the horizon.
It never failed to stir Rob. The beauty of the glen was
haunting.

Once, he had never thought to find it so, had felt out
of place here, alien in this land where he was to build a
new life. But that was before Judith, before his bonny lady
who had changed everything.

Spurring his mount into a faster pace, he skirted the
banks of Loch Tay, impatience rising with every hoofbeat,
a solid drumming in his ears. She waited for him.

Beyond the dip of crag and hill lay Glenlyon's tower,
where he had found more than he ever dreamed possible.
His life was no longer measured by sword and strife but
by the welcoming light in a woman's eyes. It was a novel
thing, and precious to him.

He clattered at last over the old Roman bridge that

spanned the River Lyon, turned up the slope that led past the spreading yew where legend held that Pontius Pilate was born of a local woman. Ancient standing stones marked fields and hills, evidence of men long dead, a silent reminder that one day he, too, would be gone. But he would leave his mark as well, perhaps not in standing stones or an infamous name, but in ways just as lasting.

On the morrow, he and Judith would wed, All Hallows Day the annual time set aside for handfasted couples who wished to make their union lasting. While he did not need the official blessing to dictate his heart, it was important to leave no question in any minds on the legality of his heirs.

One day, he would be laird of Lochawe and Glenlyon, a great responsibility and privilege, one that he intended to administer with as much prudence and experience as he could.

A rising wind carried with it the promise of winter and the threat of rain, and he rode the last mile at a faster pace, until at last he came in sight of his square tower. It rose above the land in a pledge of safety for those within, new stone gleaming in the fading light. Atop the tower walls, he caught a glimpse of movement, a swift bright flash that made him smile.

She watched for him. Waited, ever vigilant, her love and loyalty a warmth that seeped into his bones. Impatience to be with her drove him through the gates at a canter, and before he could reach the door to his hall, she was there.

"I have missed you," she said against his mouth, her arms lifting to wind about his neck, and he swept her from her feet and into his arms.

He buried his face into the warm curve of her throat and breathed deeply. Sweet, familiar, tempting, the heady scent of heather filled his senses, seeped into him until he knew he was home again, until the tension of the past days faded into memory.

" 'Tis All Hallows Eve," he said, letting her slide down the length of his body but keeping his arms around her. "The time when witches and evil spirits roam."

"Then I shall stay inside tonight."

"Oh yes," he said with a soft laugh, "you shall indeed. I have plans for us that do not include fighting demons."

A gust of wind tore at her skirts and slapped a glossy curl of pale hair across her eyes. She shivered, but there was heat in her eyes. Taking him by the hand, she led him into the hall, and a smile curved her mouth that lent promise to the hours ahead.

"First," she said, "you will have hot food and drink and warm yourself by the fire. Then there is business that must be done before we retire. Simon awaits you."

He groaned. "Not those eternal ledgers again. The man worries a penny into a groat."

"A rare talent, you must admit."

"Decidedly, and one for which I will commend him some other time. Tonight, I have other plans than to sit hunched over ledgers and listen to the expenditures of my coin."

She had her way, of course, as both knew she would, and Simon painstakingly listed rents and debits, while Rob sat with growing impatience. Finally, he leaned forward.

"Good steward, your labors and proficiency are much appreciated and will be rewarded, but tonight, I have more to do than hear such mundane—if necessary—tidings. I bring news of king and country, should you wish to hear it."

Simon promptly put down his ledger and quill. "Och, aye, of course I do."

Rob sat back, stretching his legs out in front of him to

let the fire warm his feet. "Envoys from King Edward met
Bruce at Norham to speak of lasting peace. Negotiations
went well, and Bruce has drafted a letter dictating his
terms. He demands that the kingdom of Scotland will be
free, quit and entire, for himself and his heirs forever,
without any kind of homage to England."

"And Edward has agreed?"

"He has little choice. His position is weak. This last
campaign cost them over seventy thousand pounds, and
the September parliament at Lincoln refused to finance
further war efforts. Should Edward persist, he will lose
his northern counties to the Bruce." A smile of satisfaction
lingered as he added, "He was advised to sue for peace,
which he has now done."

Rob glanced at Judith. She sat quietly, hands folded in
her lap, her wine untouched. Did she have regrets? It was
so hard to know her mind on this, for she grieved still for
the constraint with her brother. They had been close once,
but now there was only enmity between them. He understood.

It was difficult to accept still the cautious dealings with
Lochawe. Years of bitterness had not all eroded away in
their new understanding, though much had faded. United
now against Argyll, they were resolved as never before.

"So there will be peace," Simon said, shaking his head.
"I thought never to see it."

Shrugging, Rob said, "Yea, though who is to say it will
last. English kings have a way of forgetting vows made
when 'tis expedient."

Judith's head came up, a faint frown between her
brows, but she gave no argument. Firelight played over
her face, glinted in her unbound hair, and after a moment
she said, "What of Argyll?"

"He prospers." Rob flexed his fingers. "For now. He
knows the shadow of an ax hangs over his head, should

he be fool enough to betray king or Campbell."

"A kinsman," she said with a sigh, "and he has dealt so treacherously with you."

"A distant kin, but blood matters not to men like him. He cares only for his own coffers."

"Poor Mairi."

"She is safe for now, sweetling," he said softly, and he saw the fret in her eyes, the sheen of unshed tears. "Saraid and her bairns have taken to her and live within Lochawe's walls. Mairi is well cherished."

That last made Judith smile sadly. "Still, I would that she was here with me."

"Perhaps one day Lochawe can bring her to us. I will do what I can, my love." Some of the sorrow faded from her eyes and she nodded.

He stood then, and held out his hand to her, and she laid her fingers in his palm.

They trod the stone risers to the second floor in soft silence, no words needed between them. As they reached their chamber door, Morag met them. She smiled broadly.

"Ye are well come home, sir," she said. "All is ready."

"Ready?"

Judith's hand squeezed his lightly. "Morag has seen to your bath. It awaits."

Heated anticipation flared.

The wooden tub stood near the hearth, towels draped over a stool, and pots of scented soap were arranged on the floor. His brow rose.

"You do not intend that I shall smell like flowers, I trust."

She laughed, a soft sound. "Nay, though I recall times when it would have been a marked improvement."

"No," she said when his hands moved to the clasp that held his plaide over one shoulder, "I need practice in the arts of a wife. Tomorrow we will wed, and I do not want you to claim me unfit."

He held his arms out from his sides as she unfastened the clasp and began to unwind his plaide.

"You have no worry on that account," he murmured, as the blood began to beat a swifter course through him. Her hands were soft, competent, dispatching of plaide and tunic and boots until he stood naked beside the tub of steaming water. Aroused, he reached for her, but she avoided his hand and shook her head.

"Once, when I was weary in body and mind, you eased me with gentle words and touch. I will do the same for you."

Steam and flame heated the chamber, and the fire of her touch heated his soul. He closed his eyes, held tight to the fraying bonds of restraint that kept him from reaching for her when she slid her hands over his body.

He stood in the tub, water to his knees, feet apart and braced for support while she plied a dripping cloth and soap that smelled of spices over his skin. Standing on the stool to reach him, she dragged the cloth over his shoulders, scrubbing it along the aching muscle, damp heat seeping in to lend comfort. Steam rose, enveloped him in fragrant mist. Her hands were light, a feather touch over him, down his back to his flanks, then around to his rib cage. He sucked in a sharp breath when she spread her hand over his belly, the cloth a barrier, and heat ignited where she touched.

"Sweet lady," he groaned, "you torment me."

"How so?" The cloth moved lower, and his body leaped to attention. "Ah . . . I see," she said softly.

He burned. She slid her hand over his length, bare of cloth now, fingers slick with soap and water, measuring him with slow, luxurious strokes. His hands clenched into fists at his sides. His breath came hot and swift, and still she caressed him, until he could bear no more.

Grasping her wrist, he stared down at her through slitted eyes. She smiled at him.

It was invitation and challenge, and he saw no need to delay. Water splashed as he stepped from the tub to scoop her up, ignoring her laughing protest that he was getting her wet as he crossed the chamber floor to their bed. Curtains shrouded it, and when he jerked them back with one hand, he saw the bundles of dried heather hanging inside, a bower of fragrance.

"So that you will never forget me," she whispered into the angle of his neck and shoulder, and he shook his head.

"Dearest heart, I would as soon forget to breathe."

Surrounded by heather and shadow, he murmured of his love, easing himself inside her, taking her with him as they soared higher than the peaks of the Highland crags.

✝

IT WAS RAINING. Drops struck the glazed window with a steady patter. Judith lay in his arms, darkness beyond the bed, her heart so full she thought she could not bear it. Tomorrow they would wed, in the eyes of man and God, and all that she had ever wanted in life would be hers at last. There had been sacrifices made, on her part and his, but the rewards were so great that she could only feel gratitude.

Rob's hand lay on the swell of her belly as he slept, so strong and sure she felt like weeping again. Their child would be born in the spring, a new life. A new beginning.

Turning, she pressed her face against him and breathed in the scent of spices and heather. They mingled, as did his blood and hers, Scottish and English, to create a new world. She prayed it would be a more peaceful world for all, but the truth lay somewhere in the dream.

And the dream became truth the next morning, when the day dawned bright and clear, a cool wind shredding the last of the clouds.

Sheaves of bound wheat scattered the steps of the kirk, and pennies were handed out to those who came to see their laird wed to his lady. This last caused Simon no little pain, but he smiled good-naturedly, even while he shook his head at the cost.

A great crowd assembled, with MacCallums and MacGregors standing shoulder to shoulder with Mac-Neishes, peaceful now though later they would no doubt raid each other's cattle, another time-honored tradition. Laughter was loud, a ripple through the crowd, celebration of the day shared.

Not far from the ancient yew, the stone kirk with a new roof of thatch hosted the wedding party. The visiting priest was still not allowed by the pope to perform marriages, as the interdict over Scotland had not been lifted, but that made little difference to those gathered. His presence signified the unofficial blessing of the church.

They stood on the wide stone steps, and Judith thought her Highland laird had never been more handsome. Sunlight gleamed in his black hair, lit the angles of his face. The ravages of his time spent in Argyll's prison were nearly gone now, and there was no grimness in his eyes.

Tears threatened, ever ready these days, and she blinked them away as the priest lifted his hands to begin. The words were a blur, drifting to her through a haze of joy and hope, and then Rob was making his pledge.

Silvery eyes gazed down at her through the thick brush of his black lashes, and in them she could see all the love she had ever wanted in her life, a bright gleam of hope and strength. He smiled, and his voice was deep and husky, rich with promise.

"With this ring I thee wed, with this gold I thee honor. . . ."

Dazzled by the sunlight, warmed by his love, Judith knew whatever the future brought them, they would face it together.

Glenlyon

✝

SCOTLAND
June 1328

CONTENTMENT BANISHED THE shadows that lurked beneath the tower keep, rode shafts of sunlight that spread warmly over the rolling crags and into the courtyard.

The laird of Glenlyon sat upon a stone bench with his wife and son, a rare moment of rest. He watched as Judith crooned a soft song to the swaddled bairn in her arms, her hands loving and tender as she caressed the downy cheek. A light wind blew, stirring an errant tendril of her hair.

Beyond, sitting beneath the shade of a slender oak, young Mairi played with one of Morag's granddaughters. They whispered and laughed, sunlight gleaming on the curves of childish cheeks.

Angus had brought her, a welcome surprise to Judith, though the child could stay only until old enough to wed the earl's son. Still, it was a concession, hard-wrung by Angus Campbell. Argyll must know he had pushed Lochawe to the wall and dare not tempt his wrath—and retribution.

" 'Tis said the Bruce tends his gardens these days," Angus said, a comment that held more weight than mere idle conversation.

Rob turned to look at him. Though their tension had eased, the sense of constraint was still between them at times. Perhaps it would never entirely fade, but it was a beginning.

Nodding, Rob smiled faintly. "I can understand the lure."

Lochawe laughed. "Aye, so ye can, lad. So ye can. Idle times, these."

"Yea, a most welcome peace." He glanced back at Judith, whose attention was focused on the bairn. "The wedding of Bruce's little son to King Edward's sister set the seal on the peace treaty between England and Scotland."

"Aye." Angus scuffed a boot through the grass that grew between stones, and squinted up at the sky, a faint smile on his mouth. "Neither man could bring himself to attend the wedding. Ye know why I did not come to yer wedding, I ken."

"Yea, I do. Fergal is feeling better now?"

"Aye, he has Auld Maggie to tend him, poor sod. But he's a tough old dog." Angus glanced down at the brindle hound that lay at Rob's feet. "Rather like Caesar, I think. The bairn said he pined for ye, so we brought him."

Rob's hand drifted down to fondle the dog's ears, and a wet tongue washed his knuckles. "We spent many a day hunting together. He'll be content enough here to lie in the sun."

"Och, lad, little ye know about it. Old dogs are never content to just lie in the sun. Look at the Bruce. He plans to go on Crusade in that heathen land. 'Tis said he enlists men to go with him. The Black Douglas will go, of course."

Judith's head came up, and Rob felt her sharp gaze on him, though she said not a word. He let the information rest for a moment.

"There is much glory to be won fighting the heathens," Angus said, "and wealth. 'Tis said they have houses made of gold. Think of the fortune to be made by going with the king to fight the heathens."

Glancing at his wife, Rob smiled. "I have all the wealth I need here. Perhaps not a house of gold, but of good Scottish stone. I am content."

Lochawe's brow rose. After a moment he said, "Aye, lad, I see that ye have all ye need or can want from life."

Judith leaned against him, and the sweet scent of heather drifted from her as she lay her head upon his shoulder. Looking up at his father, he smiled. "Aye, all I could ever need or want is right here."

Author's Note

✝

WHILE I'VE TAKEN some liberties with this book, using historical fact as a background for my fictional characters, it's intriguing that truth is indeed stranger than fiction. In 1499, Iain Calder, Thane of Cawdor, died. His daughter, four-year-old Muriella Calder, became heiress. John of Lorn, the second earl of Argyll, sent Campbell of Inverliver on Lochaweside all the way across Scotland to abduct her. Campbell took with him a huge camp kettle, carrying it two hundred miles across the width of Scotland, for what reason history does not record. However, on the wild return to Argyll, the kettle was put to good use when that wily soldier inverted it and charged his seven sons to guard the empty cauldron with their lives. They did, and all were killed. Upon delivery of Muriella to Innishonnel Castle, the chief Campbell seat at Loch Awe, the question was asked of him if the loss of his sons would be too heavy a price to pay should the little girl die. Inverliver is reputed to have replied that Muriella Cal-

der could never die so long as a red-haired lassie could
be found on Loch Aweside. (History also records that the
child's nurse had bitten off the tip of her little finger so
she could be identified if necessary, so it's presumed that
Inverliver would have done the same to another child
should the worst happen.) The worst did not happen, however, and eleven years after her abduction, Muriella was
married to Sir John Campbell, third son of the Earl of
Argyll. The Campbells still hold Cawdor today, in the
capacity of the sixth Earl of Cawdor.

There was a real Campbell of Lochawe during this time
period, Sir Neil Campbell, married to Robert Bruce's sister Mary. In 1327, there was no earl of Argyll, the area
in western Scotland that encompasses Loch Awe. I used
for my story a description of Kilchurn Castle, situated on
the banks of Loch Awe, though this keep was not built
until the fifteenth century. It was located, however, upon
a site long used for a fortress, probably by the MacGregor
clan, so logically, there may well have been a peel tower
there long before Kilchurn was erected. It is fact that
builders took advantage of previous occupants and de-
fendable sites through the ages.

History records that the MacGregors once held lands in
Glenlyon and indeed, in Perthshire and Argyllshire, before
the powerful Clan Campbell relieved them of their prop-
erties. There was much intermarrying in those days, and
brides were frequently abducted to acquire their lands.

The raid in Weardale by James Douglas and two hundred picked men was told much as it happened, with of
course, literary license taken in including my fictional
hero, Robert Campbell, as well as Judith's brother.

On a final note, King Robert Bruce did not get to go
on his crusade to fight the heathens. He died on June 7,
1329, a little short of his fifty-fifth birthday. Before he
died, he asked James Douglas, Black Douglas, to carry

his heart on the crusade for him. This James Douglas did and was killed rescuing a comrade from the Moors in Spain in 1330. He still wore the Bruce's heart in a silver casket hung around his neck, token to a beloved king. The body of James Douglas and the Bruce's heart were returned to Scotland by their companions.

I hope you have enjoyed *The Laird*.